ALL
IN
BAD TIME

The Wisdom Court Series

Book Three

❖

Yvonne Montgomery

Book design by eBook Prep
www.ebookprep.com

Cover and Book design by eBook Prep
www.ebookprep.com

December, 2016
ISBN: 978-1-61417-995-5

ePublishing Works!
www.epublishingworks.com

DEDICATION

For DB and the crew at Bear Mountain

ACKNOWLEDGMENTS

It takes a group of sympathetic, tolerant people to birth a novel. My deep appreciation to Misty Ewegen Morehead for her enthusiasm and ideas over the course of this book, and for the times she pulled me back from the edge. My heartfelt thanks go to Shane M. Ewegen for his careful copy-editing and cogent comments.

Special thanks go to Doug Hawk and Carol Caverly for their clear-eyed readings and valuable corrections and suggestions.

Readers Betsy Cox and Judi Ruder provided helpful feedback at such useful times in the process. Margot Rounds Holmes has been a valued sounding board, always enthusiastic about Wisdom Court.

Thanks and love to my husband, Bob Ewegen, always in my corner.

To friends, family, and acquaintances who've told me of their own ghostly experiences, I thank you.

Many thanks to Karen Ryan, who works magic to free ideas.

I appreciate the ongoing support of Rocky Mountain Fiction Writers and Colorado Authors League.

My thanks to Nina Paules and Brian Paules, as well as the entire staff of ePublishing Works! for their wonderful work in bringing my books to fruition.

TIME OUT OF TIME

The small room looked as sterile as a laboratory. In the bluish light of the computer screen the shelved books and figures placed among them were no more than featureless lumps. Frames on the walls reflected light from the screen.

A slight woman sat at the desk, her hands moving over the computer keyboard before her. Strands of her blonde hair caught moonlight shining through the gap between the curtains and were rendered white. She was asleep.

Evie, wake up.

Her eyelids trembled, then stilled as her breath sighed out through pale lips. Her head tilted toward one shoulder in an oddly coy gesture as her fingers produced the clicking music of the keyboard.

The air thickened, grew heavy and cold. A scratching sound came from the bookshelves against the wall. Her hands paused above the keys but still she slept.

Evie, wake up.

Eve Stewart opened her eyes. Light flashed from the monitor and she jerked to attention, her breath caught in her throat. She gaped at her hands as they kept typing at a steady pace. Jerking them into her lap, her gaze veered toward the window and then to the door. The hush pressed against her ears as she turned back to the computer. She started to push the chair away from the desk but the jab of pain in her left knee forced a groan and she waited for the sharp ache to subside. She hunched her shoulders against the cold.

"There's no one here." Eve heard the fear in her voice and shuddered. There was never anyone here.

Since the accident she'd been plagued by strange doubts and hazy memories she couldn't bring into focus. But the last three nights had been the worst. Now she was typing in her sleep. She forced herself to look at the screen.

There were words grouped together and sentences separated by periods, but she couldn't recognize a single word. She used the mouse to scroll through the pages, one…two…three…

She saw English and leaned toward the screen.

…and the followers shall be women. Their paths have been separate, but when they are brought together, the reckoning shall…

That was all she could read. She scrolled to the end of the section, unable to decipher anything else.

Eve leaned back in her chair. What was the origin of the passage? How had she come to be typing it? Had someone been sending messages to her? Messages in an unknown language, sent to her while she slept and typed. Not one of her saner theories. She winced at the very idea of a mental problem. She was going through a rough patch, but her mind was sound.

And she was arguing with herself in another internal dialogue. *All writers talk to themselves*, she told herself for the hundredth time. *Not all of them wake up one day uncertain of whose voice is answering*, she returned.

Eve slid off the chair, hand reaching for the back of it to brace herself. She stood long enough to allow her knee to adjust to the pain and turned slowly away from the desk. She caught movement from the corner of her eye and inhaled sharply.

"Mrroauw?"

Eve's breath swooshed out in relief. "Danica!" She bent clumsily toward the cat, holding out her hand to her. The animal ignored her, pacing lion-like from beneath the window, leaping onto the desk. The cold light of the moon silvered bits of white fur in her dark coat. She settled beside the keyboard and stared beyond Eve's shoulder, eyes intent.

Eve limped to the futon and sat down hard, grimacing at the throb in her leg. She waited for the pain to ease and tried to work out a plan. As she rubbed her knee she wondered if going to Wisdom Court now would be the best thing. They weren't expecting her for another few weeks, but she hadn't actually set an arrival date. She recalled the kind words of the Director, Rose Hertzberg: *Your collection of delightful blog posts captured the fancy of the Wisdom Court Board, and we're all looking forward to your presence here. Several of your short stories have stayed in my mind, especially the one about the seven roses, and I'll enjoy talking to you about them.*

"I could start packing my books tomorrow," she murmured, leaning into the back of the futon. Her eyes closed as she considered her options. She was so tired of being alone.

As if she'd heard the thought the cat meowed.

"I know." Eve murmured, "We're a team." She told herself to go back to bed, but the pain was easing and the futon was comfortable. She lifted both legs onto the seat and settled her head onto the fat pillow beside her. Her breathing deepened and her mind slowed.

Evie, wake up.

She sighed and shifted her position. Danica jumped off the desk and leapt up beside her, pressing against her belly. Eve snuggled against the cat.

He's coming for you.

CHAPTER 1

The morning sun shone on the thrusting pink slabs of sandstone know as the Flatirons. They guarded over the three houses of Wisdom Court nestled at the base of the Foothills. In the valley below, Boulder was awakening to the blue skies and autumn leaves of a breezy October day.

The sun elongated Brenna Payne's thin body into a stick figure crossing the brick courtyard from the west associate house. She missed the sound of the fountain at the center of the square. It had been damaged the day before and was unusable as a result. She paused to examine the water still oozing from the broken brick wall. She was responsible for that destruction.

Brenna shivered in the air currents tossing her short dark hair about her head. She'd lived through a nightmare yesterday, setting free her grandmother's spirit. Of course, she and Dink had almost been killed when the pickup smashed into the fountain wall. No one had been in the driver's seat. Such things were happening more often now at Wisdom Court. At least they'd found a metal box in the ruins, in it another journal belonging to Caldicott Wyntham, the founder of Wisdom Court. They would read it today.

Brenna realized she was standing near that fountain wall. A breeze flung her hair across her face again and she pushed it out of her eyes. Her hand was shaking, and seeing that, she jammed both hands into the pockets of her jean jacket. She had to swallow back her fear.

"Dammit," she whispered. Now she didn't have Dink to watch her back. She'd gone with him to the Denver airport early this morning after he'd received a call from the manager of the restaurant where he worked.

"I wouldn't go back so fast if he hadn't gone out of his way to get me here in the first place." Dink's arms tightened around her as she'd pushed his curly brown hair to the side of his forehead. "Everybody else flaked out on him and with the rubble from the kitchen fire, he's up the creek. None of us will have jobs if he can't get some help. I can't say no."

Brenna's deep brown eyes softened at the memory of his lingering kiss before he ran to catch the plane to L.A. "I'll come back as soon as I can. I love you. Don't forget that." One more bone-crushing hug, the scent of his balsam aftershave against her cheek, and then he was gone.

Now she was alone again. She thought of the other Wisdom Court associates. Okay, she wasn't alone. They were in this strange, haunted place together, all of them determined to find the source of the supernatural disturbances happening nearly every day. If they were unsuccessful, Wisdom Court might very well come to an end.

"We've come this far," she whispered. "We have to go the distance." Problem was, she couldn't begin to imagine where that distance would lead them. It was hard enough to deal with the messiness of everyday life, let alone the lingering effects of old sins and long-ago crimes. Until they knew the details behind Caldicott Wyntham's tragic love story and what had happened to the stolen money she'd taken with her from England, they were vulnerable to Heaven knows what.

"To Hell knows what," whispered Brenna. "I don't think Heaven has anything to do with it."

"Rose…Rose?" Aura Lee leaned around the lintel of the backstairs and cocked an ear for any sounds. Silence was her reward.

"By the Goddess, where has she gone now?" Aura Lee turned back to the kitchen just in time to catch an impression of movement near the ceiling rack where shining copper pots hung. On a gasp she patted the purple dragon across the front of her magenta sari. Slowly stepping backward, she eased around the counter and made her way to the door leading to the dining room.

"What are you doing?" whispered a voice from behind her.

Aura Lee shrieked and fell against the wall.

"Holy hell." Brenna grabbed the older woman's shoulder and helped her to the nearest chair.

Aura Lee slumped onto the flowered cushion. "You scared me to death!"

Brenna dropped heavily onto the adjacent chair. "You scared me first, backing in here like you'd just set a bomb or something. I was afraid to say anything out loud."

"I saw something in the kitchen." Aura Lee took a wad of tissue from one roomy pocket and dabbed at the sweat dotting her forehead. A hank of her brassy hair hung over one ear, and her ankh earrings were trembling. "I thought getting out of the room was better than trying to find out what it was. Wait a minute," she added hurriedly as Brenna got to her feet and took a step toward the door. "Let's wait until the others show up. Then we can check it out."

Brenna frowned at her. "By then whatever it is will be gone. We've got to be brave, Aura Lee. You're the housekeeper, for heaven's sake. If you don't have backbone, nobody does."

"Humph." Aura Lee levered herself off the chair and adjusted her flowing sari. "I'll show you backbone."

Together they stood in the doorway and peered around the big kitchen. "What did you see?" Brenna whispered.

"Movement near the ceiling, on the pan rack." Aura Lee brushed by her, squinting up at the wooden fretwork holding copper pans. "It was small, I think. Might've even been a mouse."

She didn't see Brenna's cynical smile. "Oh, sure. You know how many of our little disturbances have been as ordinary as a mouse."

A bit of light sparked momentarily and then winked out. They both smelled the now-familiar odor of ozone.

Noreen gasped. "Did you see that?"

"Yeah." Brenna took a couple of steps closer to the rack. "What do you think it could've been? Is there an electrical outlet up there?"

Aura Lee shrugged, but her hand plucked nervously at her neckline. "Maybe a poltergeist?"

"Really? Just what we need," Brenna muttered.

"What do we need?" Rose asked from the other door. When they both wheeled toward her, her shoulders drooped. Her silver curls had suffered from the breeze, and the black tee shirt she wore over gray yoga pants drained the color from her cheeks. "Something else is going on, isn't it?" She carried in the cloth bag hanging from her other hand and set it onto the table. "Just another normal day at Wisdom Court."

Brenna and Aura Lee exchanged a cautious glance. Rose reached into the bag and pulled out a jug of brandy and set it on the counter. At the silence from the other two, her lips tightened. "If things go on as they have been, I'll be ordering this by the barrel pretty soon."

"Now, Rose," Aura Lee began, "we can't let this get to us." Rose turned to face them. The intrinsic serenity that made her such an effective director had been shaken over the last months, and the combination of anger and edginess replacing it had Brenna feeling sad at the loss. "How did you sleep last night?" Rose asked her abruptly.

Brenna lifted her shoulders in a shrug. "Oh, you know, a stray hour here and there. I kept waking up, thinking someone had come into my room." She shook her head at Rose's appalled expression. "It wasn't anybody—anything. Dink was with me and I knew he was leaving. I was missing him in advance, I guess."

Aura Lee smiled. "I like that young man. It has to be hard being away from him."

Brenna pushed the sadness aside for when she was alone. "I like having him around, can't deny it, but I'll get back into finishing my film and we'll see each other at Halloween, if not before." At Rose's frown she added, "It's our favorite holiday. We always spend it together."

Rose turned back to her shopping bag. "I shudder to think what Halloween will be like here this year."

"We'll be all right," Aura Lee said stoutly. "I'll concoct some protective spells and we'll see what kind of strategies Max can come up with."

"I'm so tired of this," Rose said, her voice grim. "The emanations, the icy cold, the strange sounds and wandering lights. What makes you think you'll get any work done on your film?" she asked Brenna. "Nobody's able to work on her own project with all the spirits and—and—" She waved her hands in a frustrated gesture. "—all the eerie nonsense going on here. Finding Cottie's journals just adds to the sense of disruption. Is discovering what happened to her in England going to change what we're dealing with here? The whole purpose of Wisdom Court has been undermined. If her legacy is destroyed…then what's the point of anything?"

Brenna moved to her and put an arm around her shoulder. "Hey, slow down a minute. I know you've been dealing with this for months and it's obviously getting to you. It's okay to blow off some steam. In fact, it's essential, but you have to remember you're not alone with this. We're all in it together, right?" She could almost feel Rose relaxing. She turned her gently toward the kitchen table across from the cabinets and walked her to the end chair, pulling it out for her. Aura Lee came with them and sat beside Rose.

Brenna faked an encouraging smile. "We still have the new journal to read. Waiting all night for that has made us edgy, but we couldn't start it without Max and Kerry here."

A sudden phone call from Max's office in London had come soon after the discovery of Caldicott's diary in the fountain wall. He hadn't told them what it was about, but his look of suppressed excitement had hinted at its importance. He and Kerry worked through the evening gathering documents and photographs and had left for Denver well after dark. Max's car was parked outside Kerry's associate house this morning, but they hadn't surfaced yet.

"For right now," Brenna said gently, "let's have some breakfast." She glanced at the clock. "Or call it brunch. We'll all feel better for some food." She met Aura Lee's troubled eyes. "If you'll start it, I'll come help in a second." She shifted her gaze to the ceiling rack. They'd all promised Max they would record anything unusual in the incident file. She needed to write down Aura Lee's impression of movement on the rack and her own sight of a light blinking out, and the subsequent odor of ozone.

Aura Lee got to her feet. "What sounds good to you, Rose? I could make some chicken salad and use up those late scallions from the garden. That would be easier than omelets. Or," she said after a quick glance into the refrigerator, "I could make a batch of French toast." She turned toward her. "Which would you rather have?"

Rose was rubbing her forehead, her eyes closed. "What? Oh, I don't care. Anything will do."

"I'll be right back." Brenna headed for the living room, releasing a sigh as she left the tension in the kitchen. "There'd better be something good in that journal," she muttered as she reached for the notebook on the fireplace mantel. Caldicott's legacy wasn't the only thing that would be destroyed if the paranormal happenings at Wisdom Court didn't end soon. The associate activities had ground to a halt. She thought longingly of the screening room in her studio. She still had three or four reels of film she hadn't viewed, and the day promised little time for her to get to it.

Brenna opened the spiral notebook and pulled the ballpoint pen from its spine. She turned the pages until she found a blank one, pausing to read Max's cramped handwriting on the other side. He'd described yesterday's dream, as she'd detailed it. How her grandmother had begged her to help release her from the spirits holding her. Brenna flashed on the terror she'd felt.

Her sleepwalking and the discovery of Cottie's second journal in the wall of the fountain were further proof of the growing power of the paranormal forces at work at Wisdom Court. Brenna paused, pen in hand. Neal was supposed to be fixing the fountain today, but she hadn't seen him outside when she'd come to the house. Maybe he'd had to get more materials to complete the job. Or maybe he was sick of always having to deal with paranormal crises, she thought before she could help herself, since he was the Board member in charge of the physical plant. What if he'd left because he didn't want to be around it anymore? She thought of the expression in his eyes every time he looked at Andrea. No, he wouldn't go anywhere. Not for long.

Brenna wrote a brief account of what she'd seen and what Aura Lee had told her and then closed the notebook. Squaring her shoulders, she headed back to the kitchen, hoping Kerry and Max would show up soon. Then they could read the journal and find out what Max had sent to London. Maybe she'd even get the time to get some work done.

CHAPTER 2

A ura Lee had opted for cooking to express her emotional turmoil. The kitchen was fragrant with the scents of French toast and peppers from the chicken salad, and a batch of cornbread was nearly ready to come out of the oven. Andrea and Neal arrived hand-in-hand from the back door as Aura Lee was dishing up, and the warmth in the glance they exchanged drew a sigh of envy from Brenna.

Noreen came through the dining room door five minutes later, easing past Strudel, who'd parked herself near the stove to keep watch for bits of food dropping to the floor. Noreen greeted the offer of brunch with enthusiasm. "It's getting colder out there."

When Kerry and Max trailed in a few minutes later, Aura Lee got out two more dishes without asking if they wanted any.

Rose surveyed them as she got up from the table to get coffee mugs. Between the lines of fatigue on Max's face and Kerry's glazed eyes and tousled auburn hair, it was safe to assume they were both short of sleep. Max pulled a chair out for Kerry and bent to kiss the top of her head as she sat down.

"What happened to you two, or dare I ask?" Rose set coffee in front of them and moved the china cream pitcher within reach.

Kerry yawned and brushed her bangs out of her eyes. "You'll never guess."

Max seated himself beside her. "The drive to Denver was complicated by dreadful winds. We had to slow down to keep on the road."

"Why did you go?" Neal asked. He lifted his fork and stabbed a chunk of chicken.

"I'd put in a call to the British Consul." Max took a drink of coffee and sighed in pleasure. "They agreed to send a package with the diplomatic pouch and the plane for London left at eleven-thirty. I wanted to get the samples to my people in London for testing as soon as possible."

Neal frowned. "What samples?"

Kerry slanted a look at Max. "He's still convinced the gooey stuff we found in Brenna's rooms is ectoplasm."

"It has to be studied," Max said, his blue eyes patient, "and I've been unable to find anyone here to do it. We arrived in good order at DIA and came back here after. Then we were entertained by unwanted guests."

"More ghosts?" Andrea cupped her hands around her cup with a grimace. She flipped her shoulder-length chestnut hair impatiently.

Kerry leaned against Max's shoulder as he reached for his spoon. "Max and I figured as much. It started off like a light show with orbs floating near the ceiling in the living room. They were multi-colored, pink and blue and a nasty acid green."

Noreen glanced up from the notebook where she was recording details. "Did you experience the usual cold?"

Max shrugged. "Kerry turned down the heat before we left, so it wasn't warm, but we didn't feel the kind of iciness we've come to expect. Rather pleasant, actually, watching the lights, almost hypnotic, and we were both nodding off when the tenor of the thing changed."

"Oh, dear," Aura Lee stirred more sugar into her tea.

"It started with a knocking sound, so real that I went to answer the door." Kerry took a sip of coffee. "Nobody was there, and the knocking stopped, but then I was able to hear a hissing sound, like steam escaping. We wandered all over the place trying to find the source, even into the hallway, but we didn't see anything unusual.

"We went back inside and that's when it got creepy. We heard a low voice, barely above a whisper, repeating the same thing, over and over. Like chanting." She dug a folded paper from her pants pocket and opened it. "I wrote it down the way I heard it. *Fortitudo mea, et ab ignibus, qui facturus est.*"

Andrea looked at her blankly. "Do you know what it means?"

Kerry nudged Max in the side.

"*My strength comes from hellfire and its maker.*" Max spoke the line in an even voice, but his eyes were uneasy. "That's a rough translation, of course."

Noreen wrote for a moment then glanced up at Max. "*Ignibus qui* what?"

He swallowed more coffee. "*Ignibus qui facturus est.*"

"Interesting." Absently she ruffled her hair into a standup brush as she reread the words.

"I don't like this," Rose said grimly. "It sounds like some kind of spell, doesn't it?" The look she cast Max was worried. "What do you make of it?"

"It could be an incantation, especially given the repetition." Max frowned into his dish. "Or it could be a line from a bleeding rock song. Perhaps someone was playing an iPod somewhere near."

Aura Lee tapped her lips, thinking. "I'll see if I can find it in one of my magic books," she said finally. "I don't have much material about the dark arts, but I've seen some Latin chants, and I can check through them."

Kerry fought back a yawn. "It sounded like it was on a loop, repeated again and again."

"And the voice?" Neal's face was alive with interest, his eyes intent. "Could you tell whether it was male or female? Young or old?"

Kerry shook her head.

Max said, "To me it sounded sexless, emotionless. It was barely loud enough to be intelligible. The cadence was prayerful, but so much of Latin is when you read it aloud." He lifted his fork to his mouth and noticed it was empty, as was his plate. "Hmmph." He set it down.

"I can get you some more." Rose rubbed at her forehead. "We've got plenty."

Max thought about it. "Perhaps I'll have more coffee, if there's any." He yawned.

Rose nodded and passed the carafe across the table.

The timer went off and Aura Lee got up to deal with the cornbread. When she opened the oven door, scented heat poured out into the room.

Andrea sniffed the air in appreciation. "How long did the chanting go on?"

Kerry and Max glanced at each other. "Hours. We finally covered our heads with pillows so we could get some sleep."

Brenna made a face. "Have you noticed how new kinds of incidents are cropping up almost every day? Just to make things more interesting, I guess."

"That's true, certainly since I've been here. It's the first time I've experienced the light show business, having observed more *scenes,* if you will, in the hauntings I've encountered previously." Max stirred sugar and milk into his coffee.

Brenna's eyes narrowed. "What do you mean?"

Max took a gulp of coffee. "I've come to expect set pieces featuring spirits who go through the same motions each time they appear. Rather like a film clip, such as the Roman soldiers at the Treasurer's House in York. In some spots they look as though they're walking on their knees because the Roman road they travel is a good foot or more under the floor of the house. I grant you, I haven't witnessed many such displays, and some were fragmentary, but I've not seen anything like the seeming spontaneity of the manifestations at Wisdom Court."

"Roman soldiers?" squeaked Kerry. "You saw the ghosts of Roman soldiers?"

Max lifted one shoulder. "Only once, and it was interrupted…" His self-deprecating voice died at the fierce look on her face. "Yes, I did. It was bloody awesome."

"But you say Wisdom Court beats that for hauntings," Rose said after a moment of stunned silence. "Wouldn't you know we'd be special?"

Kerry swatted Max on the arm. "How many of these stories do you have? And why haven't you told me more of them?"

Max rubbed at the back of his neck, eyelids drooping with weariness. "Too much happening and I am trying…to be accurate about what occurs here. Telling about my previous experiences doesn't help bring clarity here and now." He looked around the table as he spoke. "You don't understand how *incredible* the events here are. I realize you're all terribly frightened. *I'm* frightened and astonished at the complexity of what happens here. I don't know if there have ever *been* phenomena to match the ones at Wisdom Court. The disheartening thing is, I don't know what to do about them."

"It's okay." Kerry slipped her hand into his. "I can't blame you for being excited about what's happening. None of us do. But I think it would be so helpful if we could figure out how to do *something*. The feeling of helplessness is driving me crazy."

Max put his arm around her and rested his chin on her head. "I know it, and we'll work together to learn what we can. I'm not myself after so little sleep and—"

"Young man, you've been a pillar of stability in the last few weeks," Noreen announced gruffly. "I believe no apologies are necessary."

Rose nodded. "She's right, Max. Relax for a while if you can and then we'll go on doing what we can do, which is to gather more information." She glanced at the briefcase beside his chair. "I hope you've brought the journal Brenna found yesterday. We need to read it and I'm hoping there'll be more information for us. We have to find out what happened to Caldicott and what's behind these haunting events."

"I did bring it." Max pulled the diary from his briefcase. In Caldicott's first journal, they'd learned about her life as Clara Trinder, the illegitimate daughter of an English barmaid. She'd deliberately used a false name for herself, as well as for the people she'd written about. Her greatest concern had been preventing danger to all concerned, including the women at Wisdom Court.

Clara's life had been changed forever upon meeting Duncan, the son of an earl, in the early months of the war. Their sudden attraction had grown rapidly into a love brought to an end by his father, a Nazi sympathizer. Duncan had kept Clara a secret, concerned for her safety. Ultimately he'd stolen German bearer bonds from the earl and arranged passage to New York City for Clara to ensure her wellbeing. Having discovered his father and his followers were Satan worshipers bent on using their knowledge of the occult to affect the outcome of the war, Duncan stayed in England to fight their efforts.

The first journal had ended with Clara's escape from England with the bonds. She'd also carried with her the powerful talisman Duncan had taken from the occultists. Clara hadn't known of it until a Romani wise-woman had put a protection spell on the odd stone.

Max noted the strain in their faces. "I suppose we could wait for a while to read this if you'd rather."

"I don't think delay is an option," Neal said in a harsh voice. "It might give us information we can use."

Max handed the book to Kerry. "Do you want to do the honors?"

"Yeah. Okay." Kerry opened the journal slowly. She smoothed the page and shook her head. "As much as I want to get the whole story so I'll be able to complete Caldicott's biography, I can't help but feel things worsen the longer we keep going. Every time we learn something new, we get a bigger, stronger reaction from them. And after last night, I'm so not enjoying the thought of any more of it."

Neal raised a brow. "Them?"

Kerry looked around the room and shivered. "*Them.*" She looked down at the book and began to read.

I waited in New York two months before I heard a word about Duncan. And then it was a dog-eared letter sent and forwarded multiple times from the friend who'd hidden me in his flat and then smuggled me out of England. The man who knocked on the door of my tiny flat in the garment district amused me at first. Swathed thoroughly in a smoky gray overcoat, his face half-hidden by a fedora pulled low, his clear intent was to make no impression with his physical appearance or the sound of his voice. My amusement died as I realized how frightened he was. He wouldn't tell me his name and when I asked him if he wanted tea, his look of amazement and distrust convinced me of the uselessness of trying to make our encounter resemble anything like a social occasion.

He pulled an envelope from his coat pocket and held it out to me. His nails were bitten to the quick and his hand trembled. I reached for the letter and as soon as I touched it I knew Duncan was dead. The very feel of the envelope told me, the scent wafting from the paper told me, the fist clutching my heart told me. "What do you know of this?" I didn't recognize my own voice in the rasp I heard come from my throat.

He shook his head and backed toward the door.

"Wait!" This was the last connection I had to Duncan and I had no other names, no other contacts to make. "Tell me something—anything."

I don't know if he heard the raw appeal in my words or if he was innately kind, or any of the other reasons behind his choice to speak to me.

"Madame, two people die before this letter come to you. The son of the Ambassador was first. The one who found him said you must be told."

David, who had joked about playing spy when he managed to get me onto the airplane to New York? He was Duncan's friend, had told me a little about their banding together to survive public school, and their later exploits at Oxford. He'd been so kind to me, giving me what he could of Duncan's story for me to hold onto as I left England for America. He was dead?

I couldn't see the envelope for the tears in my eyes. "Who else," I choked.

"A Gypsy," he said with reluctance. At the shock on my face, he shrank closer to the door behind him. "The old lord, he not learn who you were, but he look, he look hard. Among the Gypsies someone whispered and a man in camp was taken. I do not know his name."

"Andras?" He was Duncan's friend and had helped him smuggle me out of the village.

He shook his head. "Someone who passed on this letter. All I know."

He reached behind him for the doorknob and turned it, pushing it open slowly with his back.

"Thank you," I said. I fumbled for my handbag. "May I give you something for your trouble?"

He shook his head in fierce denial. "I do this for cause."

"Thank you," I said again, but he was gone.

I opened the letter and began to read. "Clara, I couldn't contact Duncan after I returned from London, having seen you onto the plane. I telephoned, of course, but the servants fobbed me off, and when I reached the earl, he claimed Duncan hadn't been seen for several days. It was through secret communication with several of the house servants loyal to Duncan that I was able to piece together what probably happened. His father discovered the theft of the bonds before Duncan returned from spiriting you away. The earl attacked him, demanding to know what he'd done. No one is clear on what eventually took place, but none of them saw Duncan again. They were told later that he'd left to join the air service. To my knowledge, no one has seen him since that interview with his father. I've followed up

*with everyone I can get hold of. Given his feelings for you,
given how earnestly he wanted to join the RAF, I must
conclude that he is dead."*

Kerry looked up from the page, eyes turbulent. "The old
bastard killed Duncan and David. You know that's what
happened!"

Max put his arm around her shoulders and kissed her
cheek. "It is supposition. A safe one, I think," he added
quickly when Kerry took a deep breath to answer. "I'm
sorry, darling. It's a rotten story."

Kerry nodded and bent her head to the pages in her lap.

*I don't recall much of the next few days. Never before,
even when Mum died, had I felt so cut off from the world. I
was in a strange land and I was alone. Would be alone
until I decided what to do and where to go.*

*The morning I woke up feeling hungry, I knew I would go
on without Duncan. I wasn't sure why, but as I cooked
porridge and ate it, I knew I had decided to take what I had
and make something of it. The money Duncan had given
me was in the two banks he'd told me to contact upon
arrival in New York. There was enough to keep me for the
rest of my life. People had died as a result of my being
given that money. I had to make it count for something.*

*I didn't want to die the way the others had. Out of loyalty
to Duncan or hatred of his father, they'd put themselves
between the earl and me. Had he killed his own son? As I
wept yet again at the thought of Duncan, my feelings
hardened. What would the old man do to find me? How far
would he go for the return of his money? No, my money now.*

*If I sent it back to him, I wondered, would he lose interest
in me? Would I be safe to live my life without his shadow
hanging over me? I didn't think so. It wasn't just money
that had dictated his actions. He was hungry for power,
and not just the power of this world. He would want the
talisman. Nor would he forget being bested, let alone
forgive the person who'd done it.*

I would have to remain hidden while he lived.

I started to plan after a few more days. I needed a new identity, something untraceable that wouldn't show my arrival in the States. Duncan or David, or someone ordered by one or both of them had set up the bank accounts as foundations and I was the only signatory on the accounts. I would have to find a way to change my access information, which also was contingent upon a new identity. When I'd accomplished these things, I would decide what activity to take up in order to fade into my surroundings.

I found a comfortable apartment near one of the colleges located in the city, and when the fall term began, I enrolled there. Mum had long encouraged me to improve myself and at last I had the means to do so. I was older than many of the students, but I made some friends and had a life of sorts. I never forgot I was a hunted woman as long as the old earl was alive. I hired a clipping service to send newspaper articles about him and the other villagers by way of a post office box. As the war wound to an end, he was less seen in public. There'd been questions asked about his activities as England fought to survive the war. I read nothing about consequences for his actions, but his absence on the scene hinted at an exile of sorts.

The greatest difficulty for me was to avoid hatred for Duncan's father. That huge amount of money was available to me and some days I imagined taking it to use for revenge. How I wanted to kill him! For months I was obsessed with the idea, but something finally made me abandon the rage inside me. I remembered the hatred Duncan described in his father. He'd caused me such pain and I knew I was not the only person who'd suffered at his hands. I began to fit into the community of students and was able to enjoy the subjects I studied. I decided to do something valuable with my time and energy and in that way to create a memorial for Duncan. Only I would know about it, and that would have to be enough. Duncan had lived. Duncan had loved me. Through him I had a new life and I could change other people's lives, help make them *better. I had a goal at last and I began to research ways in which I could bring it to reality.*

Kerry let the book settle back onto her lap. A tear rolled down her cheek. "No wonder she kept putting off the big reveal."

Noreen shook her head, not understanding.

"No biography would've been complete without her telling all of this: Duncan, his father, the bonds. She couldn't face opening it all up again. It was so painful to live through, she couldn't deal with talking about it."

Aura Lee dabbed at the tears in her own eyes, her lips trembling as she struggled for control.

Andrea frowned. "That doesn't make any sense."

"Her pain," Kerry said. "The pages are thick with it. How could she bear to tell us about it?"

"Then why have you come here?" Brenna's arms were folded, her chin resting on one hand. "I'm with Andrea on this. Everything I've been told about Caldicott Wyntham, including the passages from her own journals, indicates her strength. And she said in the first journal that she had to protect all of us. She had to let us in on what had happened to do that."

Kerry jumped to her feet, letting the journal fall to her feet. She rubbed her hands over her face and glared at them. "We've gone through freaking hell to get this far in the *journals she hid from us.*" She walked back and forth, clenching and unclenching her hands. "And look at the places she hid them. It's a miracle we've seen one word of them!" She spun to confront Andrea and then Brenna. "These are not the actions of a woman bent on coming clean with the world."

Rose let out a tired sigh. "Calm down." When Kerry looked at her in frustration, she smiled. "On the face of it, Caldicott is sending mixed signals, but you've said yourself that she wanted to protect us. She still wants that."

Max reached up to catch Kerry's hand as she passed his chair. "I'm afraid she's right, darling. Remember, Caldicott was smuggled away from Duncan's home county hidden in that caravan. It may sound a bit romantic now, but imagine the sheer terror Duncan must have felt to use such means to remove her from danger." He tugged gently and Kerry dropped back into her chair. "Even if Caldicott has been visiting us as a ghost or shade, or whatever form she is able to take, she's still trying to protect us from that evil. We don't yet understand all of her choices."

Neal stirred and reached for his cup. He found it empty and picked up the coffee carafe. "We've already discussed the possibility that supernatural means are being used to this day to find the money Caldicott escaped England with."

"And the talisman," Aura Lee added in a low voice. "I'm certain he wanted to get hold of that as much, if not more, than the money. The way it was described in the first journal made it sound so powerful."

Noreen forked her fingers through her hair, creating her usual hedgehog bristle. "And the old earl was hell-bent on using it to affect the outcome of the war."

"Hell-bent." Max let out a bitter laugh. "Good word choice. If the old bastard is dead now, and by rights he should be, maybe he's directing his followers from hell."

"To think such a thing could be possible shows how far we've come to explain this whole crazy story." Rose looked around the table at each of them, her gray eyes dark with worry. "What we haven't talked much about is what we would do if the old earl, whose name we don't even know yet, is still pursuing Caldicott from the grave."

Noreen set down her pen and shook her hand to loosen her fingers. "Odds are almost overwhelming that he's dead by now, but as we've come to know, death isn't necessarily the obstacle it ought to be." She shrugged her shoulders as if chilled. "I don't want to encounter that man, living *or* dead. But I'm beginning to feel as if we're destined to, given Caldicott's efforts to escape him."

Rose leaned against the back of her chair and sighed deeply. "Every once in a while it occurs to me that finding the journals and learning what happened in the past might be triggering a rebuilding of the links these people had with each other while they were alive."

"Listen to yourself." Neal looked at her in amazement. "You're saying old animosities could rekindle among the dead?"

Rose shrugged. "I'm saying we might be creating ripple effects. Once the door has opened to the supernatural, new rules come into play. When people die and are really dead, the things they did, the plans they put into effect, die with them. Only memories are left behind. But if the old earl's coven is still active and if, through paranormal means, its members continue to search for the talisman and the money, are we targets? As best I can determine, there's no expiration date on bearer bonds. So," she asked them, "what do we do? If we stop trying to find out what happened, will it end the manifestations we've encountered? Or, if we continue seeking the truth, will the haunting events continue—even increase? And how could we fight such a powerful evil with the weapons we have?"

Max regarded her with respect. "That is the crux of the issue, isn't it?"

"Several cruxes," said Rose, "but no answers. We always come back to the same question. Someone or something is manipulating us to find out what happened in Caldicott's early life, but why? We've discovered she was a part of something horribly evil, but why?"

"So we can end it." At the silence following her statement, Aura Lee looked at them, resignation in her eyes. "Why else? Isn't that the reason behind every ghost story ever told? Evil has to be met head-on, but before you can do that, you have to dig it out and expose it to the world. Cottie is trying to give us the ammunition we need to do that."

Rose sighed. "You're probably right. I just wonder when we're going to have a clear idea of what to do. I wish she'd told us while she was alive." She turned to Kerry. "Are you tired of reading?"

Kerry shook her head.

"Keep going, please," Brenna said. "I want to know what happens next."

Before she could begin again, the doorbell rang. Neal pushed his chair back from the table. "I'll see who that is. Are we expecting anyone?"

Rose frowned. "Not that I know of."

Andrea stood up. "I'm coming with you. Remember the rule: nobody goes anywhere alone while we're under siege." Neal caught her hand with his and they headed toward the front of the house.

"Did Dink get away all right?" Rose asked Brenna.

She nodded. "He called me after he got there. He's up to his ears in repair work, but all's well otherwise."

"That's a relief. I was half afraid he'd take an assortment of ghosts back with him to California."

"So far he's okay." Brenna turned at the sound of voices from the doorway. Neal carried a suitcase and Andrea had a tote bag under one arm. A slight blond woman followed them slowly, hampered by a serious limp and a cat carrier in one hand.

"Rose, this is Eve Stewart," Andrea announced.

"Eve Stewart?" Rose exchanged a confused look with Aura Lee, who shook her head.

"I'm the new Wisdom Court associate," Eve said. "Remember? The writer who broke her leg?"

Rose's mouth opened in surprise. "Oh, my." She stood up and came around the table to extend her hand to Eve. "Of course. I'm sorry. We've been caught up in…a situation and we've lost track of details." She frowned, trying to remember. "Didn't you say you were coming after you healed? In another four to six weeks?"

Eve Stewart's lips tightened. "Yes, that's what I said. But some very odd things have been happening to me and I decided I'd be safer here than at home."

To her obvious surprise, several of the women gaping at her began to laugh.

CHAPTER 3

I *should've called first,* Eve thought in dismay. She wondered for a panicked moment if they would let her stay. She'd felt a sense of homecoming when the cab let her out. The big old farmhouse was across the brick courtyard from two two-story buildings parallel to each other. They had to be the associate houses. The lights in the windows, the last of the summer flowers, and the big old trees swaying in the piney breeze spoke of a home for ideas and accomplishments. Was that impression wrong?

The young Irish-looking woman waved her hands, trying to quiet them. "She thinks we're laughing at *her.*" She came closer and patted Eve's arm. "Trust me, we're not. So many weird things are going on here. All you can do is laugh at the idea of Wisdom Court as a safety zone." She extended her hand and Eve shook it warily. "I'm Kerry Tomlinson, here to write the biography of Caldicott Wyntham, who founded Wisdom Court. This is Max Steadman, a genealogist and expert on the paranormal." The man beside her looked in his mid-thirties, a hint of boyishness in his thin face thanks to a thatch of light brown hair over his forehead. His blue eyes crinkled at the corners as he smiled.

The dachshund at Eve's feet chose that moment to recognize the scent of cat. Her head jerked toward Eve, and she walked stiff-legged to the carrier, sniffing in growing outrage. When the cat shifted inside, the dog planted her front paws and began barking like a hound of hell.

"By the Goddess," groaned the woman wearing a magenta sari. "Strudel, stop it! Stop!" She bent down to grab the dog's collar just as the room went dark. "Rose," she said in a scared voice.

Strudel's barks became even more hysterical and Eve took a step back from her.

"Stop it, Strudel!" Rose commanded. "Hush!" But the maddened yapping escalated into a howl.

The kitchen was pitch black, even the windows were without light, as if the world had fallen into a black hole.

"I can't see anything out back," someone muttered. "Do we have a flashlight?"

"Working on it," said Rose. A drawer was pulled open, the sound followed by a shuffle of objects knocking against each other. "Got it." A click produced nothing, another click nothing more. "Dammit." The drawer thudded shut.

"Hold on a minute." Neal's voice was moving across the room. "I'll look for one." Something thudded against something else.

"Oof!" It was Rose. "Slow down."

"Sorry." The sound of a chair sliding against the floor was followed by an oath. "Everybody stay put a second, okay?"

Eve could feel the dark pressing against her like smothering folds of black cloth. She tightened her hold on the cat carrier, struggling to breathe evenly, trying to stem her growing desire to run away. On the thought a flash of pain burned from her left thigh down through her knee and she made a strangled sound. God forbid she should begin screaming.

A hand wrapped around her arm and she almost did scream. "It's me, Andrea," said a voice. "Neal will get us a light. He's on our board and oversees maintenance, so he ought to be able to find one. It won't take long."

"My leg." Eve was afraid she'd collapse in a heap. "I need to sit."

"Let me get a chair."

The pressure of Andrea's hand left her arm and Eve stood amidst the maelstrom of yelping, thumps, and thuds, counting under her breath, until she felt a touch on her shoulder.

"Eve?"

"Yes." She felt the edge of a chair against her legs and eased down gratefully. "Thank you."

"No problem. You still have the carrier?"

Eve felt the plastic handle across her palm. "Right here."

"Okay. Sit tight. Noreen," Andrea called, "can you reach Strudel?"

"I'll do my best," came a voice. "Not that I can see to take her out of here."

"Okay, let's—"

A man stood in shadow at the back doorway, flashlight in hand. The powerful beam illuminated the kitchen, stirring more shadows along the edges of the room.

"Neal. Thank goodness." Rose was leaning against the counter. "How on earth did you find it?"

Eve watched Neal edge around the sari-wearing woman, whom he addressed as Aura Lee, on her way out of the room with a very unhappy Strudel. "I went out to my pickup. I knew I had one there."

"But, the dark…" Andrea began.

"It's still afternoon out there. I could see just fine. It's dark only in here."

"How screwed up is that?" Kerry muttered.

Beside her Max was still, his gaze on the wall behind the kitchen table. She turned to see what he was looking at.

"Neal," Max said, "would you shine the torch on the wall over there?" He pointed.

Neal complied and Andrea inhaled sharply at the words scrawled in black across the cream-colored paint.

YOU WILL ALL DIE

Someone gasped. Neal snapped, "What the hell?" He turned to the small older woman near him. "Did you see anything to explain this, Noreen?"

"It was dark as pitch. What it says is undeniably true," Noreen said crisply, casting the scrawl a contemptuous glance. "What a pointless remark."

Eve couldn't choke back the laugh rising in her throat like bile. To her horror, it was followed by several more sounds she'd not heard from anyone, let alone herself.

Andrea snatched a glass from the cupboard and groped in another for a bottle. "Why we're not all raging alcoholics by now, I don't know," she mumbled as she splashed brandy into the glass. She gave it to Eve. "Here. I'm sure we'll all join you when we get the chance."

Eve took the glass, but it shook in her hand and Andrea had to guide it to her mouth. "All of it," she said. "It'll help."

She threw back the drink and coughed. When she could speak, she croaked, "Who wrote on the wall?"

"That's the question, isn't it?" Andrea said with bitterness.

The lights flashed on. Through the windows they could see the yard.

"It's about time," grumbled Aura Lee as she came back into the kitchen. "Why do spirits have to be so rude?" Her gaze went to the words scrawled on the wall and she squeaked in outrage. "I've had about enough of this!" She looked up at the ceiling and yelled, "Gods of peace and light, protect us from the vermin!"

Max masked a laugh with a cough and shot a look at Kerry. "We'll check if any other graffiti was added while we were in the dark."

Kerry nodded and tugged him toward the door. "We'll be back. Stick together, okay?"

"Spirits?" Eve said in a faint voice.

The young woman with the black hair in a pixie cut stopped beside her chair. "Do you feel faint? Or is it just your pale skin?" She registered Eve's uncomprehending expression. "Sorry. I see life in terms of movie types, being a moviemaker. You look like the last act of *Camille* at the moment: pale, wan, and with your lovely blond hair. Oh, I'm Brenna Payne. Welcome."

"Um," began Eve, but before she could say anything else, Rose addressed them from the far side of the table.

"I'm going to the living room, so if we're supposed to stick together, you'll have to come with me." She picked up the brandy bottle and headed out the door.

Neal grabbed Andrea by the hand and they followed Rose. "Oops, the cornbread." He started to turn back.

Brenna waved him on. "Got it."

"Don't eat it all, Brenna. You either, Noreen," he added with a wink and Brenna bared her teeth at him as she picked up the platter and trailed behind him and Andrea.

"Neal acts as if we're twelve years old." Noreen had come to stand in front of Eve, offering her hand. Eve took it and stood up, feeling odd at being taller for once. She forgot the issue of size when she recognized the fierce intelligence in the woman's eyes.

"I'd be happy to transport the carrier. Or brace you so you can walk, if you like. Forgive me," she added, "I'm Noreen Prescott, author of a quotations book, women's quotations."

Eve eyed her with gratitude. "Thanks. It's a pleasure. I'll be fine if you'll take the carrier. Danica isn't very heavy."

"Danica. What a lovely name. It means *morning star,* you know. From the Greek."

"Yes. Even as a kitten she'd wake me up at the crack of dawn, so she named herself."

Noreen glanced down at the feline face peering through the mesh window of the carrier. "I'm sure she's a wonderful kitty. Don't worry, she and Strudel will soon come to an understanding."

Eve followed her into sprawling room, amply endowed with places for everyone to sit. At the far end was a large fireplace where flames burned brightly. Pillows and throws in a multitude of colors overflowed from a large wicker basket beside the hearth. Rose had already tucked herself into a plaid blanket, her feet resting on the hearthstone.

Noreen surveyed the inhabitants on the sofas and overstuffed chairs like a general viewing her troops. Her eyes narrowed at the sight of Neal wedged in the corner of the gold sofa, Andrea in the circle of his arms. "Neal, you'll have to relinquish your place. Eve needs to stretch out her leg in front of the fire."

"No," protested Eve as Neal stirred and pushed himself up. "You mustn't move on my account."

Neal hoisted Andrea to her feet and nudged her toward the fat blue chair nearby. "No worries," he said with a grin. "We'll have better cuddling over here. Make yourself comfortable. And welcome."

Eve lowered herself to the sofa, and leaned against the arm with a sigh. She lifted one leg, then the other, to the thick cushions and closed her eyes. "Thanks. This is wonderful. Do you think it's okay if I let Danica out?"

"Of course," Rose said. "She can explore." She blinked sleepily. "I wonder if we have any cat litter somewhere around here."

"I brought a small bag." Eve unzipped the carrier top and folded it to the side. "She'll come out when she feels comfortable."

Rose stiffened, an apologetic look on her face. "I haven't even introduced myself. Rose Hertzberg, Wisdom Court director. I'm so glad you're finally able to be here."

"I liked your acceptance letter," Eve said and Rose smiled.

Brenna had set the cornbread onto the coffee table and gone to the basket by the fireplace. She pulled out a fringed purple throw and brought it back to Eve. "It tends to get cold in here, so let's put this over your legs."

Eve blinked, mortified that her eyes were dampening. The combination of warmth and kindness was almost too much, and she had to fight off the desire to let out the fatigue and pain she'd been living with. "Thank you."

"You've had a hard time, haven't you?" Aura Lee had returned from seeing to Strudel, slipping into the big chair near the sofa.

Eve took her extended hand, nodding, viewing the splendor of the lavender robe Aura Lee had put on, complete with gold ribbon edging. Her Titian red hair was upswept, exposing gold infinity symbols dangling from her earlobes. Eve reached for the glass on the coffee table and Brenna leaned in to top it off.

"We need some of that," Kerry said as she and Max came through the door. "It's getting colder in the rest of the house." They plopped down on the loveseat opposite the fireplace and Kerry shot a hopeful glance at Brenna. "Please, sir, may we have some and then some more?"

Brenna sniffed. "Pathetic Oliver Twist."

Kerry wrinkled her nose. "No one likes a critic."

"How cold?" Rose asked, an edge to her voice.

"Not icy," Max assured her. "At least, not yet." He took the glass Brenna held out to him and handed it to Kerry. When he had his own, he lifted it in a salute. "To peace in this world and the next."

Noreen blinked at him. "*Without hope life is but a barren garden of regret in an arid land.* Samantha Porter Simmons, eighteen thirty-three to eighteen eighty-nine."

"Cheerful." Aura Lee sipped hot tea and smiled at Eve. "How did you come to break your leg?"

Eve roused herself to answer. "A stupid accident. I've specialized in them for the last few months." She didn't catch the flicker of interest in Rose's eyes. "You know, misplacing things, losing others. Breaking my leg."

"What kind of things?" Max asked.

Eve smiled in pleasure at his British accent. "Hmm? Oh, keys, jewelry, the usual."

She fell silent and closed her eyes. When Andrea cleared her throat, she jerked upright. "Sorry. Can't help drifting off sometimes." She took another drink of brandy. "To make up for what I lost, I started finding things, too. Where they came from is anybody's guess." *Probably talking too much*, she thought and then mentally shrugged. *Have to keep the conversation moving.*

"And what sort of things were those?" Noreen asked in a gentle voice.

"A small bag of herbs or something, like potpourri, was on my kitchen window sill one morning. I didn't remember buying it."

Brenna blinked. "Potpourri?"

"Too big to be a teabag. Didn't like the scent of it so I threw it away." She wrinkled her nose. "Too pungent." She sipped again, enjoying the floating feeling creeping up her legs. And her pain wasn't as bad as it had been. Who cared if they had weird spirits writing on their walls? The pain was actually fading.

"What else did you find?" Aura Lee asked. She hadn't taken a drink, just held her glass tightly.

"Not much. In my bag, an odd little…doll, I guess. I went by a playground on a walk. A child could've dropped it in my bag by mistake." She made a sad face at the memory. "Hope it wasn't a treasure. No way to return it."

"Rose?" Aura Lee began in a thoughtful voice, but subsided at the look Max gave her.

"This happened recently?"

Eve shook her head. "Months ago. I had it propped up near my computer."

"What does it look like?" Max smiled when she looked at him in question. "Just curious."

"It's handmade, a kind of ragdoll, I think. Muslin body the shape of a person, stitched along the edges. One of the legs is torn; I keep forgetting to mend it. It's stuffed with greenish straw. Yellow yarn hair tied in a bow." She frowned into her glass. "Did I bring it with me?" She blinked. "I don't think so."

"How was it you broke your leg?" he asked. "Auto accident, perhaps?"

Eve smiled. "I don't drive much, get too distracted. I was carrying a laundry basket down the basement stairs and skidded on a patch of water on the first step down. The basket fell in front of me and luckily that's what my head landed on. Otherwise I'd be crazier than I already am." She glanced at her legs with a grimace. "My leg twisted under me and I hit hard at the bottom of the steps. I'm such a klutz," she added lightly, glancing up at them. They were all staring at her. "What?"

Neal was frowning. "Where did the water come from?"

"The water?"

"On the step. Were there pipes in that area? Were they leaking?"

Eve frowned back. *Strange guy.* "I don't know where the pipes are." She summoned a hazy notion of the plumbing in her basement. "The washer's along the wall opposite the stairs, I think."

"So where did the water come from?"

Eve gazed at him, stomach tightening. She hadn't given it a thought, what with lying in a hospital bed with her leg in traction. She hadn't examined any of the things happening over the last months, not until the strange words showed up on her computer the last few nights.

"I don't know." She met Neal's gaze. "Do you have any ideas?"

"Maybe." He glanced at Rose, raising a brow in question.

Rose shrugged and Aura Lee leaned forward. "Your peculiar little doll could be a poppet. They're used to personify someone the maker wants to affect with a spell."

The nerve on the side of her leg throbbed and Eve rubbed her hand along it, face tightening with pain. "So what does that have to do with me?"

Noreen cleared her throat. "You said one of the doll's legs was damaged. Which one?"

Eve felt her expression freeze. She took a short breath. "What are you getting at?"

"Which leg, Eve?"

She hadn't seen Max retrieve his notebook from the table, but he was already uncapping his pen.

"The left," she whispered.

Aura Lee was looking at her with concern. "You've heard of voodoo dolls, yes?"

"Ah, let's leave all that for later," Max interjected. "Don't look so nervous." He smiled at Eve with sympathy. "We're attempting to identify patterns in order to explain the situation at Wisdom Court. If what has happened to you is in any way connected, we all need to know about it."

Eve felt pressure against her ears and had the sensation that she was slowly falling. He—they—were serious. "What is the situation at Wisdom Court?"

"Ghosts," Aura Lee said promptly. Her face fell as Eve stared at her. "It's true. We've all experienced them."

"I told you strange things have been happening here." Kerry flicked a look at Max. "You saw what was written on the kitchen wall."

Eve closed her eyes. *I shouldn't have had the brandy. I'm stuck with these crazy people and I'm too tired and tipsy to leave.*

"Eve?"

She flashed suddenly on the sound of another voice calling her name. It had been a man and this was a woman's voice. He'd called her *Evie.* Before she could follow the thought, she felt a touch on her arm and she stiffened.

"Eve, are you okay?"

She opened her eyes. "I've had too much to drink."

Brenna was standing beside the couch, looking down at her with a frown. "We shouldn't have talked about this now. You're probably tired after traveling."

Eve nodded and pushed herself up, shifting her legs off the sofa, wincing at the familiar throb. If she could just get a few hours' sleep, if she could be alone and not have to hide what she thought of these maniacs…"I'm tired, not tracking the conversation well." She tried for a light laugh, but sounded to herself as if she were choking. "A nap would be good," she added hurriedly. "If you can put me up for the night, I'd appreciate it. I can leave tomorrow, since so much is going on here."

"Eve." Max was standing beside Brenna. "You don't have to be afraid."

"And yet I am." She wanted to bite her tongue, should've bitten it before she opened her mouth. "Sorry. I need to get some rest."

Rose got out of her chair and came to the sofa. "Of course you do. Hush," she said to Max as he began to protest. "She's exhausted. All this will wait until later."

Eve accepted Rose's help in getting to her feet.

Andrea came around the coffee table and picked up the cat carrier. "I'll take you upstairs to my room." She glanced at Neal. "You can flex your manly muscles and carry the suitcase."

"Always happy to serve." Neal picked up his flashlight and snagged a couple of glasses off the coffee table. "Dishwasher?"

Aura Lee nodded. "Have a good nap," she told Eve.

Noreen leaned back in her chair. "I wouldn't mine one myself. See you later, Eve."

Eve waved a hand at them and followed Andrea out of the room.

TIME OUT OF TIME

His eyes fixed on the shifting flames, tracing the wisps of smoke hiding amongst them. *He had detected the woman's psychic trail more strongly than ever.* Inside him power dragged at the leash, sending heat through his veins. He felt his eyes change. The yellow film overlay the coals.

"Sir?"

He whirled at the sound, a feral snarl twisting his mouth. In the doorway stood his servant, his face blanching in fear.

"Never interrupt me here! How many times have I told you?"

The man stepped back. "My apologies, sir, but—but you instructed me to announce Mr. Fitch when he arrived." Edging into the hall, he added, "He is in the drawing room." He closed the door behind him. The latch clicked.

The struggle to harness his mind held Severn still. *Damn him, damn his ignorant soul.* His breath centered him and the raging subsided.

He cursed himself for crossing into the opening of the ritual. He had to control all aspects of the practice or disaster would result. He could not allow himself to be seduced. He approached the keyhole desk and pulled open the center drawer. The silver knife he withdrew flashed in the light and he turned his head away from it. Although his full alteration had been averted, the process had begun and he could not force the initial effects to disappear. He must contain them.

He drew the blade across his palm, breath hissing at the sharp pain.

His voice ground as the blood began to flow.

> *Emissary, breed the fear.*
> *Shake the nerves, obscure the clear.*
> *Carve the message, twist the knife.*
> *Make the victim fear for life.*
> *Create once more the need to flee.*
> *As it is now so mote it be.*

He held the knife in front of him like a crucifix, hilt on top, lips curving in a terrible smile as light flared from it again. Cruel satisfaction bubbled in his veins even as his hand shook.

"Maintain the control." He clenched his teeth and sliced again. "Maintain the control."

Joy burnt like lava under his skin. The servant had seen. He must die.

CHAPTER 4

T *he sand stretched all the way to the horizon. She fought to keep her balance, but the box she carried was big, and too heavy. She had to place her feet perfectly into the large, deep footprints in front of her but it was so hard to see around the box. A presence was behind her, hunting her. Her foot disappeared into an imprint and she struggled to move her other leg forward. The menacing sound was closer now.*

Evie, wake up.

She couldn't see the next footprints and she couldn't remember where she was going. She had to get away. If she didn't bad things would happen. Terrible things.

Evie, wake up!

Eve gasped, a voice ringing in her ears, and felt the weight across her legs shifting sideways. She opened her eyes to a shadowy room and reached toward her knees. Her fingers brushed against her laptop, now headed for the edge of the bed. Grabbing it, she held it tightly to her chest. She hadn't been using it before she fell asleep. Had she? *Who spoke to me? Where am I?*

The laptop hummed and she fumbled to open it. Lines of type were marching down the screen. *We are coming for you. We are coming for you.* The words rolled down the page like a waterfall.

What was she doing in this room? She struggled to recall how she'd got there but her mind was foggy with dream remnants and a deep fatigue.

The surface of the cheval mirror glimmered, sparking her memory. This was in Andrea's room at Wisdom Court. She'd come to take a nap because she'd been so tired. She'd had too much brandy. The weird people downstairs had talked about ghosts and hauntings. Eve shivered and closed the laptop, pushing it aside, wrapping herself in the thick comforter. She didn't want to go back down there, didn't even want to walk across the carpet. Staying in bed was the only protection she had. She snuggled into returning warmth. She knew hanging her hand over the edge of the mattress would let an appalling something grab it and pull her under. *But under what?* She floated between time and sleep. *Under everything.*

Her eyelids were growing heavy and despite fear she sank closer to sleep. Her mind lapped against the edges of the dream, and she turned onto her other side, burrowing further into the comforter. *I don't want to be afraid anymore.*

Don't let them in, Evie. It was the voice from before.

No one calls me Evie anymore. She drifted into slumber.

The morning sun was wrapped in ragged clouds, cold and gray as a street beggar. Sparrows vied for seed from the feeder hanging outside Rose's workroom, marauding squirrels whipping their tails about as they gleaned what fell to the ground below.

Rose finished the email to the Wisdom Court membership committee and reread it, wondering again if she was doing the right thing. She clicked on the send icon and closed the server. At the tap on the door she called, "Come in."

Noreen entered, teacup in hand, and saw Rose at the computer. "Sorry, am I interrupting?"

"No." Wishing she could stop second-guessing herself, she glanced at Noreen. She'd been an administrator—in spades—serving as headmistress of a girls' school. "I asked the membership committee to email Eve Stewart's paperwork."

Noreen perched on the chair beside the desk. "Why, if I may ask?"

"She came here with no warning." Rose's tapped her fingers against the desktop in a reflexive motion. "I woke up in the middle of the night wondering if she is who she says she is. Her story about the poppet and the sachet…it freaked me out. Don't you think it was awfully…convenient? Something to tell us that would undercut any suspicions we might have? The more I thought about it, the more uncomfortable I felt."

"Hmmm, it shows how different people's reactions can be. She struck me as fairly straightforward." Noreen paused to sip her tea. "Do you really think anyone would try to break into Wisdom Court to confront us?"

"Anyone? We're already dealing with fifty shades of haunting. Why not a person? Of course they'd try."

"I suppose so." Noreen considered the birds outside the window, flapping wings at each other for access to seed. "If we surmise an organization intent upon regaining the money Duncan took from the old earl."

"I'm not so worried about the money. Much of it has to have been spent. It's the talisman I'm afraid of." The black stone with a glowing red oval at its heart was described in Clara's first journal and its image had begun to haunt her dreams. "The old Romani woman's sheer terror at the sight of it is what sticks in my mind. If I really want to obsess about something, I spend time wondering where it could be hidden. Add to that what we've read so far in the second journal, especially Clara's belief that the earl would still try to find her. If we're somehow in the crosshairs of the group that worked with the old earl to sabotage England's war efforts, then we need all the paranoia we can muster."

The lines on Noreen's eyes deepened, and Rose thought about her age. She was the oldest of them, another worry.

Rose lowered her voice. "We don't know Eve. Most likely she's legit, and I hope she is. But I'm going to double-check with the committee to make certain."

"That's good strategic thinking, my dear. After hearing her describe what she's been going through, I'm having difficulty being objective." Noreen moved her head in a sharp little nod. "Considering the possible results if she *isn't* what she seems, I'm glad you're in charge and I'm not."

Rose felt the familiar burn of frustration in her gut. "I wish I knew why Caldicott didn't tell us about what went on in her earlier life. She should have warned us! Everything that's happened in the last few months has put us in greater danger. Why did she leave us so vulnerable?"

"My dear…" Noreen began, her voice troubled.

Rose rubbed at the ache in her temple. "It's not a question we can answer right now. We have to keep following the trail she left, and that's made harder by having to delay reading the rest of the journal as a group. We can't," Rose added at the question in Noreen's eyes. "We don't dare trust Eve until we've checked her out. We'll have to get in touch with whoever recommended her as an associate. What if the Board has been infiltrated, too?"

"Rose, this is getting worse by the minute." Noreen regarded her with dismay. "Take that notion to its logical conclusion and soon we'll be turning on each other!"

Rose recognized the truth of her words. "You're right. We've got plenty to be suspicious about, but we *have* to assume that at least the Wisdom Court community is okay." She tried to smile. "Talk about paranoia."

"I wouldn't be against taking a look at whoever nominated Eve," Noreen added, "but more for information about her than anything else."

"I'll get on it right away." Rose wrote a note on the pad beside her computer.

"About the new journal…" Noreen frowned. "We can't afford *not* to read it, but it's going to be awkward."

"Taking turns is probably how we should do it until Eve has moved into her own rooms."

"You'll let her stay?"

"What else can I do for now? She's been accepted as an associate. I'd like to get hold of her driver's license, though, just to make sure she has one."

"Tell her you need to record her license number for insurance purposes."

Rose regarded her with respect. "Good idea." She pushed herself out of her chair. "I'll talk to the others as I can, and you do the same. If we're doing Eve an injustice, I'll apologize later. We're in survival mode and we can't let any enemies behind the lines."

Noreen got to her feet. "When I think of the efforts Caldicott took to mask identities, and how she hid the journals, my blood run cold. If Eve is a plant from that misbegotten group of devil-worshippers, she could do severe damage."

"We'll keep her out of the loop." Rose put her hand on the doorknob and paused. "It's all we can do for now. With any luck we'll have her cleared sooner rather than later. Let's get back and make some excuse for not continuing with the journal."

"Eve has to settle in. Aura Lee needs to prepare her quarters and you already have your routine for processing new associates."

Rose smiled. "We keep on keeping on. I feel a little steadier now."

Noreen's smile was austere. *"Martial preparation produces little blood, but the blades will cut more cunningly for the time taken in honing them."*

Rose waited for the attribution. "Who said it?" she asked finally.

Noreen gave Rose a sidelong look as she went out of the room ahead of her. "A woman who fought as a man and refused to be known as either."

Rose watched the small woman walk down the hall, wondering if she'd ever find out the source of her quote. They didn't know everything about each other at Wisdom Court. Realizing that today was disturbing.

Eve cut the omelet on her plate into smaller pieces. When she noticed Kerry watching her, she lifted the fork to her lips. A drop of cheese fell onto her napkin and she looked down, then glanced quickly around to see if anyone was still looking at her. Rose's eyes jerked toward Aura Lee when their gazes met.

Something was seriously out of synch. Ever since she'd come down for breakfast, she'd felt the atmosphere cooling. At first she didn't know if it was because of her or something else she wasn't aware of. Could Andrea be upset because she'd stayed in her room all night? She waved away Eve's apology this morning.

As the awkwardness of the conversation became more evident, she came to think she'd made a mistake by confiding in them. They were regarding her with suspicion. But for what? If she couldn't tell them the truth and be accepted, there was no point in remaining here. Her heart sank at the thought of trying to find another place to stay.

"What do you think, Eve?" Aura Lee asked.

Eve's gaze swung toward her and she must have looked as blank as she felt because Aura Lee smiled. "You're still tired out, aren't you? You might like to go to your rooms and get yourself situated. I think we've taken care of everything as far as checking you in. I imagine your kitty is settling."

Eve returned her smile and nodded. If she had to be on display much longer, she'd lose it. The apartment they'd given her was comfortable and quiet. She seriously needed quiet.

"That's a good plan," she said. "I'm still feeling punch drunk from the trip. It'll probably help to unpack and get myself set up."

Rose forced a smile. "Sounds good to me. I'll go get your driver's license and the welcome list we give everyone. It has the phone numbers you might need. Pizza places to order from and such," she added woodenly as she pushed away from the table.

"Like we ever need to do that." Andrea took the last bite of her omelet and set down her fork. "I still think I'm going to weight three hundred pounds before I leave here."

Aura Lee laughed. "We'll all be thin as rails if we keep hunting for Cottie's journals," she said. Then her face fell and she shot a look at Noreen. "I'm sure the cold from the manifestations are making us burn calories like crazy."

Kerry coughed into her napkin, hard enough that Andrea pounded her on the back. "Are you all right?"

"Bite went down the wrong way," she finally gasped.

Eve looked at her bleakly. "Sounds like you might've caught something." She got out of her chair and pushed it carefully under the table. She draped her flowered napkin over the chair back. "I guess I'll see you all later." She gave them a meaningless smile before turning and leaving the room.

They heard Rose speak to her in the hallway and a few minutes later the front door closed.

Kerry emerged from her napkin with pink cheeks. She shot a look at Brenna. "That went well."

"Don't start." Aura Lee met Noreen's eyes. "I forgot we're not supposed to talk to her about the journals. I'm absolutely no good at intrigue."

"That's in your favor, my dear."

As Rose came back into the room, Noreen searched her face. "Have you found out anything yet?"

Rose shook her head. "Margery, the board secretary, is supposed to call me back this afternoon. She's going through Eve's file, and her paper trail ought to be clear. We'll just wait and see."

"I hope she gets back to you quickly," Noreen grumbled. "I dislike this subterfuge. It makes me uncomfortable and

Eve is obviously picking up on it. I hope it doesn't create a gulf between us that can't be bridged."

Kerry nodded. "I don't like it either, but Rose is right. We have to be extra careful now. After the creep-out with the lights going out yesterday, I'm even more nervous about what's going to happen next."

"Knock on wood," Aura Lee said abruptly.

They stared at her and she huffed, "Do it. Knock on wood. Where do you think the old superstitions come from?" she added as they complied. "People were warding off evil eyes and bad luck long before we came along. Which reminds me," she said slowly. "I think we all need protection amulets." Her expression lightened. "I have a lovely new book of protection spells and charms that came yesterday. I'll get right to work." She got up from the table and headed out of the kitchen.

"Make sure they're not stinky," called Kerry after her. She caught Brenna's look of surprise. "Apparently the bad-guy spirits frequently have to be warded off with the nastiest odors."

Eve climbed the curved brick steps to the outer door of the west associate house. A chilly wind was sliding down the hillside and it scurried through the dry leaves scattered across the courtyard. She slid her key into the lock and pushed her way into the hallway, letting the door shut behind her.

She'd thought being upfront with them would establish her presence with little or no pretense. She was so tired of pretending. What if they wanted her to leave? Where could she go? Thanks to the hospital bills she'd almost run through her savings. If she stayed at Wisdom Court—*all expenses paid!*—she'd be fine, but if it required her putting up with the chill she'd encountered today, she wouldn't last a week.

She walked along the carpet runner down the tiled lobby and reached the door to her apartment. As she unlocked the door, the wall sconces flickered several times. She heard a fluttering sound behind her and air moved against her cheek. She wheeled around, heart in her throat.

A large gray feather with black slashes on it floated lazily to the floor. *What in the world?* Eve cast her gaze all around, but couldn't find a source. The high windows near the ceiling let in gauzy light, blurring the edges of the apartment doors facing each other.

When she bent to pick up the feather, the lights faltered again. She spun back to her door and turned the key in the lock, pushing inside, shutting the door behind her. Breathing rapidly, she waited—for another sound, another sign—but the foyer was quiet. Switching on the lights, she laid the key on the small table beside the door and looked for the feather. Not on the table, not on the floor.

Eve peeked out the peephole and could see nothing. Summoning her courage, she opened the door and looked at the floor around the door. No feather.

She heard the fluttering sound again, felt the breath of air on her face, and groped for the doorknob. She swung the door shut and listened to echoes of the knock of wood against wood. She leaned against the door for a long time, trying to explain to herself why she was so frightened.

CHAPTER 5

―――◆―――

"I'm missing some ingredients." Aura Lee trailed in from the dining room, a large leather bag in one hand. Her brows were wrinkled in an abstracted frown.

The others were still at the kitchen table, working on their second and third cups of coffee. "What ingredients?" Andrea asked lazily.

"For the amulets." Aura Lee shook her head in resignation. "I was talking about them not fifteen minutes ago."

"The protection amulets, right?" Brenna shot a glance at Kerry, pleased she was on top of something for once. "Of course I remember. And you don't have enough ingredients?"

Aura Lee pulled out her chair and sat down. "Isn't it always the way? I'm all out of leek and fleabane, and I don't have enough cinnamon to make even three of them. I'll have to get some this afternoon or tomorrow."

"Fleabane?" Noreen examined Aura Lee with suspicion. "You are joking, aren't you?"

"On the contrary." Aura Lee leafed through a worn book she'd pulled from the bag. "Here it is. *Fleabane will protect the home by denying entrance to evil spirits.*" She glanced at Kerry, mischief in her smile. "If you sprinkle the seeds on sheets, it will result in chastity."

"I wish I'd known that when I had over a hundred schoolgirls in my charge." Noreen folded her lips in a line. "Life would have been much simpler."

Kerry grinned. "I don't believe it."

Aura Lee frowned over the list she was composing. "Turmeric would help." She looked up from the page. "So would yarrow, since it's strongest if you carry it. I don't know about larkspur, though. It keeps ghosts away and we don't want to get rid of the ones we've made contact with."

"Why not?" Brenna recalled with a shiver the icy cold she'd suffered while in the company of a ghost.

"Because some of them are trying to help us." A wounded expression darkened Aura Lee's blue eyes. Her voice softened when she added, "Including your grandmother. And dear Cottie."

The heat in her cheeks made Brenna feel like a guilty child. "I'm sorry. I wasn't thinking." She would do anything to keep from hurting her grandmother; no matter she'd been dead for nearly a year.

Aura Lee extended her hand across the table and Brenna clasped her fingers. "I understand. It's hard to keep in mind how different things are here because of our spirit visitors."

Brenna nodded, but the snarl of emotion in her gut whenever she thought of the woman who'd been more to her than a mother put her on the edge of tears. When she felt the touch of a hand on her back, she turned and saw the sympathy in Andrea's eyes.

"Even though I can't make the amulets right this minute," Aura Lee was saying, "I can tell you about the herbs and objects I'll be using. I know how interested you are in the magical traditions I use."

Kerry shot an alarmed glance at Noreen. "I thought we'd read from the journal. It's hard enough to get everyone together, without trying to keep one of us out of the loop."

Aura Lee paused. "Well, it would be a good time since Eve isn't here." She lifted her brows at Rose. "What do you think?"

She was already out of her chair. "It's in the sideboard. I'll get it."

"What about Max and Neal?" Noreen asked. "Where are they?"

"Max is presenting his credentials to a librarian at the university." Kerry took the journal from Rose and flipped through the pages to the scrap of paper she'd used as a bookmark. "They have a rare volume on witchcraft and he wants to check it out." She glanced at Andrea. "What about Neal?"

"Appointment with a plumbing contractor, right, Rose?"

"We want to get the fountain fixed as soon as we can. Those open holes are making both of us twitchy about libel."

"Whereas I feel twitchy about Eve. Why are we keeping her from reading the journal?" Brenna looked from Rose to Noreen.

"We're waiting until we know for sure she's legit," Rose said uncomfortably. She gathered her silver-blonde hair atop her head and stuck a pencil through it to hold it. "We can't afford to let her in on what we've learned until we do."

Noreen intoned sadly, "'*Conspiracy stains the fabric of discourse and no soap but truth can erase it from the weave.*' Prudence Wyatt Bellwether, eighteen-something to eighteen something."

"Thanks," Rose growled.

Noreen pursed her lips. "I know, I know. I signed off on this, too, but I feel as though we're doing something nasty."

"We are." Kerry snatched up her cup. "But I don't see what else we can do, given the circumstances."

"It's a gut feeling I can't shake." Rose said. "The story she told us last night threw me. The longer I thought about it, the more precarious everything felt." She poured cream into her coffee and stirred swirls of white into a mocha color. "What she described is similar to what's happened here and it rattles me to think of her being connected to the haunting before she even arrived. We have to make sure she is who she says she is before we share details about Caldicott's early life."

Brenna shrugged, but her eyes were troubled. "What she told us is bizarre, but not any more so than what I went through. Or what any of us has experienced, for that matter. We're already in deep shit, pardon my French."

Rose sighed deeply. "I know. That's the point. I'm hoping we'll be able to clear things up fast, and work together. I don't think I'd be so worried if she hadn't just shown up. It got my natural paranoia going, and I started thinking about how gullible people can be. Somebody appears and acts as if she knows what she's doing. Is that enough to go on? And then the total darkness in the kitchen…" She drank from her cup. "And you and Max see floating lights and hear voices…all this just hours before Eve gets here. All of it really bothers me."

"That could be sheer coincidence," began Brenna. "We had a freak show here long before Eve showed up."

"Let's table Eve for now and read the journal while we can," Rose pleaded. "We have to find out what's in it."

"Agreed," Noreen said dryly, "but Eve won't stay tabled for long. Trying to keep her isolated while she's in the middle of everything won't be easy."

Rose nodded and passed the journal toward Kerry.

I graduated college at the end of the winter term of 1946. It was a milestone for the whole class, but I envied the open happiness and relief reflected by those in my group. Jane Putnam insisted we celebrate at her digs and as I drank the cheap wine, I couldn't help but think of the past. Would Duncan have been proud of me? I wanted to think he would, but we'd known each other for such a short time, not long enough to talk about what either of us wanted from life, let alone what he thought about women's higher education.

The thought of Mum's pride at my achievement lasted but a short time. It was her wish that I marry, have children. The lengths to which she'd gone to ensure that I improve myself were focused on the ultimate goal of getting a man to marry me.

Jane was the one person to recognize my mixed feelings and she asked me to stay behind as everyone hurried to the next celebration. "Come with me to a meeting tonight," she said. "There are some people I want you to meet."

She'd been after me to attend political gatherings for the last year. This night I didn't want to be alone with my thoughts. After we'd straightened up her apartment, we set off for Greenwich Village.

The meeting was in a small labor hall crowded between a greengrocer's and a tobacco shop. The people at the door looked me up and down, but Jane pulled me in as she greeted several of them. Her assurance was the only ticket we needed, and she led me to the front of the hall, where we found seats.

The speaker was dreadful, his monotone draining every bit of life from the socialist views he apparently believed in deeply. After five minutes of his flat voice, I was ready to leave, but Jane leaned forward in her seat with intensity, clearly caught up in his rhetoric. Bored, I let my gaze wander about the crowd, surprised at how many people had come to hear this man.

My eyes fixed on a balding fellow toward the left side of the hall. He had a small mustache and a pasty white complexion. He looked familiar and I spent several minutes trying to decide if he'd been in one of my classes. Then he turned his head and looked straight at me. My heart caught in my throat as I recognized him and I let my gaze move over him, striving to keep my expression blank. The last time I'd seen him was from Duncan's car when we'd driven through the village on our way to a county dance. The man had been opening the rear passenger door of the earl's limousine, and I'd assumed he was a chauffeur. I'd said nothing to Duncan at the time about seeing his father, not wanting to spoil our short time together.

I sat still as a statue as my mind raced. What was the man doing here? I peeked at him from the corner of my eyes, trying to make certain I'd identified him correctly. If he was the chauffeur from years before, was he still employed by Duncan's father? Had he discovered I'd come to the States? Was I in danger from him?

Eventually I was able to tell Jane I wasn't feeling well and we left. A few days later I arranged an appointment at a salon where I had my hair changed from light brown to auburn and I asked for instruction in altering my features with makeup. Soon after I found a different apartment in uptown and let my connection with Jane fade. She'd begun a new job and it didn't take more than a few months for her to become a part of my past.

"Bathroom break." Brenna scooted back her chair and headed for the one across the hall. "Don't say anything important 'til I get back."

Kerry yawned. "Do we have any brownies?" Her voice was wistful. "I need some sugar and ice water, too."

"I'll go see what I can find." Andrea stood up and stretched her arms over her head. When Aura Lee shifted in her chair, she patted her shoulder. "Sit still. I've got it."

Brenna came back in time to help and they fortified themselves for the next round.

"I knew Caldicott was a strong woman," Rose said as she set the newly full coffee carafe onto the trivet. "She's gone through so many losses so far—her mother, Duncan, and the promise of Duncan as a bridge to a new life. But look at her. She gets her degree, and you can't tell me that wasn't a big deal at the time. She figures out how her enemy might be able to find her and makes countermoves to avoid it. She was a strategist, cool and on the ball."

"It's no wonder she never wanted to talk about any of it." Strudel wandered into the kitchen and Aura Lee reached down to pet her. "Secrecy was necessary, but to me it seems as if she moved only one way and that was forward. She didn't give up or give in; she took one step after another and kept on keeping on. We haven't seen an inch of give in her approach to life."

"You're right about that." Noreen's smile was off-center. "I miss her something awful, and reading about her earlier

days makes me admire her even more than I already did."
She glanced at Kerry, just finishing her brownie. "Do you
want one of us to take up the reading?"

"No, thanks, I'm good." She found her place in the
journal and began to read again.

*I had enough money to last me the rest of my life, but I
couldn't openly access it without drawing attention. If the
old earl was looking for me, I reasoned, his efforts would
be aimed at finding a person who had no visible means of
support, but also who had plenty of money. I had to present
the appearance of a woman who depended upon her own
efforts. David had arranged for most of the bonds to be
placed in two safety deposit boxes, each one at a different
bank. He'd cashed in some of them to create a foundation
that would send me a check each month to cover my
expenses. I was the foundation in that I alone could convert
other bonds into cash to replenish my personal coffers.*

*Whilst I was in school my source of support was no one's
business. Now I must appear to be supporting myself. I
began to look for a job in earnest, not an easy task in 1946.
I'd had the good luck to finish my classes in January,
gaining a small advantage over those graduating in the
spring.*

*My degree was in business, but I found few openings in
established companies. I was a woman and my accent was
a disadvantage. If I had to speculate why, I'd guess at war
weariness amongst the managers I spoke with. I was a
reminder of the war and no one wanted to think about it
after four long years. I found myself seeking out smaller
companies advertising in the classifieds.*

*Most of the places I went were family businesses, and I
became adept at recognizing which positions were laid
with landmines. As was happening in bigger companies,
soldiers were leaving the armed services, yearning for
nothing more than to return to their former places in the
world. Of course, no one could ever find things the same.
Too many things had happened to all of us.*

I was employed at a furniture manufacturing company on the edge of Long Island, and it appeared that all would go well. The owner was a kind man and his wife went out of her way to make me feel welcome. Difficulties arose when their son was demobbed from the army. He was handsome, and intelligent as well. His return cheered his parents tremendously and after a while we were all working well together. His wife was the problem. She'd seen out the war working in a defense plant, and by the time Junior returned, she'd lost her job. Moreover, her husband had changed from the lighthearted chap described to me. Now he was determined to build his life into something that would make his sacrifices, and those of his fellow soldiers, worth what they'd cost. Many returning men felt the same way.

Mrs. Junior wasn't happy with the man who worked twelve-hour days and talked of expanding the business. Soon she was complaining and resentful of me in particular. I was the new person there so I must be responsible for the changes in her life. Loathsome whiner. They let me go to preserve peace in the family. I never found out for certain, but I'll wager the couple divorced before the year was out.

I was fortunate to have money, as I had no luck in finding other work for more than six months. And it was through the job I finally secured that I met Arnie Zdretzer.

When I walked into his small storefront in Brooklyn, I felt as if I'd traveled through time to nineteenth century London. It was a bookstore lined with shelves of books, every kind, large and small, most of them used. The advertisement had been for a clerk, not the kind of job I'd ever looked for, but I was becoming nervous at being out of work so long. When I shut the door behind me the bell attached to it rang so cheerfully that I smiled and glanced back at it.

When I turned around, I saw the old gentleman seated behind the oaken counter, nearly obscured by a large brass cash register festooned with ornamentation. "Good morning." He had a thick accent, Slavic, I thought, and I returned his greeting.

He looked jovial, smiling and harmless with his white hair and unruly beard. But his eyes measured me carefully and one hand was out of sight beneath the counter. He made me feel nervous, and I half-turned to leave.

"You need books?" He made a point of looking around at the full shelves. "I have them, as you see. All subjects."

I shook my head. "I came about the job you advertised."

He stroked his beard and looked me over more thoroughly. I noticed the yarmulke atop his head. "What is your name?"

"Anna Collins."

"You are British?"

I nodded.

"You come here after the war?"

"Just before America got in it." I couldn't tell if my nationality was a plus to him or a sticking point. Something had caught his attention and he was pondering it.

"I have a bachelor's degree in business," I said briskly. "Do you want me give you my work history?"

Again he stared at me in that searching way. "Tell me this," he said after a while.

I waited.

"Tell me who is your favorite author."

I looked at him in surprise. He stroked his beard and I saw his hand was missing the ring finger and pinkie. "Marcia Davenport."

He looked down at the counter, but not before I saw interest spark in his eyes. "Indeed. Her biography of Mozart?"

"The Valley of Decision. And her radio work on Czechoslovakia." I'd followed her work closely during the war. She was one of the few people writing who'd told the truth about what was really happening in Europe.

"I see." He still studied the counter.

I lost patience with him. "I have other things to do today. Do you want me to fill out an application?"

His gaze moved over my face. "I think not."

I was absurdly disappointed.

I turned to go as he added, "Not necessary. You are hired. When can you begin?"

I wheeled around. "Are you quite certain?"

He nodded. "I have determined you are smart and you want to work. These are important things. You want the job?"

I hesitated. Could I trust him? Did he have ulterior motives to hire me?

A small smile curved his lips. "Let us say we have trial period...of one month. At end of that we both decide if we want to continue. Yes?"

What was luck if it was never tested? "Yes."

At first I was merely a glorified clerk, but after a fortnight, Arnie began to instruct me in the inner workings of the shop: the ordering and delivery process, sometimes fiendishly complicated; the filing arrangement, and his odd accounting system. I learned he was known for his ability to obtain rare and hard to find books—in nineteen forty-six no small achievement. Many books had been lost— destroyed—during the war, and many of the people who had owned them had disappeared. Due both to an encyclopedic memory as well as his apparently prolific contacts, I suspected he was as abreast of the state of the book world as anyone living.

It was during my third month there that I began to get clues about the other activities behind the buying and selling of books.

"What a name she picked," Kerry groaned. "Anna Collins? How boring can you get?"

"How forgettable, you mean." Noreen pursed her lips, nodding wisely. "Who would ever remember a name like that?"

Kerry shrugged. "Okay, you've got me there. It's not as though she wanted to draw attention to herself."

Arnie Zdretzer was a widower and he lived above the bookshop, they learned. He'd been in America since the end of the First World War and was, despite the apparent modesty of his shop, a well-to-do man. Many of his clients were formerly wealthy, having escaped from Germany or Italy—or any of the smaller European countries ravaged by the war—with only their lives. As time went on, Anna discovered that some might have also had a few jewels sewn into items of clothing, or bits of gold hidden inside the heels of shoes or tamped into hatbands and hairbrush handles. Books were brought from family libraries, sometimes hidden inside larger books, and manuscripts from churches and synagogues were rolled into narrow tubes and slipped into hollow canes and suitcase handles.

Arnie greeted the people who came to his shop with courtesy and, many times, with the names of those who would help them adjust to life in the United States. More often than not, this category of customer was given dollars in trade for the goods they'd brought and presented.

"You're receiving smuggled goods!" I announced one morning when I arrived at the shop in time to see a throng of people lined up in front of his office. Our trial month had come and gone and I was in charge of much of the bookstore's workings. I'd had nothing to do, however, with Arnie's people business.

He rubbed at tired eyes. "So. You have observed, but do you understand?" As the heat rose in my cheeks he smiled. "Yes, you are right. But you do not see all. I have done this for many years, have been—how do you say it—point of exchange for those who have escaped from hell."

I didn't know what to say to him. The newspapers and newsreels had been full of the pictures from Auschwitz and Buchenwald, Dachau and Treblinka. I doubt the people who'd come to him had been in those places, but it was all too likely they knew people who had been. "I'm not condemning you."

"That is good." His smile wasn't real but he tried. "I am using what I have and what I can get to help the ones who

are left with nothing. The people you saw here are not destitute. Many of their countrymen are." He raised his hands and she wondered again about his missing fingers. "I am doing what I can."

The year passed by and the numbers of people who came to Arnie began to dwindle. "Many are emigrating to Israel," he told me when I asked about it. "But there will always be some who seek me out. There is no homeland for the Romani."

When he said that, I thought of the Gypsy woman who had put a protective spell on the talisman I still possessed. I suddenly realized something very important about Arnie's activities. He helped people start new lives. He could do the same for me. I had valuables and I had a nemesis. Arnie Zdretzer could help me with both.

CHAPTER 6

Eve leaned back in her desk chair and closed her eyes. Had she ever felt so worn out? Had she ever had such strange dreams? And what she'd thought would be her refuge, Wisdom Court, had become a replay of so many situations in her life. Here were numerous women who apparently didn't like her. Ever since middle school she'd had a thing about that.

Danica rubbed against her leg, her squeaky purr filling the silent room. Eve opened her eyes and looked about the office space. This, at least, made her feel a lot better about being here. The sun cut through the window, warming the air surrounding her. Small crystal beads were strung from a dowel hanging in front of the curtain rod and the sunbeams caught the multicolored facets, sending bits of light across the wall behind her. She wondered if her predecessor— what was her name? Elizabeth somebody—had hung the little sun-catchers. The lights scattered over the books she'd unpacked that morning, and she'd taken pleasure in placing each of them with care on the empty shelves. Gazing over her collection she felt the lovely, familiar sense of wealth in having so many books. Still, there were spaces for the animal figurines she'd brought with her. She couldn't work without them.

It was the task of a few minutes to set up her laptop and hook up the printer/scanner. She had her tools, now she'd have to actually work. A blog post was due and she needed to contact several of the websites where her stuff frequently ran. She loaded her browser and soon was answering emails. The most interesting was from her friend in Boston, who'd recently reviewed a book about the human brain and wanted to share a section suggesting a connection between meditation and autoimmune response.

Eve smiled as Danica jumped onto the desk, then up to the printer. She turned around three times and curled up for a nap. Her noisy purr revved like a tiny motor until she fell asleep.

Eve's fingers flew over the keyboard as the sun shifted position and the afternoon shadows lengthened. I'm so tired, she thought, but made no move to refill her coffee cup or to stop for a rest. In the distance a car horn blared, but Eve continued, the soft clicking of the keys the only other sound.

When she awoke, she was reclining against the chair back, her arms hanging at her sides. The room was beginning to dim, the sun having slipped halfway behind the mountain, spreading shadows outside her window. Eve saw the dark screen of the computer and glanced at the printer where Danica had slept. She wasn't there.

Pushing the chair away from the desk, Eve started to stand up, but fell back in her seat as dizziness overtook her. *What's wrong with me?* She let her head move forward to her chest and breathed, trying to anchor herself. Presently she looked up and saw her cat staring at her from the windowsill. "Danica?" she whispered and held out her hand. The cat hunched away from her and turned, clumsily jumping to the floor.

"Kitty-kitty?" She clicked her tongue at the cat, but she bounded into the hall. Eve stood up, a little off-balance. The room felt different, more angular and with sharper colors. There was a sound, a fluttering of some sort.

Hesitating, she took a step, looking from one side to the other to find its source.

As she neared the door, she noticed the lights were out in the living room beyond it. Something slammed to the floor behind her. She spun round, her heart pounding wildly, and saw a thick book lying open on the wood floor. She bent toward it, glancing around to see what had caused it to fall. Picking it up by its spine, she read the title printed in gothic letters across the deep green leather cover: *The Punishment of the Disbeliever*. Under the words was an embossed drawing of a devil pointing a pitchfork at flames shooting from the base of an ancient tree. His mouth contorted in laughter and his tail curled in an elaborate coil.

Eve had never seen the book before. Frozen, she stared at the tawdry illustration, mind skittering over possibilities: the book was already there (but the shelves had been empty when she put her own books away.) Someone had brought in the book while she was working—someone she hadn't heard or seen. This possibility bothered her, but she did tend to zone out while she worked. Or, the book had appeared out of thin air. At that thought, she glanced up the bookshelves and found a space where it could have been, a gap in a row of books lined up like teeth. *Why would someone bring it here while I slept?*

Eve carried the book into the living room and set it on the coffee table, wiping her hands along her slacks. The volume was ugly and made her feel as though she'd touched something dirty. On the thought she strode into the nearby powder room and turned on the hot water. She scrubbed her hands with lemon-scented soap and then re-soaped them. The framed picture of a prairie dog watched her from the dark green wall.

"Creepy, creepy," she muttered as she rinsed, and turned off the faucet. Maybe the book was part of a hazing ritual or something. She thought of the Wisdom Court women she'd met and threw out the idea. They might not care for her, but they weren't likely to pull a stunt like that.

She shook her head in resignation. All she could do for now was try to figure out what was up with her cat and go on with the day. She glanced at the darkening windows. Or evening. A drink would be nice. She turned on the lights as she went through the living room.

From the office she heard the printer go on. The familiar whir of papers continued as her nerves tensed. There was no reason for the printer to be working.

She forced herself to walk back to the room, pausing at the open door. The printer was spitting out page after page. She stepped close enough to pick up one.

The words crawled across each white expanse.

We're coming for you. We're coming for you. We're coming for you. We're coming for you...

"What in the bloody hell?" A memory nibbled at the edge of her mind. Her hand crushed the paper as she began to recall. Last night she'd awakened from a dream. Had she seen the words then? Yes, the words flowing down the screen of her laptop.

Evie. She could hear again the husky voice. Someone had called her Evie. No one but her mother had ever called her that. Except last night someone had.

Had it been the first time? Was someone here pulling pranks on her? Was that what the oddball behavior at breakfast had been about? Were they already judging her, finding her wanting?

A hot mixture of hurt and anger rose in her. Had they given her the onceover last night and decided to fake her out, to frighten her into leaving? The careful courtesy and stiff conversation were so different from the kindness they'd shown at first. She thought they'd accepted her, but beginning with the mean girls in school and extending beyond to women in groups there was a certain standard she'd never been privy to. They wanted her to *fit in*. It had happened more than once. Was it the same thing now at Wisdom Court, too? Was she always going to have to fight for a place at the table?

"Screw them," Eve growled. She'd show them it wouldn't be as easy as they thought. She might be a loner and a crazy writer. Her own mother had called her that. But she wasn't a coward and she wouldn't let a bunch of jerks drive her away.

The doorbell rang several times and then the sound of thumping came from the front door. Everyone except Brenna had come back for cocktails and conversation about their work during the afternoon.

Rose started to get out of her chair but Andrea was on her way out of the living room before she could get to her feet. "I'll go see who it is."

Kerry closed the notebook where she'd been making notes from the day's reading. "Could be Max. He'd wonder about the locked door."

They heard a loud slam and the sound of voices coming closer. "It's Eve," Noreen murmured.

It was an Eve they hadn't seen before.

Flushed and furious, she planted herself in front of the fireplace and drilled Rose with accusing eyes. "I want to know if you are trying to get me to leave Wisdom Court."

Rose's mouth opened in surprise but before she could answer Eve went on. "Too many things have happened since I got here, so if you took one look at me and decided to disinvite me, you've overplayed your hand."

"Wait a minute," Rose said as she stood up. "We have not *disinvited* you. What are you talking about?"

"All the tricks with the sounds and the stupid things written on my computer are what I'm talking about." Eve threw the papers she carried onto the coffee table. "More of the kind of thing that was going on back at home is what I'm talking about."

Kerry picked up one of the pages and scanned the words, looking up in surprise. "Definitely threatening." She let it fall to the table. "I don't blame you for being upset."

"I'm sure." Eve's voice was heavy with sarcasm. "I don't suppose you heard my name being whispered."

Kerry shook her head, eyes wide. "Whispered? Not me."

Eve clenched her fists. "Ever since I arrived—no—ever since I told you about the stuff happening to me at home, you've backed away from me like I have Ebola." She shifted her gaze to Rose. "I wasn't making up stories and I wasn't lying. But I could *feel* you withdrawing. I'm not willing to put up with whatever game you're playing. If you want me to leave, tell me. I'll leave." She turned to go and then whirled back around. "And I know damned well you locked the door to keep me out."

They watched her storm out of the room.

"Eve, wait!" Aura Lee called.

Seconds later came another resounding crash as the door slammed shut.

Eve's tempestuous exit slowed to discouraged plodding.

They had some nerve. Especially Kerry, trying to make her believe she actually sympathized with her. Fat fucking chance of that. She trudged up the associate house steps, mind still struggling to come up with better comebacks to the reactions she'd gotten. *Too late now.*

She halted in front of the main door and fumbled with her key. Damn them, anyway, for spoiling her acceptance at Wisdom Court. She'd been invited! She was as good as any of them.

The key slid into the slot and she pushed her way into the hallway. A few steps took her to the door of her flat and she heaved a sigh as she let herself inside. *I'm so tired of being alone.* Nope, she couldn't afford to wander down that road. She smashed the keys onto the foyer table and marched toward the kitchen. Self-pity couldn't be an option.

"The sun's over the yardarm somewhere," she announced in the empty kitchen. A glance out the window showed the outside lights had been lit—the somewhere was here. "Well all right, then." She grabbed a tumbler from the nearest cupboard and reached for a bottle among the several standing behind an empty ice bucket in a corner of the counter. Brandy. *Hmmm. It tasted pretty good last night*. The cork slipped out with a satisfying *pop* and the liquid gurgled into the glass.

She sniffed the heavy scent and raised the glass in a toast to the old farmhouse across the courtyard. "Here's to the off chance of my being able to stay here." Her hefty swallow sent fire down her chest and into her belly. Coughing, eyes watering, she set down the glass and grabbed one of the barstools tucked under the island. Leaning against the polished wood surface, she waited for the effect to fade, a slow grin spreading across her face. *I could get myself into so much trouble with this stuff.*

Eve heard a scratching sound and swung toward it. Danica was in the office across from the kitchen and appeared to be readying herself to climb up the archway molding, digging her claws into the wood and stretching her body into the shape of a furry ski jump. She pulled her paws toward her again, leaving long scratches in the wood grain.

"Shit, what're you doing?" Eve pushed off the stool and lurched across the polished floor and into the room, heading toward the cat. "That bunch across the way already wants to boot us out of here. Now they'll make me replace the molding before they do." She snapped her fingers. "Danica, Dani, stop it!"

With supreme disregard, Danica dug in her claws again and pulled them toward her, leaving more deep grooves in the wood. Eve bent to grab the cat, her fingertips brushing along the furry back. She heard a heavy metallic click and the floor disappeared from beneath her feet.

She fell, her good knee striking something hard, and she yelled at the spearing pain. The back of her head scraped an edge as she dropped. No time to think. She hit stomach down on a hard surface. Everything went black.

The throbbing in both knees woke her up. Eve lay still as consciousness returned, mind trying to put together pieces. She had to get up; it was time to work. Eve licked her lips and tasted brandy. Had she passed out? She turned her head from side to side to deny it and felt the stab of pain from her scalp. "Oh, God." When she opened her eyes she froze.

It was utterly dark. She squeezed her eyes shut and counted to ten. Reopened them. The absence of light was complete. She could see nothing.

For a split second her mind reached for an explanation, but panic flared like wildfire and she cried out. No light, no shadows. No hope. From childhood it was her worst nightmare. Yesterday in the kitchen she'd gotten through the dark because of the people with her. But today, here— where was she? Her breath stuck in her throat as she remembered her cell phone. Madly she patted at the pockets in her slacks. Both were flat.

"Help me." Her voice was small, timid. "Help me!" Louder now. A full scream erupted from her throat, shocking her, but she couldn't stop it.

"Help me, oh God, please help me."

Her voice was swallowed in the close, dank air. Her sobbing intensified, building between hitching breaths, the sound of it hurting her ears, spurring on her horror. *I'mblindI'm blindI'mblindI'mblind—*

Evie?

She caught her breath on a sob.

Evie?

"Who's there?" Her voice cracked. "Is someone here?"

She couldn't hear an answer. Waiting in an agony of fear and hope, she moved her hands at her sides, patting the surface where she lay. Her fingers recoiled from the damp, gritty feel of it. *Where am I?*

Eve pushed both hands against the ground and forced herself into a sitting position. Something grazed her cheek and she brushed instinctively at her face, fingers tangling in gauzy strands. *Spider webs?* She whimpered at the stickiness on her skin. She could be surrounded by webs and not know it. One hand twitched with an impulse to flail at whatever hung around her, but she fought to control it. The idea of bringing down swaths of web onto herself made her want to start screaming again.

Eve forced herself to breathe. Her sister had nagged her over the phone, wanting to help her deal with her broken leg. "Yoga's the thing, it'll calm you down, and it'll help you concentrate. You just breathe."

Yeah, that's what I need. I'll just breathe and the webs will go away and the lights will blink on. Everything will work out fine.

The air was musty and smelled of dead vegetation. Her breaths were coming faster. Hysteria bubbled along her nerves. Eve took a choppy breath and let it out, did it again. She was going to lose it and when she was found—*if* she were found—she'd be raving. Somehow she had to hang on.

That's my girl. She couldn't hear the voice; she could *feel* it, inside her.

"Who's there? Where are you?" She slapped both hands against the ground. "Dammit, answer me!"

After a long moment she got a response.

You can call me Charlie.

A laugh burst from Eve's throat and another crowded after. The next was a cough and soon she was heaving short, sharp sounds that made her even more frightened.

She could feel bile rising in her throat and knew she'd be vomiting any second.

Evie, stop it. Take hold, girl. You must stop.

The edge of desperation in the voice brought her up short. She grasped every shred of self-control she could muster and wrestled with the need to scream. If she could do nothing else at this moment, she could control her response to where she found herself. The silent battle went on for a long time.

As her breathing steadied and her heart rate slowed, she let her head sag, felt her spine relax. The storm had passed.

"I did it, Charlie." She tried to ignore the rasp of her voice. "Why don't you get me out of here?"

As she waited for a response, her muscles began to tighten.

"Dammit, you can't *not* be there. I need you. I need your help," she added thickly.

I'm trying, dear heart. Are you able to be very still? I'm trying to get through, but it means you're waiting a bit.

"I don't understand—"

And I can't explain right now. Please, work with me. Stay calm and try not to broadcast your feelings. I'm having a bit of bother with trying to get a message through.

Eve felt a tear move down her cheek. "All right. I'll try."

You're amazing.

Eve could feel he was no longer with her.

TIME OUT OF TIME

———◆———

Severn waited until the kitchen maid shut the back door behind her. He'd hung in limbo while the house settled, until the staff wandered off to their own pathetic lives. His brain bubbled with resentment that they could impede him.

He gave another five minutes to allow for stragglers. At last he sidled out the library door and made his way to the stairs to the ground floor. If anyone appeared, he was getting a glass of milk to settle his stomach. The strain of measuring every action, of filtering every comment, was beginning to wear at him. He was surrounded by parasites.

"Sir?"

Severn nearly slipped on the stone step. Using every ounce of control, he turned slowly to the man behind him. "Yes, Simms, what is it? I thought you'd retired."

The butler was as immaculate as he'd been at seven that morning. He bowed. "It pains me to admit I was remiss in getting a message to you, sir. Reynolds was responsible for it, but he has not been seen today."

"Reynolds?" Severn bit back a smile at the memory of the noise his body had made when he'd tipped it into the marshland near the upper fields.

"The under butler, sir. When I discovered the envelope, I felt it incumbent upon me to give it to you as soon as possible."

Severn ground his teeth. The man never said anything simply when a soliloquy could be made. "You're most conscientious, Simms." He took the envelope from him. "Now you must get some rest. It's been a long day for you."

Simms nodded, unsmiling. "No longer than most, sir. Goodnight."

"Goodnight." Severn waited until he could no longer hear the man's footsteps and went swiftly to the door hidden at the back of the huge fireplace. Modern appliances had taken the place of kitchen hearth tools. Handy for him.

He pulled on the wrought iron lever beside the left bracket supporting the spit. With a muffled rumble, the stone door opened and Severn eased his way into the passage. He pushed the switch on the wall and waited as the heavy door closed. He slipped the torch out of his coat pocket and shone its light along the rough stone of the floor and then down the carved stone steps. In a matter of moments, he was outside the locked entrance to the grotto below the house. He listened for any foreign sounds, but only the faint drip of water from the caves further down the tunnel could be heard.

The key slid into the lock easily and the large metal door swung inward, triggering the automatic lights. Severn entered and pushed the door shut, relocking it.

"Finally." This was his true home, not the pile of bricks and possessions stacked above it. He went to the big fireplace across the room and flicked the switch to turn on the flames.

He poured himself a large whiskey and lifted it toward the ceiling. *To Reynolds.* He seated himself in the leather chair hearing the crackle of paper and reaching for the letter Simms had given him. *Pompous prick.* He tore open the envelope and pulled out the one sheet of paper. He read the message scrawled across it, read it again.

A transmission to the woman has been intercepted, source unknown. Await orders.

"Goddamn it." He gulped his whiskey and got out of the chair. There would be hell to pay for this and he would see to it personally.

He crumpled the letter and pitched it toward the fire. As the flames spread across the paper, the words curled and were consumed.

CHAPTER 7

The air nipped at Kerry's exposed skin despite the morning sun, a giant disc in the bright blue October sky. Water from the fountain still oozed into gaps in the courtyard bricks, reflecting the light into her eyes. She swore as she tripped over the rough surface, keeping as far away as she could from the holes above the collapsed tunnel. Neal was supposed to be fixing this.

Her ankle turned on a broken brick and she struggled to keep her balance. The backpack she carried slipped out of her hand, landing in one of the puddles and splashing the hems of her jeans. "Damn."

"Watch your step, or you'll end up part of the brickwork." Brenna took a big step over a larger area of water. She pulled her hoodie more closely to her and stuck her hands in her pockets. "As short as her legs are, I wonder how Noreen manages this."

"Good question." Kerry trudged behind her toward the back door of the old farmhouse. The grass was tipped with frost, and some of the yellow and rusty mums were rough around the edges. "I sure hope it doesn't snow anytime soon."

"You and me both. I haven't had a chance to get any warmer clothes." Brenna led the way up the steps to the back door and grabbed the knob, pulling it open. Warm air scented with spiced pumpkin poured out like a benediction. "That smells so good."

Kerry nudged her forward. "Go on in to the kitchen. Now I'm starving."

"You're letting the heat out," called Rose.

Kerry pulled the door shut behind her and glanced at the earlier arrivals. Noreen was sipping from a steaming cup, pulling back her elbows to allow Aura Lee to slip a plate in front of her. Another went to Andrea, snug in her brown turtleneck and jeans. She reached for a muffin from the almost overflowing basket in the center of the table.

Noreen grabbed her own muffin and neatly pulled the butter dish out of Andrea's reach.

"Hey! No fair." Andrea pulled a hank of hair out of her coffee cup and waited while Noreen slathered her muffin.

"*All's fair when the sun shines as long as the enemy is otherwise engaged,*" Noreen quoted indistinctly, having stuffed a chunk of the pastry into her mouth halfway through.

Kerry laughed and slid into a chair. "Who the heck came up with that one?" She poured coffee for herself and leaned against the table to reach the muffins.

"Sybil Maris Mayhew, eighteen forty-four to nineteen thirteen." Noreen chewed with great enjoyment. "She was a school teacher for much of her life and wrote a memoir about her Civil War adventures."

"Sounds more cheerful than some of your others." Brenna drizzled honey onto her muffin, waiting until the stream of gold came to a stop. She let the last drop fall on her finger and licked it off.

"She ended up marrying a dashing lieutenant in one of the Pennsylvania groups. He survived the war and they had seven children. A happy ending, I think."

Rose slipped into her chair and reached for her cup. To Kerry she looked a little smoother today, as if she might have actually slept through the night.

Rose's smile died when her glance came to the empty chair. "No sign of Eve, I take it."

Kerry shook her head. "Her curtains are open but I didn't see any activity."

Brenna poured more coffee into her cup. "How are we going to clean up what happened yesterday?" She glanced at Noreen. "Or are we going to let her leave? It would solve the problem of possibly having an enemy spy here."

Noreen pursed her mouth as she considered the issue. "It would be an easy way to remove her until we can be sure she's legitimate."

"You sound like a hit man, sort of." Andrea picked up another muffin and bit into it absent-mindedly. "Doesn't feel right." Her sidelong glance at Aura Lee took in the other woman's distress. "Feels like we ought to talk to Eve and tell her what's going on."

Rose stood up and headed toward the door.

Andrea raised her brows at Brenna, who grimaced and shook her head. "Where are you going?"

Rose glanced back over her shoulder. "I'm going to call Margery, the Board secretary. I can't stand sitting around waiting for shoes to drop. The info I asked about Eve," she explained in irritation at their blank faces. "Surely by now she's had enough time to look into Eve's nomination and acceptance. Along with her entire history."

Aura Lee frowned into the space in front of her. "I wonder what Eve meant about someone whispering her name. That sounded so strange."

"No stranger than you seeing a hand reach through your perfume tray." Noreen ruffled her hair in distraction. "From what she told us yesterday, Eve's been under attack for a while. She must have been hoping for a break now that she's here."

"No such luck," Andrea muttered. "When I began sketching ghost images after I first came here, the support I got from everyone was what kept me from going nuts. Even you, Kerry, and you were still little Miss Skeptical at the time." She rolled her eyes when Kerry stuck out her tongue. "We all leaned on each other and it helped us figure out what was going on. I can't help but think we're working against ourselves if we don't have the same solidarity with Eve."

Aura Lee nodded. "You're right. Just because she came here before she was supposed to doesn't mean she's involved in a plot against us."

Rose trailed back into the kitchen in time to hear her. Her shoulders drooped and her eyes were shadowed with frustration. "Margery's in a meeting for the next couple of hours. Damn," she groused as she dropped into her chair. "I want to get this taken care of. I hate feeling guilty." She glanced around the table. "I suggest we work separately until Margery calls me back."

Andrea glanced down at her hands. "I assume you mean the Wisdom Court investigation."

"Right." Kerry's voice was dry. "Sure. Who'd want to pass that up?"

Rose shrugged. "Except for Eve's arrival, things haven't changed much. We still need to look for accounts of earlier hauntings in the files of former associates."

"And don't forget finding possible explanations for the hauntings *we've* experienced." Aura Lee continued to turn the turquoise ring on her forefinger. "I'd still like to know why that hand reached through my perfume tray. It's such a random thing to do."

Brenna sighed. "Somebody hunting for new nail polish?"

"Didn't have the right shade inside the tray," Kerry snickered. "Couldn't get a ride to the mall."

A giggle burst from Andrea and she slapped a hand over her mouth.

Noreen groaned. "*Frivolity rarely masks fear, but rather heightens it to the point of discomfort.* Agnes Corning Poindexter, eighteen twenty-seven to eighteen eighty-three."

"Really?" Kerry rolled her eyes. "That has to be a ringer. No way did anyone ever say that. Especially a Poindexter."

Noreen's smile was smug. "*Au contraire*. She lived near Philadelphia and ended up marrying a traveling minister who undoubtedly buried her in children and admonitions."

Kerry pushed away from the table. "I give up. Max is due back in a bit. I'll find out if his witch book has anything interesting in it. I'm out of here." She headed for the back door, Brenna close behind her.

"I've got things to do, too," Brenna said. "See you later." Cool air rushed into the kitchen as the two left.

"Was it something I said?" Noreen asked, the innocence in her voice undercut by the mischief in her eyes.

Andrea picked up cups and saucers and carried them to the sink. "Do you need anything from the little store?" she asked Aura Lee. "I'm going to walk down that way."

"No thanks, dear. You have a nice walk." Aura Lee waited until the door shut behind Andrea and turned to Rose and Noreen. "I have to tell you something I don't want the others to know yet."

Rose registered the trouble in her voice and frowned. "What is it?"

"It's about a dream I had last night." Aura Lee caught the glance exchanged between Rose and Noreen. "Listen to what it was before you start judging."

"Sorry." Rose dropped back into her chair. "What kind of dream?"

"It was short, thank the Goddess." Aura Lee took a deep breath and said quickly, "We were all together here at Wisdom Court, but we'd been fighting. Someone was crying—I couldn't tell who it was—and then we were running away." She paused and her hands trembled. "I knew we were trying to escape someone—or something—terribly dangerous. A sudden explosion knocked us all to the ground and smoke was everywhere. And then..."

When she didn't continue, Noreen touched her arm. "What?"

Aura Lee wiped at tears filling from her eyes. "I heard someone say, *Oh, God, she's dead.*" She choked, "That's when I woke up." She looked from one to the other in fear. "What if it was one of us?"

The hours crawled. Kerry had undertaken global searches of Wisdom Court alumnae and was both surprised and disheartened at how lackluster many were. While a good number of former associates had used their experiences at the institute as springboards to rewarding careers, she continued to stumble across names sunken in obscurity. Or bizarre lives, she thought with a shudder. Like the woman who'd given up a fellowship in botany for her own five-acre botanical garden in Central America. The photo of her smiling from a chunk of rain forest, tattered hat and vines curling around her shoulders, depressed her. "Maybe it's the crazy in her eyes," Kerry muttered as she finished her notes and moved on.

When the landline buzzed, she pounced on the receiver. "Tell me something good."

"Were you sitting on the phone?" Andrea exclaimed.

"I'm bored out of my tiny mind." Kerry waited a nanosecond. "So, come on, why did you call?"

"Rose heard from the board secretary. All is clear on the western front."

"Huh?"

Andrea sighed. "Eve has been cleared of nefarious intentions."

Kerry looked at the pile of notes she'd made about earlier associates. "She may be the only one that's ever happened with."

"What do you mean?"

"Tell you later. What's the plan?"

"We're supposed to meet outside Eve's place. We're going to talk to her and make nice."

"What time?"

"How's now grab you?"

Kerry was already turning off her computer. "Suits me. See you in a bit."

Within ten minutes most of the Wisdom Court women had crossed the courtyard to gather outside the west associate house. The sun was hovering above the Flatirons and the late afternoon air was chilly.

Andrea's jean jacket was obviously too light since she clutched her arms in an effort to stay warm. Her chestnut hair swirled around her face in the rising breeze and she grabbed at it to keep it out of her eyes. Her hands were speckled with paint.

Brenna pulled her hoodie over her flyaway black hair. "Are we waiting for Rose?"

Noreen glanced beyond them. "Here she comes. Aura Lee, too."

"That's all of us." Kerry rubbed her hands together. "Let's get this show on the road."

Rose approached ahead of Aura Lee, hearing Kerry's last remark. "That's my intention." She waved them up the steps to the house. "After you." She pulled a key out of her pocket and opened the outside door. "I'm not looking forward to this."

Andrea patted her shoulder. "You had to check her out. Nobody has a quarrel with that. It's your job."

Kerry held the door for Brenna and Aura Lee and slipped in behind Noreen. "Here's hoping Eve will see it that way."

Noreen rapped on the door and they waited. She knocked again but nothing happened. "Well." Rose turned to Aura Lee. "Did Eve say anything about going out?" She turned her head to the door. "Did you hear that?"

"What?" Kerry took a step closer.

"Meowing. It must be her cat." The sound came again, this time more loudly.

"Danica." Noreen made a face at the surprised look from Brenna. "It's her cat's name. Danica."

As if she could hear her name, the cat meowed again and then began yowling.

"Wow." Kerry bent toward the door. "Kitty-kitty?"

The wail was repeated, and a soft thud against the door was followed by another plaintive cry.

"You think something's wrong?" Kerry used the side of her fist to hammer on the door. "Eve! We need to talk to you."

The following silence was oppressive.

Rose sorted through the keys, pulling out one and sliding it into the lock. At the click of the latch the door swung open. Eve's cat was at their feet, and it was clear she was trying to communicate with them. She rubbed frantically against Noreen's slacks, purring loudly. Brenna knelt and smoothed the cat's black coat until the creature slowed down.

"Poor kitty," Brenna said softly, stroking the cat all the while. "Poor little kitty."

Kerry slowly moved past them into the living room. "Eve," she called quietly. "Are you here?"

There was no answer.

"I'm going to check upstairs." Andrea ran up the steps and returned in a couple of minutes. "Nobody's up there."

Together the women searched the rest of the apartment.

"Will you look at this?" Aura Lee was standing beside the archway molding to the office. "Big gashes in the woodwork."

"How strange." Rose rubbed her fingers over the scars. "Could the cat have done this?"

"I suppose." Aura Lee cast a dubious look at Danica. "She has long claws."

"I have a friend whose cat sharpened his claws on wood." Brenna glanced down at Danica, calmly licking her paws. "She found him another home after he ripped the hell out of her antique rosewood desk."

"That would tend to kill the joy." Kerry knelt on the floor beside the molding. "I can't believe Danica's had enough time to do this much damage." She scratched at the wood with one fingernail. "Huh. This stuff is softer than pine. Maybe she has been responsible for all the damage."

"It's only in this one spot." Aura Lee surveyed the rest of the woodwork. "I wonder what possessed her to scratch here."

Kerry stood up just as the door to the apartment swung open.

"Kerry, are you here?" called Max.

"In the study."

As he approached, her eyes widened at the grim expression on his face. "What's wrong?"

He pulled her into his arms and held her to him for a moment. "I need you to come with me. All of you," he added over her shoulder.

Rose drew closer. "What is it?"

Max took Kerry's hand and started tugging her toward the living room. "I'll tell you as soon as we're out of here. Something's wrong in this place. I got a message about it."

"A message?" Noreen eyed him keenly. "What kind of a message."

Before he could answer, Aura Lee shouldered Noreen aside. "Was it from the Other Side? Did Cottie get in touch with you?"

Max's face softened at her eagerness. "Let's go to the main house and I'll tell you about it."

At the sound of scratching, they turned and saw that Danica was once again sharpening her claws. She meowed loudly as she moved her paws over the molding. She dropped to all fours and scrabbled at the baseboard.

"What's all this?" Max asked. He bent to stroke the cat's fur.

"She was yowling when we got here." Rose looked around the room in frustration. "It's as if she's trying to tell us something."

Brenna exchanged a wry glance with Kerry. "Timmy's fallen into the well again!"

"Oh, stop it." Aura Lee shivered dramatically. "Something's going on in here. We just can't see what it is."

"Which is why we need to leave now." Max herded them out of the office. "I'll tell you what I know and we'll try to figure out what to do."

When they got to the door, Andrea looked behind them. "What about the cat? Should we leave her here?"

Noreen frowned. "Perhaps not. I'll go get her." She called for Danica as she walked back to the study.

Aura Lee shivered. "Do you smell ozone?"

Rose sniffed the air. "The faintest bit."

"I don't smell anything." Kerry raised her brows at Max. "You?"

He shook his head, frowning. "I want to leave. Why is Noreen taking so long?"

"Here she comes."

Noreen wasn't carrying a cat as she came toward them.

"Where's Danica?" Brenna asked, frowning in concern. "You look like you've seen a…"

"Ghost? No." Noreen kept walking, leading them out of apartment. "I didn't see the cat, either. I hunted around a bit but she was nowhere to be seen."

Their footsteps echoed in the hallway. Max pushed open the door and held it for them as they filed out onto the steps. "You appear to be upset."

Noreen nodded. "I checked the bathroom near the office and went back to look under the desk again. On the floor was a thumping thick book with a devil on the cover. *The Punishment of the Disbeliever* it was called. It frightened me."

Kerry looked puzzled. "Just a book?"

Noreen smiled sourly. "Just a book that hadn't been there two minutes before. Just a book I didn't hear fall from a shelf." She marched steadily toward the main house. "I hope that little cat is all right because something else is in that house with her."

"But where is Eve?"

Noreen shook her head, still walking to the door. "I don't know, but I don't want to stay there while we try to find out."

CHAPTER 8

The small scraping sound awoke Eve and her eyes popped open. The dark pushed against her like a sentient being only waiting for her to return to awareness. The smell of dirt and musty leaves was familiar now, as was the thick silence. Her stomach growled and she fought against knowing how hungry she was. But hunger couldn't compare with her thirst.

"Charlie?" she whispered.

Nothing answered.

How long was it since he'd been there with her? She had no way of knowing. She didn't want to think about the other question in the back of her mind: did Charlie even exist?

Eve moved her hands over the ground on either side of her, feeling clods of earth and pebbles rolling against her skin. She sat up, recoiling immediately at the brush of strands against her cheeks. Oh, God, the spider webs.

With reluctance she waved one hand over her head, grimacing at more contact with whatever was hanging over her. How big an enclosure was this place? How would she ever find her way out?

Eve pushed herself to her feet, biting back a groan at the pain in her knees and shoulders. But it was bruising pain, not the agony she'd felt when her leg had broken. Maybe, by some miracle, she wouldn't have to use a boot again, or a cast.

She tried to ignore what now felt like sheets of cobwebs touching her everywhere. The prickly feeling against the back of her neck made her think of crawling legs. In an instant her imagination supplied huge spiders hanging from the ceiling—was there a ceiling? "No spiders, no spiders," she muttered. "There can't be any spiders."

The scraping sounded again. Eve turned toward it. "Hello?" She took a clumsy step. "Is someone here?"

In the next instant her heart jumped. She was looking into two glowing eyes. As she watched, they blinked and then slowly moved closer to her.

She put one foot behind her, then the other, praying she wouldn't trip on a rock. The eyes blinked again and continued toward her.

Her breath came faster and her heart thundered in her ears. She reached from side to side with her hands, touching nothing but webs. "Charlie," she whimpered, taking another step back. "Charlie, Charlie, Charlie!" Her scream filled the space, filled the world, tearing from her throat.

Her foot came down on something and her ankle turned. She felt herself starting to fall. "No!" She would be at the mercy of whatever was stalking her.

She landed hard.

"Max, we're wasting time. We've got to find Eve." Rose was pale and kept worrying the nail on one thumb, peering out the kitchen window every few minutes to see if Eve was coming across the courtyard. They'd gravitated to the kitchen, Andrea and Noreen sitting at one side of the table, Brenna and Aura Lee at the other. Max and Kerry sat beside each other at one end, but as the minutes crawled by, the gap between them widened. Max had convinced them to return to the main house to await further information. In the last largely silent half-hour he'd reverted to the stiff stranger he'd been upon first arrival at Wisdom Court.

"What was the message you received about Eve's apartment?" Rose asked again. "Where did it come from?"

"I don't feel I can rightfully tell you where the message came from."

Kerry slapped one hand on the kitchen table. "That's bullshit. We've looked all over for Eve. You charged over to her place to get us out because of some undefined danger, from some unidentified source, but what about her? What are we supposed to do? If you know something, you have to tell us."

Max ran his hand through his hair. "It's one of the Society's most guarded studies. We're sworn to secrecy on this, Kerry. I'm sorry."

She visibly bit back her impatience and reached for his hand. "Can you tell us anything? Is someone at your Paranormal Society aware of what's happened to Eve? Trying to help her?"

He searched her face, cupping her cheek. "It's been over an hour since I received the message, and there hasn't been another. I can assure you that we don't leave people in harm's way. If there's anything to be done, my…associate is doing it. That's all I can tell you right now."

Aura Lee stood up and came around the table to where Max and Kerry sat. "We've been working together for weeks against whatever is attacking Wisdom Court. You're one of us." Her voice roughened and she paused to regain control. "Your loyalties are divided between us and your colleagues at the Society, aren't they?"

Max nodded, guilt darkening his eyes.

She patted his shoulder. "You have to help us, Max. The Goddess only knows what's happening to Eve right now. If you can't side with us on this, I don't know what we'll do."

"Aura Lee—" Kerry sighed heavily. She let go of Max's hand and got to her feet, brushing impatiently at her eyes.

Max observed the gesture with dismay and stood up, too, stepping toward her. "Kerry, I can't just—"

She shook her head. "You have to." When he moved closer she held up her hand to stop him. "No, Aura Lee is right. You have to choose."

Max caught her hand and pulled her into his arms. "I choose you, luv, every time." He held her to him and looked at Aura Lee over her head. "A colleague has been in contact with Eve."

"In touch with her! Is she all right?" Rose asked quickly.

"What do you mean, in contact?" Andrea frowned at him, eyes narrowed in suspicion. "How can that be?"

Max nudged Kerry into her chair and put his arm around her shoulders as he sat beside her.

The teakettle whistled and Brenna hopped up to turn off the burner, bringing the kettle to the table and setting it on the pumpkin-shaped trivet. She fixed Max with a cold look. "How has your colleague been in touch with Eve?"

"It's complicated," Max began, but was stopped at a fierce outburst from Noreen.

"Codswollop!" she snapped. "Hurry up and tell us."

Brenna and Kerry exchanged an impressed glance.

"Go, Noreen," murmured Andrea. Noreen cast impatient eyes at her and her smile died.

"As I started to say," Max continued in a steely voice, "there's a certain amount of explanation required in order to answer your questions. First, do I have the promise from each of you that what you learn here will not be repeated to anyone?"

"Who the hell would we tell?" Brenna asked in surprise.

"Very well." Max took a breath and let it out. "It has to do with remote viewing. Have any of you heard of it?"

The room was silent. Rose frowned and ventured, "Wasn't that a thing during the cold war? Something about using ESP to spy on the Russians? Or they on us?"

Max nodded. "That's roughly it. It's been a subject of controversy for decades. The NATO governments researched the theory, but the Russians were far ahead of us in testing the practice."

"Expand a bit," Andrea leaned her chin onto one hand, interested. "How did it work? Would you hand me the tea stuff?" she asked in an aside to Rose.

"May I have some as well?" Max looked back at Andrea. "The notion was to identify certain individuals with the extra sensory perception, or ESP, to be able to view places far away from them. They'd focus on geographical coordinates and draw or describe what they saw whilst focusing their energies. From what I've read, they'd aim for a trance state for the duration of their viewing efforts."

Brenna reached for a muffin and began to strip off the paper liner. "Did it work?"

Max took the cup Rose offered. "Thanks. The arguments over the efficacy of the procedure are many. Some evidence indicated impressive achievements and some did not. The United States government funded several research projects, so clearly there were enough elements to arouse interest. The funding was discontinued in the nineteen eighties."

"This is all very interesting," Noreen interjected, "but what has it to do with our current situation?"

Max's lips tightened. "I'm getting there." He reached for the milk pitcher and splashed a bit into his cup. "Since psi or psychic ability frequently arises in regard to paranormal research, we at the Society have tried some experiments of our own, and my colleague—you can call him Charlie— has proven particularly adept at the procedure."

He took a drink of tea. "At my behest, Charlie began surveillance on Wisdom Court earlier this year. Via remote viewing, I mean." His eyes met Rose's gaze. "It was after my car accident, when I was in hospital. I'd corresponded with Ms. Wyntham and was concerned at the delay in helping her."

"Behest." Kerry grinned at him. "You are so cute."

Max's ears turned red, and Aura Lee took pity on him. "Kerry, stop it."

His rare smile flashed. "I'm happy to be appreciated."

At Noreen's throat-clearing cough, he continued.

"Charlie began to search for signals, ESP, dream messages, and the like. I'd sent him photos of Wisdom Court and the location information he needed to anchor him. What he discovered early into the process were several strong energy sources. Entities were here and Charlie was able to tap into them. Moreover, one of them was Caldicott Wyntham herself."

"What?" Rose stared at him, thunderstruck, and the others were equally taken aback. "This was when she was still living?"

Max nodded.

"Cottie was an adept?" Aura Lee murmured. Her fingers tightened around her teacup and Kerry noticed the trembling her hands.

Max eyed her with sympathy. "There's no way of knowing how aware she was of her own power. Charlie said her psi scores were among the highest he's seen. But in my earlier telephone conversations with her, she was dismissive about such things. She told me she wanted me to disprove what she termed her 'fits and starts' about ghosts and other such emanations."

"She didn't believe in what she saw?" Aura Lee sounded so woebegone that Kerry jumped to her feet and hurried around the table to her. She wrapped her arms around the older woman and hugged her.

"I can't believe she denied everything." Kerry rested her cheek against Aura Lee's hair. "She just didn't have the energy to face everything head-on. You better than most remember how frail she was. She probably wanted Max to come, to bring an outsider's point of view." Kerry patted the older woman on her shoulder. "She respected your abilities, I saw that she did. It drove me crazy because I was convinced you were either pretending to tune into all the otherworldly mumbo-jumbo, or you had several screws loose."

Aura Lee had stiffened with indignation as Kerry continued. "Now you listen to me, young lady," she stated firmly.

Kerry glanced at Andrea and winked.

"Wisdom Court has been crawling with spirits as long as I've been here," Aura Lee continued. "Even you have come to see that."

Rose pushed her chair back impatiently, the abrupt motion causing tea to spill over the rim of her cup. "Stop arguing. Get to the part about Eve!"

"Eve is still here at Wisdom Court," Max said in a rush. "Charlie feels her energy quite clearly. He just doesn't know her exact location."

"Where is Charlie, anyway?" Brenna's voice was testy.

"Outside London." Max nodded as her jaw dropped. "It can be difficult to precisely pinpoint sites from the distances we have in this situation."

"There are so many places she could be." Rose's frustration was edged with fear. "We have to look for her again."

"Agreed." Max drained the rest of the tea from his cup. "I believe the best thing to do would be to return to Eve's apartment and look again."

"But you said it was dangerous there." Noreen was losing patience fast. "Do you mean we should have been at the associate house all along, looking for her?"

Max sighed. "Charlie alerted me because he felt a threat when you were all in Eve's rooms. He has a high rate of accuracy, and I didn't dare ignore his warnings. He hasn't been in contact for the last hour or so, and I'm certain he'd want us to check Eve's place again."

Andrea was staring at him with narrowed eyes. "Wait a minute. How exactly is this Charlie contacting you?"

Max looked down at his hands.

"I haven't heard any cell phones ringing." Rose assessed him thoughtfully. "How do you stay in touch with each other?"

"Well," Max said slowly.

Aura Lee let out a whoop. "You're receiving his mental messages, aren't you?" She turned a bedazzled face toward Rose. "They're reading each other's minds!"

"Is that true?" Andrea asked in a whisper.

"I suppose you could put it that way." Max smiled thinly. "It's more a shifting of information back and forth." He caught sight of Kerry's open mouth. "It's hard to describe."

Andrea looked around the table. "Am I the only one who's freaked out by this?" She glanced back at Max. "What if you're both wrong?"

"We haven't been so far."

"We are talking about some strange shit here." Brenna shook her head helplessly. "Just when you think we've seen it all at this crazy place, here comes another bombshell."

Rose stood up and shoved her chair back into place. "Our options are limited. I say we go back to Eve's place and see what we can find. It can't do any harm."

"You hope." Noreen shrugged at their surprised faces. "It seems to me that harm has been a big part of what's happening these days at Wisdom Court."

Rose walked past the coat hooks on her way to the back door, snatching a hoodie and swinging it around her shoulders. "I'm going. Come with me if you want."

"Lights, camera, action," Brenna said in a cheerful voice. "Let's go, then."

Kerry followed behind, pausing only to pull Max out of his chair. He bent to brush a kiss on her cheek.

"Do you know any protective spells for us to use?" Aura Lee asked Max as he held the door for her.

"Surely that's your department." He pulled the door shut behind him and started down the stairs to the shadowed courtyard.

"I'm chanting for all I'm worth," she assured him. "On the inside, just like you and Charlie."

CHAPTER 9

The rasp of heavy footsteps snapped Eve back to attention. Though she couldn't see anything, the image filling her mind was a huge, misshapen monster with glowing eyes. She realized she was shaking, a fine, steady trembling beyond her control. It made her angry. What are you going to do? she demanded of herself. Just lie here and let it eat you?

No. She opened her eyes and rolled to her stomach as quickly as she could, dimly aware of a sharp pain in her thigh. As she braced her hands at her sides, her mind served up one lurid picture after another, of pointed teeth dripping saliva, of thick claws aiming toward her throat. Of her blood flowing from a fresh, hideous wound.

No, she thought again. Forcing her torso up with locked arms she turned her head back and forth, seeking her enemy. There. The blazing eyes were moving from side to side, searching for her just as she sought it.

Make yourself bigger, she thought, mind flashing on advice she'd read about confronting bears. Make noise. She pushed to her feet, growling, stunned at the fierce, rough sound coming from her throat. "Get away from me," she rasped in her meanest voice. "Get the fuck out of here. You don't belong here!" She was shouting now. "Get back to hell where you belong!"

That's brilliant! Charlie's voice was inside her. *Don't stop! Yell at it! Make it go away.*

Eve took a wobbly step forward, gaze locked with the unblinking eyes burning in front of her. She could get lost in those eyes. Those eyes could kill her. Stop it. "Get out, get out, get out!" she shrieked at the top of her lungs. "Leave me alone, you piece of dung, you offal, you goddamned insult to the universe."

She couldn't believe what was happening. The eyes were dimming. Was it weakening? How could that happen? Was her rage having an effect on the creature?

She panted, gathering herself, bracing for effort. She took a deep breath and cut loose with a scream. Every shred of terror, of outrage, of the price she'd paid in this place soared out of her mouth, hurting her ears.

That's it, that's it, you're heroic! You're defeating it. You're driving it away. She was barely aware of Charlie's voice anymore. Everything in the world had come down to the noise she made and her will driving it to fill this place.

"Be my guest." Rose handed her keychain to Max and he unlocked the door to Eve's apartment. He pulled it open and took a quick step back as a howling bundle of fur burst through the widening crack and ran down the hallway. "For the love of God!"

"It's Danica," Noreen said in concern. "She's terrified." She turned and followed in the wake of the cat.

The others crowded behind Max as he entered the room. Rose paused to jerk the key from the lock. Pillows from the sofa were on the floor, several shredded, the stuffing falling out. Further inside were torn up papers scattered across the tongue-in-groove floor.

"What in hell's been going on in here?" Kerry sidestepped a mess on the floor outside the kitchen. "Yuck. Looks like cat throw-up." She headed for the roll of paper towels on the counter.

"Any sign of Eve?" Andrea peered into the office. "Look. There's that book Noreen mentioned." *The Punishment of the Disbeliever* lay open over the computer keyboard. She looked back over her shoulder toward Brenna, standing in the doorway. "I don't even want to touch the thing."

Brenna approached the desk. "It makes the Britannica look like a loose-leaf notebook. Can't be doing the keyboard any good." She grabbed two corners of the book and lifted it up, setting it onto the desk. "Ugh, it feels sticky."

"I wonder where it came from." Andrea peered at it more closely. "It sure isn't the kind of thing anyone around here would bring home. Unless I'm missing serious clues about the proclivities of our happy little group."

Brenna fought back a smile. "That might make for interesting conversation." She wandered out the door and glanced up the staircase leading to the bedroom suite. "I could check up there again."

Andrea followed her. "Let's go together. It feels creepy in here."

Before they got to the first step, Max came down the shadowed flight of stairs. "There's nothing unusual up there. Either Eve is unduly neat or she hasn't had time to deal with any of her possessions."

"Thanks for cleaning that up, dear." Aura Lee passed Kerry, dealing with the cat mess, and stepped carefully into the kitchen. "I don't see any sign of Eve in here," she called to the others. "Everything looks normal. She certainly hasn't fixed any food," she muttered.

"I don't know if normal is bad or good." Rose paused beside her and cast a measuring eye around the room. "Where in the world could she have gone?"

Noreen appeared at the open front door, arms filled with angry cat. Her hair was even wilder than usual, her face creased in irritation. "If I didn't know this poor animal was traumatized, I'd be tempted to boot her outside. She scratched me!" When she held out one hand to show them, the cat leapt out of her arms and made a beeline for the office. "Good riddance," muttered Noreen, but she hurried to close the door.

"Wash that thoroughly," Aura Lee ordered. "Cat scratches can become infected if you don't take proper care."

"Why am I not surprised?" Noreen marched toward the bathroom. "Has anyone found anything of interest?"

"No." Kerry took the soiled paper towels to the wastebasket. "Except for the mess, it doesn't look any different than it did earlier."

From the office came a low, rumbling growl. Before they could react, the sound increased in volume and pitch. When they reached the door and yanked it open, they saw Danica clawing madly at the damaged woodwork. "Stop it," Rose snapped at the cat, and clapped her hands, but Danica scratched more deeply, snarling at her.

"What is the matter with you?" Aura Lee moved cautiously toward the animal, but when she came within reach, the rumbling built into a fearsome scream that came from all corners, filling the room.

"My God, is the creature in pain?" Max asked in alarm as the shriek died away.

"That didn't come from the cat." Rose pushed past them to get closer. At the same moment, a loud click sounded near the window. A part of the floor fell away and Max grabbed Rose by one arm. The cat dropped into the hole and, before their eyes, the section snapped back into place with a thump.

"By the Goddess," whispered Aura Lee, tottering toward the once-again smooth floor.

"Don't get too close." Max released Rose's arm and followed Aura Lee's path across the trap door area. Kneeling, he rubbed his fingers over the wood surface, seeking cracks that would indicate the parameters of the opening.

"Over here." Kerry had a finger against the base of the door molding and she pointed down an almost imperceptible line. "You'd never notice it."

Max made a wide circle to get to Kerry. When he bent to check what she'd found, he nodded. "I see it. It's incredibly fine, something easily overlooked." He turned his head to check out the vertical molding. "How in hell does it open?"

Brenna's back was plastered against the wall beside the area Danica had savaged. "It's right here." She pointed out the dull gleam of metal amidst the torn wood with a delicate touch. "What if the cat triggered it with that scratching?"

"Wow." Kerry edged back and pushed herself to her feet. "That would explain the way she was acting. Feline remorse."

"Let me see." Rose leaned close enough to examine the mechanism. "Stand back," she said crisply after a moment. "I'm going to try to open it."

"But what if—" began Max, gesturing in frustration.

"But nothing. Eve must be down there, and we know the cat is."

Max nodded with reluctance. "Very well. But be careful."

Rose took her keys from her jacket pocket and picked out the multi-purpose tool on the ring. She used her nail to pull down a flat head screwdriver and used it to pry at the metal piece in the molding. After a moment of digging at both sides, a steel loop lifted away from the wood, and at the same time the trapdoor fell open. Rose jammed the screwdriver blade into the loop, barring it from slipping back into its resting place. The door hung open.

Rose got down on the floor. "Hello?" she called into the hole. "It's dark as pitch down there. Eve, can you hear me?"

They heard movement. "Yes. I hear you. I can hear you." Her voice was rough.

"Is Danica with you?" Noreen asked loudly.

After a moment they heard a shaky, "Yes."

"Is there any way for you to get up here?"

Again that slight delay, then, "No."

Rose met Max's eyes. "We have to call Neal. At a bare minimum we need a ladder and maybe some rope."

"Already on it, Rose." Andrea spoke softly into her cell phone and listened to a reply. "He's not far away and can be here in ten."

"Good." Rose turned back to the dark space. "We'll get you out, Eve, but it'll take a while. What can we get for you now?"

"Light." She coughed and spoke again. "Just get some light down here. I've got to be able to see what's down here with me."

Rose looked up from the hole in the floor, meeting Max's frowning gaze. "What's down there with her?" she repeated.

Max shook his head. "She might have hit her head."

Kerry reached the edge of the trap door. "What do you mean?" she called to Eve.

"Just get me out of here as fast as you can."

TIME OUT OF TIME

Severn picked himself up from the floor, shaking with rage. He'd spun the web to create the monster. He'd held control as he moved the creature toward her. And the burning eyes had been almost impossible. "She should have been gibbering. She should have been crushed!"

The soft knock at the door brought him up short. "What do you want—" His voice was an animal growl. He took a step away from the fireplace, shocked at the weakness in his legs. The knock came again.

Severn forced himself across the rug, grasping the knob when he reached the door. Turning it, he jerked the door toward himself and glared out at Simms.

At the sight of his face the butler took a step back. "Sir, there's a message."

The tightness in Severn's throat kept him silent.

"It's Mr. Fitch, sir," he added quickly. "He isn't able to come tonight. He's caught in a large auto accident, sir."

Severn closed his eyes, leaning against the door lintel. "He begged me to tell you, sir." Simms moved his hand to pull at his collar, dropping it to his side as he collected himself. "He insisted on it."

Severn closed the door. He listened, ear pressed against the wood, until he heard the man's uneven steps down the hallway. Only then did he let out the breath he'd held so tightly.

What went wrong? Severn reviewed the spell work in his mind, running through the sequence of elements in the casting. *I did them all properly.* He'd memorized the Latin perfectly and had counted the beats between each directive. *I have the power of the Seventh.*

She wasn't vanquished. She didn't succumb to fear. She fought back.

Again he mentally thumbed through the spell, slowing as an idea began to form among his hurried, obsessive thoughts. *Fitch. The bumbling, puffed up fool was removed from my influence while my attention was on breaking the woman.*

A wave of dizziness almost felled him. Only his will kept him on his feet.

Was it an accident? Or is there another player in this game?

Another idea made his blood run cold. *Could the woman have attacked Fitch while she was fighting off the spell? Could she know about them? Did she have the power to attack them as she chose?*

CHAPTER 10

The square of light overhead was so far away. Eve trained her eyes on it, half convinced it would disappear before they got her out of the hole. She glanced over her shoulder to see if the monster was anywhere near.

"Mrroauw?" Danica lashed herself against Eve's legs, back and forth. The familiar pattern kept Eve together. That and her arms firmly hugging herself. She hadn't noticed how cold it was when she was in the dark, but now she could feel currents of air moving past her. *They could be spirits, invisible to me.* She shut down the idea before it could gain traction. She had enough to deal with without adding spirits to it.

"Anybody up there?" she asked abruptly.

The shadow of a head appeared along the edge of the trap door. "Sure thing." It was Kerry's voice. "What, you think we all left to get coffee or something?"

"Guess not." Why was this taking so long? At the feeling rising through her chest Eve clamped on the controls again. "Just getting bored with the décor." She heard the quiver in her voice and pretended she hadn't.

"I don't doubt it." Kerry's shadow pulled back, soon replaced by a larger one.

"Eve, do you want me to send down some water?" It was Aura Lee. "You must be thirsty."

"Will I be down here long enough to go to the trouble?" She could hear the edge of dread in her voice. God knew how she sounded to the others.

"I have a bottle right here and some ribbon. You'll have it right away."

Seconds later Eve saw light reflect off a water bottle as it bobbed slowly toward her. She reached for it and clutched it to her for a moment before tugging at the loose knot around the neck. "Got it."

Aura Lee pulled the ribbon back up as Eve fumbled with the lid and held the bottle to her lips. The cold liquid filled her mouth and she was suddenly horribly thirsty, nearly pouring the water down her throat. Coughing a little, she gulped some more and then screwed on the lid.

"No choking, now." Aura Lee sent down another package, this one in a paper bag.

Eve caught the bag and lifted out a fat buttered muffin. It was warm against her fingers and a whiff of pumpkin wafted to her nose. Eve swallowed against the lump in her throat. "Thank you," she muttered. *She probably didn't hear me.* "Uh, thanks," she called more loudly, and darted another look behind her. The pumpkin scent was doing strange things to her. At a wave of dizziness, she took a step back and sat onto the stone floor harder than she'd planned.

"You're more than welcome." Sympathy was rich in Aura Lee's voice. "You poor dear. I can't imagine how difficult it's been for you there. I'm so sorry about the trap door and all. We had no idea such a thing existed and now we'll have to check every apartment to see if there are any others."

Another head appeared beside Aura Lee's. "We'll work it all out." It was Rose. Even from the floor Eve could see the shadow of Rose's hand patting Aura Lee's shoulder.

Taking a large bite of the muffin, Eve pulled off a morsel and held it out to Danica. The cat's tongue was rough against her buttery fingers.

"Neal will be here any minute," Max called down. "He stopped at his house for a longer ladder. He said to tell you to hang tough."

Eve washed down muffin with a swallow of water. "I'll do my best."

"Did you hurt yourself when you fell?" asked Andrea.

"I should've asked you earlier," Rose added. "Should I call the doctor?"

Eve rubbed at the back of her head and noted the ongoing throb in her legs. "I clipped my neck and hit my knees, but aside from some aching, I'm pretty okay."

"Goodness." It was Aura Lee again. "I'll send Brenna to the house for the first aid kit. We'll have to check for swelling. Do you have a headache?"

"I'll bet she does." Neal had arrived and was standing at the edge of the door. "Max and I are going to send the ladder down. You need to get over to the side so we don't drop it on that head of yours."

Eve forced herself to her feet, grabbing Danica as she got out of the way. She held the cat to her, feeling her purr against her as the end of the metal ladder slid down to rest on the floor. She thought about getting out of the dungeon and her arms tightened. Danica pushed against her chest and jumped out of her arms. "Damn," she whispered.

"Did it land squarely?" asked Neal.

Eve peered at the shadowy stones. "Yes, it looks stable."

"Good. I'll be right down."

"Wait a minute." Eve's eyes opened wider. The rungs of the ladder were beginning to move, twisting in place. "Something's happening." Her breath was coming more shallowly.

"What d'you mean?" Neal sounded impatient as he thrust the flashlight into the opening and aimed it toward her.

In the cone of the light Eve could see her surroundings more clearly. She caught a motion from the ceiling, blanching at the thick cobwebs billowing like sails. "Oh." A thick musty odor filled her nose and she coughed.

"What's that moving down there?" Neal demanded. The rungs looked like living snakes now, and the sidepieces were beginning to move in turn.

"It's the ladder." Eve edged toward it, extending her hand to feel it. Her fingertips touched the scaled surface and the deep cold of it hurt her skin.

"It's icy," she said, her voice shuddering. "And it's moving like snakes fastened together."

"Fucking hell. What's going on around here?" Neal grabbed at the top rung and just as quickly pulled back his hand. "She's right. It's like dry ice." He leaned closely toward the rungs. "Jesus, they do look like snakes."

"Let me see." Noreen took a couple of steps toward Neal and reached for the side of the ladder.

"Be careful," Neal protested. "This is weird as hell."

Noreen gently touched the pulsating metal and withdrew her fingers. "Aura Lee, come look at this. Have you ever heard of anything like it?"

Aura Lee came closer, pulling the folds of her caftan to one side as she peered at the top of the ladder. She stared off into space as she considered the problem. "You know," she said slowly, "I think this might be the result of a spell. I remember reading about something a bit like this." She hefted herself to her feet. "I'll be right back," she called to Eve, and headed toward the front door. "It's in one of my books!" The door slammed behind her a few seconds later.

Neal knelt next to the opening in the floor and peered down. The ladder continued to move. He edged away from it. "How're you doing?"

Eve had spent several seconds looking around her in the small area illuminated by the flashlight. The massive spider webs continued to catch the wind she couldn't feel. "Uh, okay, I guess." She glanced again at the ladder rungs, still coiling as the side supports had become thicker, now looking like small boa constrictors hooked together by the rungs. A sudden thought hit. "Neal, is this really happening?"

His short laugh was bitter. "Damned if I know." He shone the flashlight in her direction. "I'm hoping Aura Lee can help us figure it out. She's got all kinds of witchcraft shit in those books of hers." When Andrea came to kneel beside him, he grabbed her hand, and they exchanged a worried look.

"She's taking her own sweet time." Eve cast a glance behind her, feeling another presence. Had she heard something? Was the monster back?

"She's probably leafing through her tomes about magic as we speak." Neal set the flashlight on the edge of the opening. "I have a rope in my pickup. How strong are you?"

Eve's attention had shifted toward the faint rustling coming from the shadows beyond the spider webs. "Neal?"

"Yeah?"

"Shift the light to my right, will you?"

Neal turned the light in the direction she was looking.

When she saw the light reflected by a multitude of eyes, she cried out. Hundreds—no, thousands—of squirming serpents were slithering together across the ground toward her, bodies coiling and uncoiling in colonies as they spread across the stone floor of the cave. "More snakes." Her voice was nearly silent, as breathy as the sound of the serpent skins shifting against dirt.

"What did you say?" Neal directed the light beam around the chamber. "Holy mother of God, what is that?"

Eve pushed herself to her feet. "Snakes, thousands of them." She edged toward the square of light falling from the trap door where the ladder continued to writhe.

"This is nuts," she heard him say.

Nuts or not, she had to get out of there.

Eve pulled on the sleeves of her shirt, bringing the edges over her hands, holding on them with her fingers. She had two choices: stay and chat with the mob of snakes or climb the cold reptile ladder. "I'm coming up."

"Go for it." Neal pointed the light directly at the first row of snakes. "Make it fast."

Eve put one foot on the bottom rung, forcing herself to ignore the sickening fleshiness of it. As she reached for the side of the ladder she heard a small sound from the shadows she faced. Then it was louder and she turned toward it. *I forgot Danica!*

"Mrroauw."

"You have got to be kidding me." She almost rested her forehead on the scaly rung until she remembered she couldn't.

"What the hell are you waiting for?" Neal yelled. He was leaning out across from the top of the ladder. He jerked his hand upward. "Those things are getting closer. Come on!"

"I'm coming." She let go of the writhing support and turned to slip around the ladder. "Kitty-kitty," she said softly and clicked her tongue. "Danica, come." She could see the cat's eyes blink, the yellow appearing and disappearing in the murk over by the wall of the chamber. Eve snapped her fingers. "Come on."

The rustling sound was louder and Eve jerked her head around for a quick look. The writhing mass of reptiles looked like a single, horrible organism moving inexorably toward her. The sound of the snakes' hissing grew louder, diminishing the thunder of her pulse in her ears.

Eve ducked under the rungs, half expecting the touch of reptiles around her legs, but she made it from under the ladder and headed quickly toward the shadows hiding her cat.

"Eve, what're you doing?" Neal demanded in disbelief. "Get up here now!"

"Mrroauw." Eve saw the cat's head move, a pale break in the darkness. She plunged toward the motion.

"Kitty-kitty." *I'm going to strangle her if the snakes don't eat her.* "Kitty-kitty." She cast a look behind her at the snaky bodies intertwining, twisting as they flowed across the floor. She heard a shriek from above.

Danica leapt from the shadows, her 500 claws poking into Eve's skin. Clasping the cat to her chest, Eve stepped on the bottom rung and swung her body around. The sear of ice on her hands hardly registered as she grabbed the nearest crosspiece and scrambled up the ladder as fast as injured leg and panicked cat allowed. Her palms throbbed but she kept moving. As she drew near to the opening, she felt a clutching at her foot, as if many fingers grasped at her. She reached up and Neal grabbed hold of her wrist. "Pull me up! Hurry!" she cried, and he jerked her onto the floor. Danica sprung off and went running.

Eve turned to see the glittering eyes of a sea of squirming snakes twist up the ladder, heads sliding over each serpentine step until they reached the edge of the trap door. Behind her a scream ripped the air. As she bent her leg to kick, a large bird flew from the chamber shadows across the light from the trap door. *An owl?* Eve lowered her leg to the floor as the raptor caught several snakes in its beak, whipping them from the ladder. Its wing knocked the ladder sideways along the edge of the opening, sliding into a crash to the floor below. She pushed herself up to track the owl's flight, gasping as a snake dropped onto the stone.

She collapsed back on the floor, looking up to see Andrea and Neal holding onto each other.

Kerry was on her knees beside her. "Did they bite you?"

Eve turned her head back and forth, reveling in the feel of the floor supporting her. "Don't think so." She lifted her hands. "They hurt."

Noreen bent to look at one palm, horror in her eyes. "Blisters all across your palms."

Kerry cringed at the wounds. "Oh, God." She checked Eve's other hand with care. She turned to Rose, who'd fallen back at the appearance of the snakes. "You need to call the doc. She's got sores the size of quarters."

Rose nodded and came closer. "From the ladder?"

Eve closed her eyes as fatigue washed over her. "I guess. Is Danica okay?"

"She's fine." Max held the cat in his arms and came slowly across the floor. "She's a bit wild-eyed."

"Me, too." Eve just breathed for a while as she mentally went over the aches and pains she was feeling.

"Did the fall kill the snakes?" Brenna asked.

Neal let go of Andrea. "There's a question you don't hear everyday." He stepped to the trap door and looked into the chamber below. Frowning, he retrieved his flashlight from the floor and aimed the beam from corner to corner. He lowered himself onto his hands and knees, then onto his belly and sent the light about the area again. The others stood clustered around him.

"What about the owl?"

The room went still. Eve opened her eyes to find everyone staring at her. "The owl. It pulled some of the snakes off the ladder."

Rose knelt beside Eve and put her hand on her brow. "You said you hit the back of your head when you fell, yes?"

Eve struggled to sit up, finally letting Rose help her. "Didn't you see it? Any of you?" She could tell by their concerned expressions they hadn't. "Maybe it fell, too." She looked toward Neal, still holding the flashlight at the edge of the trap door. "Please look. It came out of nowhere and went straight for the snakes."

"Okay." Neal turned back to the chamber below them and slowly moved the light over the area.

Noreen dropped into a chair. Her face was as pale as snow. "This situation becomes stranger by the second."

Max shifted the purring Danica to one arm and rested his other hand on Noreen's shoulder for a brief moment. "We'll get to the heart of it."

"What d'you see?" Kerry asked Neal in a plaintive voice.

Neal cast the light over the underground area once more. "It's what I don't see I'm worried about."

Noreen made a face at his cryptic statement. "Elucidate, please."

Neal pushed himself up and got to his feet with an assist from Andrea. "There's not a single snake body that I can see."

"Shit," Brenna murmured. "They're hiding somewhere."

Neal put his arm around Andrea and rested his cheek against her brow. "Maybe. I didn't see an owl, alive or dead," he told Eve. "There's also no ladder."

"What?" Max stared at him in surprise. "You're joking."

"Afraid not. Take a look if you don't believe me. I saw dirt, a few cobwebs, and skid marks from the ladder supports. That's it."

The front door crashed open and they all jerked toward it in time to see Aura Lee, several books clutched against her chest, charging into the room. A smile of relief spread across her face when she caught sight of Eve. "Thank the Goddess you're all right."

Eve closed her eyes again.

Aura Lee handed a book to Rose and another to Noreen. "There are a couple of pieces I found about the transformation of matter through complicated spell work." She registered their surprise and weariness as disbelief. "I'll point out the pertinent passages. Some sophisticated work has been done here. It's not every day you see an aluminum ladder changed into snakes, or into the appearance of snakes."

Rose looked up from the book she'd been handed. "How could it have been an illusion? Eve has blisters on her hands from touching the rungs. And she felt the snakes on her ankles."

"What are you talking about?" Aura Lee's face crumpled in consternation. "There were other snakes, too?" She wheeled toward Eve. "Were they apparitions? Looking real but not?"

Eve shook her head slowly. "I could see them, hear them, hell, I even smelled them."

Aura Lee bent to look closely at Eve's hands. "Oh, my dear. This puts a different complexion on everything." She stood up abruptly and snatched up the multicolored cloth bag she'd brought with her.

"What do you mean?" Noreen asked in a testy voice.

Aura Lee pulled out a necklace and bent to place it around Eve's neck. "The ability to transform or just disguise a ladder into joined snakes is amazing enough, especially since it was able to injure Eve. But to make those snakes?" Shivering, she reached again into the bag and pulled out more necklaces. "These are the amulets I made for all of you." She handed them out, cautioning them as they put them on. "You must wear these 24/7. They're waterproof, so leave them on in the shower."

Brenna held the tiny vial suspended on the leather chain of her amulet, peering at the dried leaves and blossoms mixed with a variety of different substances she couldn't identify. "These are supposed to protect us against snakes?"

"These *will* protect you, but only if you're wearing them." Her glance around the group caught the skepticism on several faces. "It's all right if you don't believe in the amulets. Wear them anyway. If we're dealing with someone with the skill and power to create these terrifying things, we need all the protection we can muster."

Max took the amulet from Aura Lee and put it around his neck. "You know we'll have to go down there to see if the snakes are hiding."

Kerry took a deep breath to argue with him, but Rose beat her to the punch.

"The ladder's gone. Why wouldn't the snakes be gone, too?"

"What do you mean, the ladder's gone?" Aura Lee was pale now, her eyes narrow as she searched Rose's face.

"Neal said the ladder was gone." She gestured toward Eve. "It fell as the snakes got near the trap door. We heard it crash on the stone below."

"And you didn't see it on the floor?" she asked Neal, a catch in her voice.

He shook his head. "I saw dirt and cobwebs. That's all."

Aura Lee clasped her hands at her waist. "Disappearing things is among the hardest skill there is in magic and in witchcraft."

Andrea glanced at the amulet on her necklace. "Why?"

"Energy. It can be transformed, but to make it disappear is almost impossible." Aura Lee moved to the overstuffed chair and sat down as if she'd just lost her own energy. "When you burn something, it becomes vapor or smoke. You kill something and it decays, releasing the energy that made it live. To make something *not be* and have no energy signature is an incredible achievement." She leaned her head back against the chair, clearly tired. "It's beyond any skill set I've encountered."

"What about the owl?" Brenna was rubbing at her brow where a headache was growing.

"Owl?" Aura Lee frowned in confusion. "What owl?"

"Precisely." Brenna held out a hand to Eve and helped her to her feet. "You really believe you saw it?"

Eve nodded. "It was bigger than any Great Horned owl I ever saw." She glanced at Aura Lee. "It flew from the shadows and attacked the snakes."

Aura Lee pondered. "Maybe a sign? Owls are powerful. Could be we have an ally in this battle."

CHAPTER 11

◆

Eve put her head under the shower, enjoying in the hot water flowing over her face. She'd taken a shower the night before, after she'd been escorted to Andrea's room for the night, but she couldn't stop feeling the brush of spider webs against her skin.

Eve hung the towel on the rod beside the tub. When she picked up the comb on the counter, she examined the skin creams and perfumes arranged there. She touched the bar of soap decorated with swirls of green and gold. Then she allowed herself to look into the mirror over the sink. The fear in her eyes was a given, but what about its source? The snakes were real or they weren't. She felt a gut-punch of terror. What if none of this was real?

As she limped down the stairs, Eve recalled the speed with which the Wisdom Court women had brought her to the main house yesterday. When she'd expressed concern at being a nuisance, Andrea had patted her shoulder. "I'll stay at Neal's. I'm always welcome there, right, cupcake?"

Neal had flashed a sexy smile. "You bet, my little kumquat."

Andrea had rolled her eyes, but the color in her cheeks deepened. "See, I've got him under my thumb."

When Eve started to argue, Andrea frowned at her. "Surely you can't believe we'd let you stay at your place after what just happened, can you?"

"Don't even think about it," added Kerry. "Who knows what'll show up next? You're not staying there alone until we figure out how to deal with the monsters. Get used to it."

"Okay, okay," she'd muttered. Eve wasn't at all sure she'd be any safer at the main house, but the idea of another night alone, wherever she was, didn't appeal anyway.

Eve caught the scent of something wonderful and followed it to the kitchen. As she stepped into the room, she was surrounded by warmth. Light glowed from the cream-colored walls and polished cabinets. The copper pots hanging overhead reflected the movements of the people as they talked and ate. The herbs on the windowsill were bathed in sunlight.

Aura Lee was flipping a pancake, glancing over her shoulder with a smile when she'd caught it. "Good morning. I hope you're hungry, because I'm making pumpkin spice pancakes." Her brassy hair was upswept, but a tendril had escaped, brushing the shoulder of her green caftan.

Eve nodded. "They smell heavenly." Her gaze went from the oversized iron skillet across the dark counter to the pottery chicken next to a pot of rosemary in the window. "This kitchen is wonderful." Aura Lee smiled her pleasure.

"Coffee or tea?" Brenna asked. A carafe and a teapot were on the table in front of her. She and Noreen were seated side by side, a spiral notepad between them.

"Coffee, please," Eve replied. She gestured at the notebook. "What are you working on?"

Noreen lifted one shoulder. Her mouth was pursed, causing wrinkles to fan out from the corners. "It's our latest attempt to make sense of events. We've been listing details of your adventure yesterday. Now you're here to fill in some blanks."

Pulling out a chair, Eve sat, reaching for the cup Brenna extended. "Thanks." She poured a dollop of cream from the glass pitcher and took a sip. "Good stuff."

"Mmmm-hmmm." Brenna drank more of her own and set down her cup. "Soon I shall take on the characteristics of a human."

"I'll catch up as soon as I can."

Aura Lee brought a stack of stoneware plates to the table and set them near Eve. "Start these around. Everyone will show up in a bit, but that doesn't mean you three have to wait for them."

Eve parceled out the plates while Aura Lee fetched a full platter. This she set at the center of the table. "We have butter, syrup, and jam. Dig in now, don't let them get cold."

"Thanks, Aura Lee." Brenna unfolded a napkin and draped it across her lap. "These look so good." She speared a pancake and put it on her plate.

Eve served herself and waited for Brenna to hand her the syrup. As she poured it, she realized the warmth she'd initially felt in the room was fading. A cool breath against the back of her neck brought out goose bumps. Before she could react, she heard a faint sound and turned to her right to see what it was. A sibilant string of almost-words were flowing past her ear, like the hissing of a snake.

Eve breathed in sharply, turning her head the other way, but the sound was only on her right side. Frowning, she took the syrup bottle from Brenna.

"Something wrong?" Rose stood in the doorway from the dining room, a halo of light gleaming on her curling silver blonde hair. She watched Eve with worried eyes.

Deliberately Eve let out the breath she'd been holding. "A sound, almost like hissing. Can you hear it?"

Rose turned and threaded her way between Aura Lee and the kitchen island, slanting a glance at the burner knobs of the stove along the way. She closed her eyes and listened. After a moment she shook her head. "I can't, but that doesn't mean it isn't there." She asked the others. "Do you hear anything?"

Brenna came round to Eve's side of the table. She was quiet, with her eyes closed as she tried to hear something. Her eyes widened and she turned her head, meeting Eve's eyes. "I do hear it! It's very low, but it's definitely a hissing."

Eve sagged against the back of the chair.

Noreen looked between the two of them. "Coming from where?"

Rose cast a look around the room. "What could the source be and why can't the rest of us hear it?" She frowned. "Do you think it might be the furnace?"

Brenna sat in the chair beside Eve and closed her eyes as she focused. She tilted her head closer to Eve. With a gasp, she put ear directly against Eve's. When she pulled her head away, her face had lost color. "It's coming from you! From your ear."

Rose stared. "That's beyond crazy. Have you ever heard of anything like this?" she asked Aura Lee.

"No." She started to say something else but spun around, lunging for her spatula. "The pancakes!" Quickly she flipped one off the griddle and turned off the burner at the same time. "Somebody get Max. Maybe he's heard of such a thing."

"Someone's trying to frighten me," Eve said in a hard voice. She put her hands over her ears and pushed hard. The sibilance grew louder. "And they're doing a great job." She straightened her backbone and scooted her chair closer to the table. "I'm going to finish this wonderful breakfast. Nobody's going to spoil it for me." She cut a chunk of the golden hotcake with the side of her fork and speared the piece, bringing it to her mouth. It tasted like ashes, but she chewed with determination and looked around at the others. "Have some. It's really good." She had a hard time hearing herself speak thanks to the noise in her ear.

Brenna moved back to her place and resumed eating as Rose took her seat and served herself. "You've got the right idea," she said to Eve. "It's impossible to know if what's happening here is real or not, but we have to live our lives regardless. I'm sorry about yesterday," Rose added abruptly. "I had to check you out, but I hated keeping you out of the loop."

Eve nodded, feeling a smile tug at her lips. "We all have to do what we think is right."

Noreen nodded sharply. "'*Keep a steady course though the waves pound against the hull. All will come aright at the end.*' Parminta Edgerston Winslow, eighteen thirty-two to eighteen ninety. She was married to a ship's captain, raised three children with him on their ship."

"Now *that* was a brave woman." Eve took a swig of coffee to wash down the pancake. "I'd almost rather be trapped with snakes than have to keep three kids from going over the side."

"Not very maternal, are you?" Kerry said from the arched doorway to the dining room.

"No reason to be," returned Eve.

Max edged around Kerry, his eyes trained on the pancakes. "Are there enough for us?" His hair was windblown and his eyes were blurry with fatigue.

"Of course." Aura Lee brought the other platter of cakes to the table. "Sit down."

"I'm glad you're here," Noreen said to Max as he pulled out a chair for Kerry and slid into his own. "We have a new…uh, symptom, if you will." She turned toward Eve. "Tell him."

Eve described the hissing in her ear as Max polished off two pancakes, his gaze focused on his plate. When she'd finished, he glanced at Brenna. "And you heard this sound as well?"

"I heard it coming out of her ear," Brenna said.

"What's that you say?" Max set down his fork and reached for his cup.

Kerry took it before he could pick it up and when he shot her a look of protest she nodded toward Brenna. "Pay attention. She said she heard the hissing coming from Eve's ear. That's just weird." She filled his cup and handed it to him.

"The sound was coming *from* her ear?"

"Yes. It was faint, like an amp turned really low, but I heard it."

Max gazed at Brenna, his thoughts busy behind his eyes. "I've never heard of such a thing," he said finally. He appealed to Aura Lee. "Have you?"

"No. Rose?"

She was rubbing one eyebrow. "It sounds vaguely like something I might've read once. I think I'll call Jerri."

"Who's Jerri?" Eve was halfway between worried about her ear and amused at the whole thing. "I've had more oddball conversations since I got here than in my whole previous life."

"Wait'll we get to the good parts," muttered Kerry.

"Jerri's our house doctor," explained Rose. "She has a practice here in Boulder."

Max had drunk half his coffee, unlocking his mental gears. "Have you ever heard odd sounds in that ear before today?"

Eve sighed. "I don't think so."

"So you haven't been diagnosed with tinnitus." Max tilted the carafe and topped off his cup.

"No."

Kerry nodded at him. "That's a good question. I wonder if you can develop tinnitus in an instant."

"What is it?" Brenna asked.

"Strange sounds in your ears, intermittent or constant. People complain of whistling, clicking, roaring like waves. It's fairly common."

Brenna reached for the coffee carafe. "I was thinking more about getting radio waves thanks to a tooth filling, or something like that." She smiled at Eve. "Great party trick."

Eve snorted. "I'm not that cool."

"Do you still hear it?"

Eve closed her eyes and concentrated. "It's gone."

"Thank the stars for small favors." Aura Lee sat at the table and served herself. "Now we can talk about what happened yesterday." She paused, her knife poised over the butter. "Did you find out anything about the snakes?"

"None of the books I brought with me have anything close." Max reached for another pancake. "Were you able to find any spells that could explain what happened?"

"No." Aura Lee frowned at her teacup. "I wish any of the books I checked had decent indexes." She sipped her tea. "I found articles about transposing matter, though many examples were obscure. Most were small things: rose petals, bugs, in a couple of cases, birds."

Kerry narrowed her eyes. "Wait a minute. You're saying those small things were sent from one place to another through magic?"

Aura Lee nodded. "According to several of my books, yes. Spell work developed by longtime practitioners."

The disbelief on Kerry's face was blatant. "Were there any trials to verify the validity of those claims?"

"Don't you have it backwards?" Noreen asked in a dry voice. "We saw the snakes, yes? How would *you* explain their appearance or presence?"

"Or the blisters on Eve's hands?" Neal said from the archway. He slipped out of his leather jacket and hung it on one of the hooks by the door to the porch. Andrea handed him her sweatshirt and headed for a chair.

Eve raised her hands to show off her bandages. "Living proof."

Neal and Andrea sat down and were given plates.

"We went on a shopping expedition this morning." Neal poured a generous stream of syrup over the cakes.

Rose eyed him with narrow eyes. "What did you buy?"

Neal took a big bite and chewed happily. "I'm eating." He nudged Andrea to continue.

She swallowed a bite and grabbed for the coffee carafe. "We bought another ladder." She caught the grimace on Eve's face. "And we're going back down to check things out." She drank from her cup. "Any volunteers?"

"I'll go." Eve poured cream into her fresh coffee as the others expressed their dismay. "I won't go alone," she said calmly. "That experience cost me something. I want to know what happened down there and why. It's the why that makes me crazy."

"It's all about Cottie," Aura Lee said. "From the beginning, everything that's happened has had to do with her here at Wisdom Court. You're the latest to arrive, but you've already had signs in your life of what's been happening here."

Eve stared at her disbelievingly. "I don't understand how she and I could be connected."

Brenna nodded in understanding. "I felt the same way, but it's happened to me, too. The connection has to do with Wisdom Court. I'll go down to the mystery room with you, but I'm bringing my phone so I can take pictures of everything."

Andrea took another bite and continued around it. "That's great." She swallowed and shot a smile at her. "We figured as our architectural expert, you might have ideas of what to look for down there."

"Sounds good to me." Brenna turned to Kerry. "You want to join this expedition?"

"You bet. Can't wait to check it out." Kerry grinned at Max. "There'll be no keeping him out of there."

"Do you think there are more rooms?" Aura Lee asked. "Cottie never said a thing about there being any."

Rose let out a short laugh. "She never said a lot of things."

Max's expression had turned thoughtful. "We could all go. We all have different vantage points. That makes finding anomalies easier. I'm hoping we can gain more information." He reached his hand to clasp Kerry's. "Evidence of where the snakes came from, for example."

"If there was any funny business about that left behind," Neal said, "there's been more than enough time to clean it up. I'd love to find a projector or bits of squirmy rubber, though."

Brenna finished her coffee and set down her cup with a thump. "So we're going to explore the secret chamber, right?"

"I guess so."

Rose looked at Neal in inquiry. "Do we have to go down the ladder?"

"Yeah. If anybody's not liking that idea, I'd suggest waiting in Eve's place until we've figured out what's what." Neal pushed his plate away. "There might be a more accessible entrance, though I can't think where it would be."

Rose stood up. "Let's meet at Eve's in an hour. That'll give us time to get ready. Any objections?"

"Only a question I always ask when I'm on a site." Brenna looked up at Rose. "Do you have any problem with my recording this trek?"

"Great idea." Rose scooped up her dishes. "We can catch a ghost or snake on film. I'd love some evidence for once."

"Of what?" Kerry stacked her cup onto her plate.

"Of anything." Rose's voice was grim. "It's about time we had a fact or two to rub against our theories and legends."

Brenna grinned. "I'll do my best."

CHAPTER 12

E ve stepped off the ladder's bottom rung onto the stone floor. She'd put her protective boot on her recovering leg and it made a scuffing sound that echoed in her ears. The air around her was dank and the walls were closer together, the darkness deeper. She fought the panic nibbling at the edge of her mind.

She felt a touch on her shoulder and jerked around.

"Hey, it's just me." Brenna lowered her cell phone she'd put into camera mode to search her face in the heavy shadows. "You okay?" With her dark clothes and black tomboy haircut, her face appeared to float in the gloom.

Of course not, Eve thought savagely. "This sweater isn't heavy enough." She wrapped her arms around herself.

"You want my jacket?" Already Brenna was pulling one arm out of its sleeve.

"No, no, don't." Eve grabbed for the sleeve and pulled it back up her arm, feeling guilty at her generosity. "No reason you should freeze in my place." She peered around, trying not to freak as her gaze touched on the spider webs. Kerry and Max were in a shadowy corner, their movements setting the strands of the things in motion heightened by the glow of their flashlights. Eve shuddered at the thought of touching them. But they were nothing compared to the writhing snakes, their glittering eyes holding hers as they slithered across her memory.

Brenna broke the spell. "Come on, let's go see what we can find."

Eve aimed her flashlight toward the end of the room and made her way over the cluttered floor, frequently pointing the beam down at the rubble to avoid tripping over anything. Beside her Brenna filmed their progress.

Neal was at the base of the ladder, holding it firmly as Andrea climbed down. When she reached the floor, he called up to the figure in the open trapdoor. "Noreen? You're next."

She waved down at him. "I've changed my mind about coming with you. Aura Lee and I will fix tea for everyone."

"Sounds like a plan. What about Rose?"

"I'm staying here, too," Rose called. "Good luck."

"See you in a while." Neal turned toward Andrea. "That'll make it a little less crowded."

Andrea fished a flashlight out of her coat pocket and switched it on. "Here's hoping we don't find any snakes." She caught sight of Brenna and Eve, now nearly at the south wall. She headed their way and Kerry and Max fell in behind her.

Neal followed them, shining the light overhead and down the rough stone of the walls. As they reached the end of the room, he lifted the strap of his tool bag and slid it down his arm. "Look at this stonework. The individual pieces have been cut and fitted. I'm not sure there's any mortar, maybe a little. The workmanship is impressive."

Brenna ran her fingers over the rough wall. "I'm wondering how long it's been here. The house is at least a hundred years old, but I can't tell about these walls. Huh, look at this." She pointed at a fissure. "It could be a crack." She knelt to examine the junction of wall and floor as Neal moved the beam of his flashlight all the way to the ceiling. She felt the area with her fingertips. "I think it's too straight to be accidental."

Her fingers rubbed gently against stone. "Interesting. Here's another crack at floor level. I can get my finger tips under this part." She demonstrated, running along the bottom. "Ouch!" She snatched her hand back and glared at the bead of blood on her forefinger. "It's sharp."

Neal bent to look more closely. "Where?"

Brenna pointed to a tiny red smear at the base of one stone and stuck her fingertips in her mouth. "It looks man-made to me."

"Let it bleed a bit," Max said. "It'll expel some of the germs." He migrated along the wall to a section with a shallow depression about a yard across. "I wonder what this is about."

Kerry leaned in with her flashlight to examine the surface of the bricks. "Creepy. It looks sort of like something pushed it in."

Neal glanced over his shoulder. "It does. It'd take a strong push to get the area to indent that way. Wait a minute. See that?" He pointed with the pry bar he'd removed from his bag. "Is that a footprint?"

Kerry dropped to her knees. "It is!" She looked up at Neal. "Where could it have come from?"

Brenna bent to grab her phone and eased her way nearer to the print. She started snapping pictures, changing her position to get every angle.

Neal shrugged. "Could be one of us left it." He glanced around the room. Eve was slowly moving across the floor away from a corner hung with cobwebs. Max was making exploratory pushes against the indentation he'd found. Andrea approached Eve, pointing at something overhead. "Maybe not. Let's take a look at the size." He set down the pry bar and his bag and walked carefully to the footprint.

As his foot came down beside the print, Brenna inhaled sharply. "It's really big, bigger than yours."

Neal looked down at the print. "Yeah. Thing is, I don't see any more of them. How come there's only one?"

Kerry was turning about, searching the area around them. "I don't see any more. Hey," she called to the others. "Be careful where you step. We found a big footprint over here. Looking for more."

Their attention was focused on the floor after that, and they all moved with exaggerated care as they came toward Neal and the others.

When Eve caught sight of the print, the size of it shook her. "What was down here was probably big enough to have feet that size."

"What did you see?" Kerry was using her flashlight to search for more prints.

Eve shivered. "Two glowing eyes is all I actually saw, but I heard footsteps as it came toward me."

"Wow. No wonder you were so scared when you came up. I thought it was just the snakes that freaked you out."

Brenna was on her knees next to the wall. "I think I've found another fissure. Look here." As Neal moved nearer, she ran one finger up the stone. "It's parallel to the first one. Check higher, will you?"

Neal felt along the area a couple of feet below the ceiling. "Yeah, there's something here."

"Given the crack at the bottom," Brenna said, excitement in her voice, "We might just have a door."

"How would we open it?" Eve asked. "There sure isn't any latch I can see."

"Grab a hammer out of that bag, will you?" When Eve complied, Neal slipped a chisel from his work-vest pocket and inserted the blade into the crack. He began to tap the handle to push it further in.

"Why are you doing that?" The sharp metallic clink stabbed at Eve's ears like an ice pick.

Neal moved the chisel blade down a few inches. "Since there's no latch or knob, I'm wondering if there's something like the trigger on your trapdoor to open this. Figured I might hit it if I pound long enough."

Eve's head ached, the throbbing keeping time with the pulse at her temples. As Brenna drew closer to film Neal's work with the chisel, Eve turned away and started back to the light coming in around the ladder.

"Look at this," Andrea said from behind her, and Eve turned in surprise. She had a fistful of cobwebs she'd pulled from a bank of them overhead, holding them out for Eve to examine.

"Ugh." Eve took a step back. "Keep them away from me."

Andrea picked through the filaments, pulling them apart and rubbing them between her fingers. "They may be fake."

"Fake? What d'you mean fake?"

"As in not real." Andrea headed toward the others, still clustered around the would-be door. "Hey, guys, check this out."

In moments they were riffling the ersatz spider webs, arguing over what the material could be. "It almost feels like dishwashing thingies made out of recycled plastic bottles."

Kerry shook her head in disagreement. "It's more like those really thin strands you get on weird Halloween lights, except softer. But I don't think it's plastic."

Andrea took back the mass she'd pulled down and stuffed it in her jacket pocket. "Whatever it is, I don't think it's made by spiders. To me that raises a question: if somebody with mad magic skills put this stuff on the ceiling, why is it fake?"

Neal was on his knees, slowly making his way to the floor with the chisel. When he'd gone across the crack at the floor, continuing part-way up the other vertical opening, he pushed himself to his feet and put his hands on his lower back, leaning back to stretch out his muscles. "Good question."

He slid the chisel into the crack and knocked it upward with hard strikes on the bottom of the handle. When nothing happened, he shot a glance up the remaining part of the fissure. "Let's try prying this thing open." He'd jammed the beveled end of the pry bar into the crack about a yard above the floor. "Come here, babe," he said to Andrea and she moved over beside the bar. "If you'll pull while I push, something might give."

Andrea put her foot against the wall and bent her knees. Neal took hold of the center of the bar, leaving room for Andrea's hands at the end of it.

Wiggling back and forth to set her feet, Andrea waited for Neal's signal. "Okay," he said, but before she could pull, before he could push, the panel of bricks popped out as if kicked open from the other side.

Neal fell on his behind and Andrea lurched backward, knocking into Max. His arms came around her, holding her upright.

"Wow." Kerry stared at the gaping door and aimed the flashlight beam into the cavern it revealed. "Another room."

Eve's head pounded. She closed her eyes and light flashed behind the lids. She opened them and walked to the open door.

"Wait a minute," she heard Andrea say, but she didn't stop. The further she walked, the louder the hissing in her ear. *Soonyousee. Soonyousee.*

"Eve, what are you doing?"

She heard the question from a distance and didn't try to answer it. She had to move, had to find the source of the pain. Step by step she entered the hollow space. Her hands groped over the wall they found, fumbling across the rough surface of crudely cut stone. Like a blind person she felt across the rock until she found the hole she knew was there.

Her forefinger slipped into the gap and she touched the smooth, cold ring inside it. As she pulled it toward her, a crumbling sound came from nearby, and a narrow panel swung inward, revealing another recess. The pain in her head ended suddenly and she fell sideways against the edge of the opening.

"Hey, now."

Eve felt a hand under her elbow stabilizing her.

"What was that all about?"

Eve opened her eyes. Brenna's face came into focus.

"The pain stopped."

Neal, shining light into the cavity she'd exposed, turned at that. "Dammit, you walked all over the footprints." He stopped, attending to what she'd said. "What pain?"

Eve wiped at the sweat on her face. "Headache, a really bad one. It got worse when the door opened. I felt something drawing me to this place. I knew the pain was coming from here."

"That's awful." Andrea offered her a water bottle.

"Thanks." Eve took a big swallow and handed it back. "Sharp pains in my temples, hissing in my ears." She met Neal's gaze, registered his scowl. "I'm sorry I walked on the prints."

Andrea frowned at her. "Why didn't you say something?"

Eve let out a long breath, giddy at the absence of stabbing pain. "Don't know. Something kept pulling me here—like a signal or tractor beam. I knew it had to do with the pain."

"Rose is going to love this," Kerry muttered from behind them. "What's in there?"

Neal put a hand on Eve's shoulder. "Don't worry about the prints. Probably weren't many." He turned back toward Kerry. "I don't see anything. Wanna have a go?"

Kerry aimed her light, scattering the shadows shrouding the room and walked through the doorway.

"Slow down," Brenna muttered, following her with the camera.

After patting over surfaces and peering closely at the walls of the cavity, Kerry pulled her head back and made a face. "Nothing I can see."

Andrea looked around with a thoughtful expression. "I wonder how many of these doors there are down here."

"Me, too." Kerry glanced around. "So what is this place? It feels like a closet."

Neal edged past her into the space, exploring with the flashlight. "Check this out," he muttered. The elongated circle of light spread to another wall about five feet from them.

"Looks like a corridor." Kerry shone her own flashlight

past Neal's and walked further into the recess. Behind her Max was illuminating the walls with his torch.

"There's a turn here." Kerry took it and was out of view.

"Wait for me, luv." Max hurried to catch up as Andrea followed behind.

Neal looked over his shoulder at Eve and Brenna. "You coming?"

Eve shook her head. "My knee's hurting. I can wait here while the rest of you follow the trail."

"Don't be silly." Brenna called to Neal, "I'm staying with Eve. You guys go ahead." When he hurried off, she turned to Eve. "I should've asked if that's okay with you."

"Of course, but you won't be able to take pictures." Eve let out a sigh. "I'm grateful you're here, though. I just want to rest for a bit. There for a while I thought my head was going to fall off. I feel fine now. Weird."

"What about any of this isn't weird?" Brenna poked around the small space. "Let's sit on these slabs and take it easy."

"Sounds good." Eve limped further into the recess and sat down cautiously. "It's cold, but it feels good to sit." She rubbed at her left knee above the edge of the boot.

Brenna leaned against the wall and took a shot of the stone wall. "How long is it supposed to take for it to heal?"

Eve shrugged. "A few weeks, according to my doc. He wasn't very happy with me for leaving to come out to Boulder." Her lips compressed as she massaged one tender area.

Brenna wrinkled her nose. "I don't suppose wandering around hidden chambers is helping much. To say nothing of falling down here to begin with."

"Yeah." Eve extended her leg, pressing the sole of her boot against the stone to try to stretch her hamstring. "God, I'm so tight," she muttered. At the same moment, with a rumbling sound, a portion of the wall they leaned against swung open. Brenna fell backward, catching herself before her head could hit the floor, clutching her phone to her chest. Eve grabbed the edge of the stone and slowed her fall, landing on her left hip. "What the hell!"

"It's a door." Brenna groped for her camera and then her flashlight, shining it through the opening.

"Did we trigger that?" Eve whispered.

"Damned if I know." Brenna pushed herself to her feet and extended her hand to help Eve. "Maybe when you put your foot against the wall."

They peered into the opening, about six feet high and three feet across. It looked like a hallway.

Brenna peeked around the edge and then glanced at Eve. "Shall we?"

Eve pushed her hair off her face and assessed her leg.

"I admit I'm wondering if it's more dangerous to sit still or to keep moving."

"We could go a little way, just to see what we find. If it's too hard, we'll come back here. Deal?" Brenna's eyes glittered with excitement.

"Yeah." Eve dusted off her jeans and stepped to Brenna's side. "Remind me not to touch anything, okay?"

Brenna nodded and walked through the gap, pointing the camera forward, Eve at her heels.

Andrea followed Neal and his bouncing light beam down the corridor, almost running into Kerry and Max. They were facing another wall made of stone, this one festooned with cobwebs. Max was running the beam of his flashlight over the rough surface.

"Dead end?" Andrea was aiming her light in another direction.

"Looks like." Kerry looked past Max at Neal. "What do you think? Another hidden latch?"

Neal was running his hands over the portion of wall beside him; Andrea began doing the same on the opposite expanse. "Anybody see any cracks?"

They all pointed their flashlights across the walls, shifting them to examine the uneven stonework. "How about this?" Kerry asked sharply.

Max followed her pointed finger with his torch, holding it

on the small hole in the grout between two stones. "Perhaps. Do you want to try it?"

Kerry started to put her forefinger into the hole. Then she stopped and turned to Max. "Not this time. Let's use something besides a finger."

Neal pulled a short Phillips head screwdriver from his shirt pocket and handed it over.

"Always prepared," Andrea murmured.

Kerry pushed the screwdriver into the hole. Nothing happened for a moment, and then a scraping came from the floor. As they watched, a row of three stones was pulled into the wall, leaving behind a rectangular gap.

"Geez." Kerry handed the screwdriver back to Neal. "What next?"

Neal lifted one hand to press against the wall and, smoothly, a section of it moved inward. "This is crazy," he muttered. "Who could've put all these doors in here?"

Before they could aim their lights into the dark enclosure, a light appeared inside it, shining from the ceiling.

Kerry stuck her head inside and the light set her auburn hair aglow. "Oh, wow."

"What is it?" Max craned his neck to look past her. "What do you see?"

Kerry pulled her head out. Her eyes were flashing with excitement. "Stairs!" She darted into the room and started climbing.

"Wait a minute. Kerry, stop!" Neal stepped into the stairwell. "We have to do this slowly. There's no telling how old these are or in what kind of shape."

Kerry looked down at him from six steps up. "I haven't heard a single creak."

Neal peered at the steps winding upward in a spiral. "Huh, looks like they're metal." He put his weight on the bottom step and looked up at her. "Okay, just go slowly." He looked out at the others grouped beside the door. "One at a time, okay? I don't want too much weight on these steps, just in case."

Andrea nodded. "You take it easy, too."

Kerry climbed up in measured steps, testing for looseness at each level. "There's another wall up here."

"Great." Neal climbed up the steps to the top and examined the wooden panel in front of them.

"Do you think it just ends?" Kerry asked in a disappointed voice.

Neal was brushing his fingertips along the top edge of the wall and over the corners. "Seems like a waste of time to me. Having this tunnel here doesn't mesh with a dead end."

"Yeah. You're right."

Andrea stepped up to the landing. "He's always right, or so he says." She peered at the blank wall. "This isn't what I was expecting."

Neal tried running his forefinger down the corner where the stone met the wood. "Bingo," he said softly.

"What?" Andrea stepped closer to him and looked up over his shoulder. His forefinger was touching a particular spot about six feet up from the landing. When he didn't respond, she crowded between him and Kerry to get a better look. "You know I hate suspense. What is it?"

Neal moved his finger. "You can't really see it, and only barely feel it. A tiny pinhole."

Kerry slumped against the wall. "What good is that?"

"Who cares about a pinhole?" Andrea chimed in.

"You'll both care in a minute, as soon as I find something small enough to stick in it." He looked down at his tool belt, swiftly considering and dismissing what he had there.

"What are we looking at?" Max had brought up the rear and was checking out the small space. "Did you find an invisible lock or something?"

"A pinhole," Kerry told him. "He's excited about it."

Neal patted his jeans pockets and then groped in his shirt pocket. "Dammit," he said, looking around as if what he needed would appear suddenly. "A needle or a safety pin, something with a point. Anybody have something like that?"

Andrea's lips curved in a smug smile.

"I love your smile." Neal bent to kiss her. "Whatcha

got?"

Andrea lifted her hands to one ear and delicately removed the rubber stopper from her earring. She pulled the wire from her lobe and handed the earring to Neal.

"Oh, baby. You want to do the honors?"

Andrea looked up again at the purported hole. "I'm too short. I can't even see it. You do it."

"Here goes." Neal felt along the wall with his finger and slid the tip of the wire into the hole. Silently the wall in front of them swung open about two feet.

"Whoa." Kerry shared a smile with Andrea. "I adore pinholes. How the heck did you know it was there?" she asked Neal.

"Been reading about hidden treasures." He measured the opening with his eyes. "Who wants to go first?"

"You found it," Kerry said. "And I don't know that I'd fit." She nudged Andrea toward the opening. "You're the smallest."

Andrea turned sideways and eased through the crack, moving the door open a little farther. Neal sucked in his stomach and pushed his way through. The other two edged around the partly open door.

Andrea and Neal stood amidst rows of canned food and bags of flour and sugar and tortilla chips. Mesh bags of onions and potatoes swung at their shoulders, and spices lined narrow shelves above them.

"What in the world…?" Kerry said from behind them.

Andrea reached for the doorknob in front of her and turned it. They came out of the pantry into the Wisdom Court kitchen.

CHAPTER 13

Eve and Brenna advanced slowly down the rough passage. It was barely tall enough for them to stand upright, and the ground was hard earth. Small lamps were recessed every few feet in the earthen walls, emitting enough light to show the floor.

Brenna lowered her camera. "I'm not enjoying this. I think it's getting more cramped in here."

Eve glanced around, measuring the shadows. "You want to go back?"

"Not yet." Brenna slanted a look at her over her shoulder. Her dark hair framed her face, pale as chalk. "It's reminding me of nightmares I had when I first got here. Of walking through endless corridors, not knowing where they went. Spooky."

Eve felt a quiver down her back. "Sounds nasty."

They kept going, watching their feet. Eve stumbled on a rock, nearly turning her good ankle. She pushed the stone over to one wall and stepped forward, right into Brenna's back. She'd stopped in the middle of the passage.

"Do you hear music?"

"What? Music?" She stopped, cocking her head to listen. "No, I don't—wait a second. I do hear something."

It was high-pitched, almost tinny. "Can you tell where it's coming from?"

Brenna shook her head, simultaneously scooting closer to Eve. "It sounds like ice cream trucks going through neighborhoods. Those tinkling nursery-rhyme tunes they play till you go insane."

Eve closed her eyes, hoping it would sharpen her hearing. The bare clink of metal on metal drifted like an idea. "It's ahead of us, I think."

Brenna followed her this time. After a few steps, the tunnel curved to the right. The only light they could see was a good three yards ahead. "You still have that flashlight?"

Brenna pulled it from her pocket and switched it on. The shaft of light bounced off water pooled on the floor. She pulled the beam up the wall, finding drops trailing like tears from the housing for a dead lamp. The two women exchanged a quick look.

"What is this place?" Brenna's whisper rustled in the close air of the tunnel. "Why would anybody build this?"

Eve lifted one shoulder. "You've been here longer than I have. Didn't somebody say something about hidden journals?"

"Sure, we've been reading the ones we've found. But nobody ever dreamed there were tunnels under the buildings." Brenna started walking again. "We need to bring you up to date about Wisdom Court and how everything got set into motion." Her laugh was short. "We haven't had the time."

They reached the next functioning light in the tunnel and saw another turn. Eve looked back the way they'd come. "Do you have any clue of where we might be?"

Brenna panned the camera around them, recording the location. "We started under your rooms in the west associate house. I figured the first door we hit was south of the trapdoor, and with the twists and turns, we could've gone west or even further south." She leaned against one wall of the tunnel and Eve heard bits of earth falling on the floor.

Brenna gazed at the arch of the tunnel above her head, her hair almost brushing against it. "There's a fountain in the courtyard. Thanks to me, a pickup truck smashed into it a couple of days ago. That might be the source of the water on the floor back there." She glanced back toward it. "It could've leaked through the cobblestones."

"Which would put us roughly under the fountain." Eve was becoming aware of a dull reverberation. "Do you hear that?"

"Yeah." Brenna put out one hand, touching the tunnel wall. "I can feel it, too."

Eve pressed her palm against the wall near Brenna's hand. "Like vibration." They exchanged a sick look.

"Holy hell," Brenna said in a scared voice. "What if water's soaked into the tunnel walls? What's to keep them from collapsing?"

"We'd better call somebody." Eve pulled her cell phone from her pocket and speed-dialed the Wisdom Court number. When nothing happened, she glanced at the screen. "No service. How about yours?"

Brenna exited her camera app and went through the same drill of numbers and waiting. "Nothing." She went back into camera mode. "I hate cell phones."

"Yeah." Eve edged around the curve in the passageway, straining to hear any falling rocks. "It seems pretty quiet ahead." If they went the wrong way and the tunnel collapsed on them, they could die down here. "We have to decide right now." Eve took a shaky breath. "We need to get out of here. Do we go back or forward?"

Brenna's eyes cut down the way they'd come in time to see several chunks of earth fall to the ground. "No-brainer," she gasped. "Forward, we've got to go forward. Run!"

Eve felt a stab of pain in her leg and then forgot about it. The sounds of falling rock were closer, like footsteps racing toward them from behind. They ran faster, using the lights along the wall as their guides.

Then the lights flicked out. "Shit!" Eve slowed, waiting for Brenna to switch on the flashlight.

As she did, a loud thud shook the ground. Brenna swung the beam around and they saw a large rock some five yards behind them. "Let's go!" Brenna spun around and moved forward.

"Come on, come on." Brenna was almost running now, so when she careened into the low crossbeam ahead of her, she dropped the flashlight and camera, falling to her knees.

Eve came to a halt and limped to the flashlight. "Brenna." She was picking up the camera when she felt something pull at her shoulder. She spun around, thinking Brenna was trying to stand up, but she was on the ground, barely conscious. Eve bent toward her, reaching with her free hand to grasp Brenna's upper arm, tugging at her with no effect. "Are you okay?"

Brenna groaned from deep in her chest. "Head, God, my head."

Eve aimed the light at her forehead, seeing the dark stain across her brow. "You're bleeding." She set the camera onto the ground and turned to help her, only half-hearing the rattle of falling stones from behind them.

"Let's get you up." Eve pulled at her, but Brenna slid out of her hold, falling back to her knees. Eve tried to keep her from hitting the ground and dropped the flashlight.

Something splashed onto Eve's jeans and when she reached for the light her fingers touched liquid. "Oh, no." Water was spreading across the floor ahead of them. "We have to get out of here." The flashlight was at her feet. She shoved it inside her waistband and grabbed the camera, then hoisted Brenna to her feet, lodging her shoulder into her armpit. "Walk," she ordered as she pulled out the light and pointed it in front of them. "You can do it. Walk!"

Brenna took a step, then another. Leaning heavily against Eve, her legs moved haltingly.

Eve half-dragged her around the next curve in the tunnel, afraid to admit to herself that the flashlight was dimming. "Oh, God, oh, God," she whispered. "Keep going."

The clatter of rocks falling behind them increased in volume. Where could they go? If the tunnel fell in around them, they were toast.

Breathing heavily, somehow keeping Brenna on her feet, Eve staggered forward, falling against the earthen wall as Brenna tripped behind her. Her shoulder jammed against the dirt and rocks and a chunk of earth fell from the ceiling. Yanking Brenna to one side, Eve held her with both hands as she fell against the wall yet again. It gave way and both fell into darkness.

"Did you call Eve and Brenna?"

Kerry dug into the bag of chips she'd grabbed from the pantry. "Neither answered so I texted them. They're probably finding another bunch of journals down there."

Max paused to let her enter the library ahead of him. "Speaking of which, are you sure you never came across any schematics or blueprints regarding underground tunnels in Caldicott's journals?"

Kerry held out the bag to him and he scooped out a handful of chips. "You read them, or skimmed them, anyway. Both of us would've noticed, don't you think?"

Max sat down at the large table. "I suppose it would have been counter-productive to describe them after building the things in the first place."

Kerry plopped into a chair. She rubbed absently at the ache between her brows. "You're assuming Caldicott knew about them. Stanley Thornton built the house. He could have put secret passages under the property." She shook her head in confusion. "Although why he would've is beyond me."

"It had to be Caldicott," Max muttered. "She built the associate houses. The secret room under Eve's apartment had to be dug there instead of a basement. The tunnels were most likely excavated at the same time."

"More hiding places for journals and such?" Kerry's shoulders sagged. "The longer we look for the pieces of this puzzle, the more we trip over. Didn't the woman ever hear of safe deposit boxes?"

Max slammed the book onto the table. "Safe deposit boxes work quite well for journals and money. Highly dangerous talismans, however, are another story."

"I suppose. But why create so many hiding places? You don't need underground tunnels and secret rooms to hide one small stone, no matter how dangerous it is."

Max looked at her with troubled eyes. "You might if you were trying to make sure no one else could ever find the thing. It appears to me that she was attempting to make discovering the talisman as difficult as possible."

Kerry nodded slowly. "Which means she knew the bad guys were on her tail long before she died."

"Exactly."

In the kitchen, Andrea pushed on the cold-water faucet handle and filled a glass. As she turned off the water, she felt it jerk under her hand. "What was that?" She ran her fingers over the fixture as she handed Neal the water.

"What was what?"

"The faucet moved, like something hit the pipe." She frowned at it. "What could cause that?"

Neal swallowed the water, setting the glass on the counter. "That's odd. Let me look under the sink." He opened the base cabinet and knelt down to peer at the pipes. "No leaks that I can see." He stood up and closed the doors. He stared at the sink thoughtfully.

The back door opened, Rose almost falling in behind it. "There's a sinkhole near the fountain and water is leaking across the courtyard."

Andrea looked at Neal in dismay. "Brenna and Eve," she said. "What if they haven't come out yet?"

"From the room under Eve's apartment?" Rose demanded. "They might be down there? We thought they were with you."

"We don't know exactly." Neal was heading for the door. "Eve's leg was bothering her, and Brenna stayed behind with her. The rest of us followed the tunnel here to the house by way of the pantry and stopped to get a drink. Get Max and Kerry. Library." He flung himself out the door and ran down the steps.

"Wait for me." Andrea took a step and stopped. "Are Aura Lee and Noreen here?"

"No." Rose crossed to the phone. "Tea and all that. I'd better get them out of there."

"Tell them to yell down the trapdoor at Eve and Brenna. Should we call the fire department? Or somebody?"

Rose was punching in numbers. "I'll take care of it."

Andrea raced out the back, coming around the edge of the house. She stopped when she saw water had reached within several yards of the front steps. Images of the walls in the secret chamber and the tunnel they'd followed filled her mind. Surely water couldn't erode stone mortared together as they were.

She caught sight of Neal as he came around the edge of the east associate house. He was carrying his toolbox, making for the fountain. Andrea skirted the spreading water and passed him as he began to splash through the puddles. "I'm going to Eve's. I'll take the ladder down—" Before he could interrupt she raised one hand. "I won't go down if there's water down there. But I need to at least yell for them, let them know what's going on."

Neal set the toolbox on an unbroken edge of the fountain. "I'll shut off the water here and get to you soon as I can."

He grabbed her for a swift kiss and turned back to his tools. Andrea ran toward the west associate house.

CHAPTER 14

Gravel moved under Eve when she rolled onto her side. It was dark and cold. Nearby rustling brought her heart to her throat. Then she remembered. "Brenna?"

A low groan was her answer.

Eve scooted flush against her, reaching forward slowly to brush her fingers against her arm. Brenna shifted. Rocks stirring against rocks made a whispering sound.

"Eve?" said Brenna in a cracking voice.

"Yeah."

Eve was patting the area around her, trying to find the flashlight, praying it would have some battery strength left. "How're you feeling?"

"Like shit." She coughed and gasped in pain.

"Your head?"

"Feels like I got hit by a truck."

"It was a support stone in the tunnel, I think." Eve felt the cylindrical shape of the flashlight. "Here goes nothing." She switched it on and a dull yellow circle reached into the dark, stopping at a wooden door, complete with a keyhole. They were inside a small room with walls made of lathe and vertical two-by-four braces. Dirt and rocks of various sizes were scattered across the earthen floor.

"Let's see how badly you're hurt." Brenna leaned toward her and Eve aimed the flashlight at the top of her head. Blood was thick in her hair but not flowing, and a goose egg was forming above her brows. Eve flicked the light off. "We need to save it for getting out of here."

Brenna didn't ask about her injuries. She shifted her weight again. "I don't know if I can walk anymore."

A rumbling sound filled the space, thundering like hail hitting a roof. "What is it?" Brenna shouted.

The roar was growing in volume. Eve put her hands over her ears and talked as loudly as she could. "The tunnel walls falling down and rocks hitting the wood." It was like being inside a drum.

In a few minutes the sounds decreased and Eve uncovered her ears. "Any idea where we are?"

"No." Brenna was breathing shakily and her voice trembled. Eve fought off a desire to turn the light back on. "We fell against a tunnel wall and the whole thing gave way. I thought I heard something as we fell, a slamming sound, maybe, especially if the door opened and then shut again."

Another round of pounding began and ended as Eve propped herself up and reached for the flashlight. "I forgot to check for water coming in under the door."

"Cheerful thought." Brenna lay back, wiping her hand across her forehead. She bit back a gasp of pain as she touched the lump on her forehead. "Well?"

"No water I can see." Eve flicked the switch and darkness fell over them again.

Eve used her hand to sweep gravel off part of the floor so she could rest her head on it. Her mind was scurrying like a mouse in a maze, considering and tossing ways they could get out. And where the hell were the others? Had they been caught up in the tunnel collapse? The possibility was so awful she tried to come up with any other distraction she could. "How's your head?" she asked Brenna.

"Throbbing like whatever's hitting that door." A scraping sound came as she shifted, trying to get comfortable. "Hope I don't have a concussion."

"No kidding." Eve's eyes were searching the darkness for any sign of light, her gaze shifting from side to side. The lack of stimulus was getting to her, so she closed her eyes and tried to calm her breathing.

"What's wrong?" Brenna asked quietly.

Eve wanted to rage at her—what wasn't wrong—but it wouldn't help. "I'm trying to keep from losing it."

"You're not alone." Brenna took a deep breath. "I keep expecting something to jump out at us. Like that snake you saw."

Eve stopped breathing. She hadn't given a thought to that prospect.

"I'm sorry." Eve felt Brenna's hand patting her leg. "I didn't mean to scare you, or us. I can't believe I said that."

Eve's laugh sounded broken. "I don't want to go there. It's bad enough without adding that to the mix."

Brenna didn't answer for a moment. When she did, her tone was plaintive. "Where are the others? Did they forget about us?"

Eve moved her head back and forth and then remembered Brenna couldn't see her. "They're probably trying to figure out where we are. If we'd stayed put in that alcove area, we might've been able to get to the ladder without any problem. Now, with the tunnel collapsing, they're not going to be able to get to us for a while."

"Yeah." Brenna thought for a moment. "I'm wondering what's on top of this room. Did you see the wood supports on both sides of the door?"

"I did." Eve pushed herself up to a sitting position. "From what I could see, this little room was fortified. I think that's the only reason we're not under a pile of dirt."

"I think you're right." Brenna paused. "Let's turn on the light for a minute. I want to check out something."

"Okay." Eve groped for the flashlight and pushed the switch. In the dim light the room made her think of the inside of a trunk. Beside her Brenna sat up and gazed around the area.

"Look. The ceiling and the walls come together in right angles." Brenna forced herself to her feet.

Eve saw her sway and scrambled up, catching her arm and steadying her.

Brenna ran a finger along the seam where the ceiling and wall came together. "It's a tight fit," she murmured. "Must be nailed together." She took a couple of steps and lifted her hand again. "I can't see any sign of water leakage, can you?"

Eve narrowed her gaze, following the angle of connection at the ceiling down to the floor. "No, it looks dry over here."

Together they slowly examined the joints. "It's nice and tight," said Brenna. "We caught a break, falling in here."

"Yeah," Eve said, "but how are we going to get out?"

Brenna turned to her with a smile. "I have a plan. Let's sit again and turn off the light. We can't waste it."

"I'm moving over here." Eve walked carefully to the wall opposite the door and sat down. "Something to lean on."

"Good idea." Brenna sat beside her and when she was settled, Eve turned off the light. The darkness tucked itself around them like a blanket.

"So, what's your plan?"

Brenna yawned. "We hit the ceiling with rocks in hopes the others are looking for us and will hear the pounding."

"Not bad," Eve said. "But I don't recall seeing any rocks big enough for that. Did you?"

"No." She was silent. "That's a bummer."

She was beginning to sound odd, Eve thought, with almost a childish lilt in her voice. "We'll worry about it later. Tell me how you came to be at Wisdom Court."

"I make movies." Brenna breathed slowly. "Got a letter from Rose 'cause she saw one of 'em. Invitation, too. How 'bout you?"

"Somebody here read my blog pieces and a few short stories I wrote." Eve blew out a breath. "I was supposed to get here when you did, I think. Then I broke my leg."

Brenna was quiet and Eve began to wonder if she'd dropped into sleep. Then she asked, "You gonna work on a book here?"

"I'd like to." Eve fought off a desire to let her feelings go—fear, anger, sorrow—all of them churning inside her. "All I ever wanted is time to write without life getting in the way."

"You have a life? That's cool." The gravel rattled and Eve felt Brenna move beside her. "I'm so sleepy," she said through a yawn. "I'll take a little nap and we'll figure it out."

Alarm clutched at Eve. What if she *did* have a concussion? She shouldn't be allowed to sleep, should she? Wasn't that what she'd read in first aid books? People were always waking up the concussed. "Uh, just rest for a bit, but don't go to sleep, okay? We can keep talking for a while."

"Okay." Brenna yawned again and Eve had to fight sliding into one of her own. "It's getting colder."

"Is your jacket zipped?"

Brenna didn't say anything, and her breathing slipped into a regular rhythm.

"Crap." Eve listened to her breathe for a while, wondering what she should do. Her imagination was gearing up, little noises hinting at squirming snakes and spiders spinning webs.

Eve grabbed for the flashlight and clicked the switch. She moved the dimming light over the walls, surprised at the amount of dust in the air. No snakes or spiders presented themselves. As she flicked the switch, the light reflected off something in the corner and she turned it back on again. She couldn't find anything at first, but there it was, a tiny flash near the floor.

Eve crawled across the floor and aimed the flashlight again, finding a small bit of metal close to where the two walls met. She scraped at the metal and caught her nail on the edge of it, pulling it toward her. A small drawer slid out of the wall silently. When she shone the light inside it, she saw a packet tied around with leather string. As she pulled it out of the compartment, the drawer slid shut.

Eve took the packet back to her resting place, pausing to shine the light over Brenna. She winced at the sight of her head wound. She sat down beside her and started to open the small package but the light was fading. Flicking off the light, she put it with the package and tucked both against her stomach as she lay on her side. She would keep guard over Brenna and wait for the others to find them. That was her last thought before sleep captured her.

Evie, wake up. Wake up now. It's important.

"What?" Eve's eyes popped open in the dark and she knew she was in the hidden chamber. The nest of snakes was near and they would eat Danica.

Evie, watch out—the drill—take cover…

"Charlie, is that you?" Eve struggled to waken, half in her dream, half unaware of where she was.

She pushed herself up, scraping her head against something behind her. "No!" At a nearby movement she sidled away, trying to escape. "No!" Her voice climbed. "Get away from me."

"Eve, it's me, Brenna."

Eve felt a hand on her arm. "Brenna?"

"Yeah. What's wrong? Did you hear something?" Her voice was as scared as Eve's.

Eve let out a sob and patted the floor around her with manic energy. "God, the flashlight, where is it?" Her fingers brushed against the cylindrical shape, closing around it tightly and she knocked it against the packet. When she switched it on, the dim light was the best thing she'd ever seen. She picked up the package and tried to put it in her pants pocket.

"A nightmare?"

"I guess. Something woke me up, I'm not sure what."

They were still in the room and the floor was dry. Nothing had changed.

On that thought, a sudden loud thump came from overhead, and dust fell from the ceiling. A second thud was followed by a cracking sound. More dirt scattered around them, some falling onto their heads.

"What is it?" Brenna grabbed the flashlight and shone it across the ceiling. "Is it breaking down?"

"Don't know."

A sliver of light appeared with another crash, more rocks and dirt falling near them.

"My God, I think somebody's trying to get in." Brenna coughed at the rising dust.

Eve shuddered at the next smash, ducking as several rocks fell close to their position. "They don't know we're here! Hey!" she yelled as she scrambled to her feet. "Stop! We're here! Stop digging!" A good-sized rock fell behind her and she spun to see if Brenna was okay. In the dim light she could see her leaning against the wall, arms covering her head.

"Neal, Rose, somebody!" screamed Eve. "Stop! You'll hurt us if you don't." The response was another stone, this one the biggest yet. She scooted over to Brenna, grabbing her by one hand. "Come on," she panted, tugging her toward the other side of the room. "Yell. Scream with me."

Brenna stumbled after her, wincing in pain. "Help! Help us," she shouted.

Eve took a deep breath and shrieked. "Help us!"

Dust rustled to the floor in the sudden silence. A muffled "Hello?" floated through the room.

Brenna turned toward Eve. "Did you hear?"

Eve nodded.

"We're here," Brenna yelled. "We're down here."

The blade of a hand saw slid through one of the cracks overhead and moved up and down over and over again, moving to an angle and rising and falling until another length was cut. When the saw appeared at the end of the two cuts and sliced across the space between, Brenna grabbed Eve's hand and held it.

Something thudded against the cuts and a chunk of wood fell to the floor. "Eve? Brenna? Are you in there?"

"Yes," they both shouted.

They heard muffled talking and then they could see a portion of a face filled the hole. Eve waved the dying flashlight at it and realized it was Neal.

"Thank God," they heard him say. "We'll get you out."

Brenna leaned against Eve, forcing her back against the wall behind them. "I'm so glad they found us," she said through sobs. "I'm really sick of this place."

At Eve's trembling laugh, Brenna laughed as well, and then cried some more. "No hysterics," Eve said as she helped Brenna down to the floor. "Lean against the wall and relax. It won't be long now."

TIME OUT OF TIME

"The membership is restless." Fitch lifted the silver dagger from the desk, shifting it in his thick hand to allow it to catch the light from the fireplace.

Severn lunged across the desk and wrested it from him, replacing it with exaggerated care. "I've told you before not to touch anything you see here." He could not show weakness in front of this buffoon. His eyes held Fitch's gaze until the man was forced to turn away. "What gives you the idea of restlessness in our esteemed colleagues?" He hardly knew what he was saying.

Fitch flushed at the contempt in his voice. "They ask for details about your plan, and several hint they'll leave the group if action isn't taken soon." An instant of pleasure gleamed in his close-set eyes. "I've kept them in line so far, but they're eager to *do* something."

"Really." Severn sat in the leather chair, barely containing his rage. Resting his hands on the polished surface of the desk he laced his long fingers together to prevent their curling into claws. "Clearly I am in your debt." He noted the smile forming at the man's lips and decided to kill him at the next half moon. He was a liability due to the attention he'd drawn in the car accident. But he was useful enough to keep around for the moment. "You assured them of our ongoing progress, I assume."

Fitch shot him a glance, his round face creasing with petulance. "They listen to me, but I need to kindle their keenness." His hand formed a fist on the arm of the chair. "It would help if I knew more about the plan. As you always say, zeal stimulates belief." He took a breath. "If they lose belief, what will fuel our efforts?"

Fear. His gaze resting on his hands, Severn was silent. "Your warning is appreciated," he said at last. A lightning glance caught the flash of relief on Fitch's face. "Our efforts have been only partially successful. If they ask, tell them the remote viewing has become more effective." He paused, considering his words. He would throw this weasel a bone to see how far afield it was taken. "This is for your ears only: I have detected another in our game, someone I've not yet identified."

Fitch frowned. "Another?"

The man's an idiot, Severn thought savagely. "I'll explain another time. We must be cautious."

Fitch had brightened at the thought of private information. "I'll keep this to myself, of course." He raised one brow and asked hopefully, "May I be of help?"

Not bloody likely. For a moment Severn feared he'd spoken aloud, but Fitch maintained his concerned expression and he knew he had not. "I'll call on you if need be." He rose to his feet and Fitch followed his lead. "Before you go, jot down the names of those who are…particularly impatient with our pace." At the arrested look in Fitch's eyes, he came around the desk, hand extended. "I can depend on you to maintain order, my friend, but I must make certain clear communications exist among all the members." *They will suffer for their doubt.*

Fitch was already nodding in agreement.

"I have another appointment," Severn added. "Simms will provide you with pen and paper. Leave the list with him and I'll look it over later this evening."

He opened the study door and ushered Fitch out into the hall, signaling to the butler, giving him brief orders. As he strode down the corridor, he heard Fitch slipping into the pompous tones he used with the servants.

Severn fell against the wall, strength nearly gone. He'd been so close. So close! He'd touched her; he'd felt the jerking of her flesh as his hand nearly grabbed hold of her.

He made his way to his chair. He could not mount another attack tonight. But soon…soon he would destroy her.

CHAPTER 15

Dr. Jerri Williamson's usually pleasant face was grim and anger burned in her eyes. "What in hell is going on here? At the rate you're going, you'll have a body on your hands the next time you call me."

"Oh, no, Jerri," Aura Lee protested. "It's not that bad."

For all her upset, Jerri's touch was gentle as she cleaned Brenna's forehead with alcohol-soaked gauze and tossed the pad into the wastebasket near the bed. "I expect you at my office in the morning," she said to Brenna in clipped tones. "An MRI is in order." When Brenna took in a breath to argue, she raised her hand. "Otherwise I'll call an ambulance and have you admitted to Boulder Community today."

Brenna subsided, a sulky cast to her mouth.

The doctor glared at Aura Lee. "Take me to my other patient." She followed her to the door where she paused to look back at Brenna. "Stay in bed. Even if you don't have a concussion, you've been through enough to wear you down. I mean it. Stay off your feet."

"Okay." Brenna's expression softened. "Thank you."

"Welcome." Jerri waved Aura Lee ahead of her. "Lead on, McDuff."

Eve was lying on the long couch in the living room. The idea of curling up by the fireplace had been too pleasant to resist. So far she'd had the additional perks of tea and cookies, along with Rose's frequent passes through the room to check on her. *I could get used to this.* Eve nestled into the cushions, pulling the blanket a bit closer, and fell into sleep.

The landscape was pitted with craters and ongoing explosions explained their numbers. She limped the best she could through the rough terrain, but smoke and dust in the air slowed her. She didn't dare fall. She'd never get up.

Dust and blood, haunted by rue,
String of guts, fear and a grue.
Hone the edges, score the skin,
Choke the breath without, within.

Eve moved her head from side to side, a grimace twisting her features. She plucked at the throw draped over her.

Sleight of hand, the eyes obscured.
Rich blood to drink, aged and cured.
Long strand of evil, then to now.
Life on the edge, to my will bow.
"Evie, wake up. Wake up now!"

Eve's eyes shot open as she let out a cry. Nearby she heard a voice and she jerked her head toward it. Aura Lee led a woman into the room and they both headed directly for her.

Aura Lee bent over her, eyes searching her face. "What is it, dear? I heard you scream. Are you all right?"

The woman beside her took hold of Eve's wrist, one finger measuring her pulse. Her square, kind face was intent. "Were you running laps in here? You're heart's beating like you were."

Eve shook her head and Aura Lee murmured, "She broke her leg some weeks ago. There's a limp."

"Bad dream," Eve whispered.

"I'm Jerri Williamson, closest thing to a house doctor at Wisdom Court."

Her eyes were compassionate, Eve decided, and she smiled tentatively. "Happy to meet you."

Jerri sat on the edge of the sofa. "I'd say the same, but I have the feeling that something going on around here is affecting everyone's health." She lifted her hand and put her palm against Eve's forehead. "You're a little feverish. The others said you were in the tunnel between six and eight hours. Does that sound about right?"

Eve stopped to think. "I'm not sure," she said after wandering through cloudy thoughts. "Neither of us had a watch and our phones wouldn't work, so we couldn't tell time." Eve closed her eyes and sighed deeply. "I'm so tired."

Jerri frowned up at Aura Lee. "Were any gas lines affected by the tunnel collapse?"

Aura Lee's expression moved from concerned to terrified. "By the Goddess, I don't know. Neal hasn't said any were, but we're not exactly sure about any of it."

"Did you hit your head on anything? Any rocks hit you?"

Eve lifted her eyelids, heavier now than before. "Yesterday—was it yesterday?—when I fell into the secret room I think I hit my neck or head on the edge of the trapdoor. *Was* it yesterday?"

Jerri Williamson stood up abruptly. "Go get Rose," she told Aura Lee. "Tell her I have to talk to her. Right now."

As Aura Lee scuttled away, Eve reached up to tug on the edge of her sweater. The rich rust color of it was pleasing, she thought fleetingly. "I'm really okay. Just reaction, I think. We haven't eaten in a while, low blood sugar. Check out my eyes."

Jerri studied her, finally resuming her seat on the edge of the sofa cushion. "All right." Pulling a small flashlight from her bag, she peered into Eve's eyes and, to her surprise, her ears. When she was finished her lips twisted in a rueful smile. "I'm probably nuts, but I don't think you're concussed. I imagine you need a good night's sleep, several, in fact, and a pile of comfort food."

"Jerri? Is anything wrong?" Rose came into the room drying her hands on a towel. "Is Eve badly injured?"

"Remarkably enough, no." Jerry slid the flashlight into her bag and closed it, then got to her feet. "Eve, I want you to get that sleep, and the food. I'm ordering you to be careful with yourself for a few days. Understand?"

Eve nodded.

"Cross your heart." At Eve's short laugh, Jerri frowned. "I mean it. I want your solemn promise to veg out for a day or two. Deal?"

"Okay," Eve returned. "Deal."

Jerri patted her hand. "Thank you." She turned to Rose. "I need to talk to you for a minute."

"All right." Rose led her toward the kitchen and stopped at the table. "You want to sit?"

Jerri was already pulling out a chair. "Got any coffee hot?"

"I'll see." Rose slid a cup out of the cabinet and put it under the urn. When she twisted the spigot, coffee flowed into it. "Here you go."

"Thanks." Jerri drank the coffee down fast and Rose wondered how she managed not to burn her mouth.

"I need to know what's happening here," Jerri said abruptly.

Rose considered her. "Why?"

"Because you've called me more frequently this past week than you ever have. Because your people here are apparently involved in dangerous things. Because I'm worried about all of you." She examined Rose with penetrating eyes. "I'm not going to blab about it; doctor patient privilege and all that."

Her gaze dropping to her hands, Rose let out a long breath. "I don't know if you'll believe me if I tell you. It's gotten pretty damned weird."

"Try me."

Aura Lee passed the doorway to the kitchen on her way to her rooms. She heard Rose and Jerri talking quietly and wondered what it was about. She shook her head at her own curiosity as the hall clock struck nine.

Charlie was in her head again. Eve awoke all the way, the end of what he'd said ringing in her ears. "Not so loud," she muttered aloud.

"I'm doing everything I can to deflect his energies, but it's getting harder. He's hell-bent on getting to you. He doesn't know exactly where you are, but he and his cretins have identified the general area. I had to carry that information to him myself."

"Thanks so much." Eve stopped, realizing what he'd said. "You mean you're working with him?"

"I mean I've infiltrated his filthy organization. How in hell do you imagine I'm able to give you this information?"

"How in hell do you imagine I'm dealing with the fact of a voice in my head, let alone figuring out what's going on?" Eve hit the sofa cushion. "Dammit, Charlie, you haven't told me much of anything."

"You can't expect me to sustain a narration of my activities! I'm risking my life just being here. If any of them finds out—"

Eve growled deep in her throat. "Listen to me. Things are happening here, stuff falling apart. You show up with cryptic messages every once in a while and that's supposed to be helpful? Well, it isn't!"

"Eve, are you all right?"

Aura Lee was standing in the doorway. Eve couldn't see her face, but she was fairly certain she was wearing her concerned expression. Inside her head Charlie was saying, *"Talk to Max. Tell him what I've told you. Put some things together, for the love of God."*

"Eve?"

She closed her mind to Charlie. "I'm all right."

Aura Lee came further into the room. "I thought I heard you talking to someone."

"Dreaming, I think." Eve pushed herself into a sitting position. "I hate to ask, but the doctor told me to eat something. I wasn't very hungry before, but now I'm famished."

Aura Lee nodded wisely. "Of course you are. Let me get you something." She turned and then looked back. "Did Jerri tell you to eat anything in particular?"

"Comfort food."

Aura Lee's laugh was full. "That's the best prescription I've ever heard."

Eve returned her smile. "Isn't it? Whatever you have will be fine."

"I'll be back in a jiffy."

Eve watched her disappear. When she heard a cupboard door and the clink of dishes, she closed her eyes and thought hard. *Charlie?* He'd been able to hear her before when she didn't speak. *Charlie?*

She kept trying to reach him, but there was no response.

What if he'd been discovered while he was communicating with her? What if she'd made him so angry he hadn't protected himself adequately? *Charlie, please hear me, please tell me you're there.* No response.

After a while she stopped trying, fearing she might be distracting him with her continued efforts. She focused her attention on the fire, nearly getting lost in the flames. Her gaze rose to the painting over the fireplace. It portrayed a woman probably in her thirties. Her chestnut hair was worn in an upsweep and her gray-green eyes held a hint of mischief under flaring brows. Eve wondered if the firmness of her mouth suggested pain. The idea of pain made her think again of Charlie.

By the time Aura Lee returned with a tray, Eve felt she'd ruined everything, even Charlie's chances of survival. Then she remembered he'd told her to talk to Max. That she could do.

"Here you are, my dear. I hope you'll enjoy it."

Aura Lee had taken the idea of comfort to an extreme. On the tray was a bowl of rich chicken soup swimming with plump dumplings. The scent of the broth alone had her salivating. An iced brownie was obviously the dessert, and a glass of deep red wine was waiting for her to drink it. "This is wonderful," Eve said, blinking back threatening tears. "Thank you."

"You're more than welcome." Aura Lee beamed down at her. "Is there anything else I can get you?"

Eve took a swallow of the wine, thankful for the warmth of it filling her chest. "Is Max around?" she asked carefully. "I'd like to talk to him."

Aura Lee looked at her thoughtfully. "I believe he and Kerry are at her place. Do you want me to ask both of them to come over?"

Eve fumbled with her spoon. "Yes, that would be fine."

Pleased, Aura Lee nodded. "I'll call them right now." She hurried from the room.

Eve took a bite of the chicken soup, closing her eyes at the blend of flavors on her tongue. No matter what happens at Wisdom Court, she thought in gratitude, we get the most delicious food.

She was fighting off a desire to lick bits of icing off the brownie plate when she heard a sound at the door.

Aura Lee bustled in, eying the tray and its empty dishes. "You really were hungry, weren't you? Do you want some more?"

Eve smiled up at her, eyes at half-mast. "No, but thanks. Everything was so good. I can feel myself healing already."

Aura Lee beamed in pleasure. "Goddess bless you, child. You look as though you might nap for a while."

Nodding, Eve settled herself a little further into the sofa cushions. "I'd like to. Are Max and Kerry coming over soon?"

Aura Lee set the tray on the liquor cabinet and turned back to shake out and smooth Eve's blanket. "Nobody answered so I left a message. You go ahead and sleep if you can. That's the best thing for you. They'll be over here before long anyway, if I know them." Deftly she plumped the pillow and slid it back under Eve's head.

"Okay." Eve smiled again. "Thanks, Aura Lee."

"You're more than welcome." Aura Lee picked up the tray and Eve caught sight again of the portrait over the fireplace.

"Who's in the painting?" she asked.

Aura Lee glanced over her shoulder. "That's our founder, Caldicott Wyntham."

"What was she like?"

Aura Lee's smile held a world of sadness. "She was wonderful." She walked toward the kitchen door. "Rest now."

Eve lay still, relishing the comfort of a full belly and a warm place to sleep. *All I need now is to know that Charlie is safe. Maybe he'll get in touch soon.* Lips curving at the thought, she drifted into sleep. When Danica landed on the spot beside her, she didn't wake up, but the purring of the little cat followed her into her dreams.

CHAPTER 16

K erry's kitchen was a cross between a badly organized
library and a squalid dorm room. Dishes were stacked
in the sink full of cold soapy water, and books of all sizes
formed towers at the edge of a paper war zone atop the
table. They'd been organizing piles of information since the
early morning hours.

Max glanced up from his notes with a frown. "My
timeline is off again. When did Caldicott take the job at the
bookstore?"

Kerry had been reading through her sequential list of
paranormal events, adding items as she compiled details
gleaned from everyone at Wisdom Court. "What?"

Max rubbed at the frown lines between his eyebrows. His
light brown hair fell over his forehead and he pushed it out
of his eyes. "The bookstore with the Russian, or whatever
he was. When did she start working there?"

Kerry cocked her head to read the titles on the spines of
the books stacked along the kitchen counter. "Here." She
drew a journal from the first pile and slid it across the table.

Max's fingers brushed against hers as he pulled the book
toward him. "Thanks, luv." He shot her a smile but she
didn't see it. Kerry was trying to remember if Aura Lee had
described music when she saw the hand extending through

the surface of her silver tray. She didn't think so, but hadn't there been sound? Oh, of course, the strange humming that had increased in volume to an ear-splitting scream.

"Bloody hell," Max said softly. He was glaring down at the open journal. "Bloody fucking hell."

Kerry's eyes blurred as she went from one list to the other, trying to find where she'd left off. It was four lines down from the top. Maybe.

Max flipped another page. "Bollocks."

Kerry lifted her chin to frown at him. "What the hell, Max?"

"You do realize we never finished reading this one, don't you?" he muttered at the pages.

She sighed in irritation. "Tell me what's got your goat or shut up and let me work."

Max's gaze scorched her. "We didn't finish reading this journal." He bit off the words, lips curled in a snarl. "We were interrupted when Eve arrived the other night. So much has happened, we didn't return to read the rest of it."

"Oh my God!" Kerry nearly pushed her chair over in her haste to get to the other side of the table. "Let me see."

Max snatched up the volume and held it out of her reach.

Kerry narrowed her eyes. "Max," she warned, her voice rising. "Hand that over right now."

"No."

He grunted when she landed on his lap, and before she knew it, Kerry was trapped in his arms. He was stronger than he looked. "I want to see it."

"No." His eyes were alight with mischief. He tightened his grip, bending his head to nibble on her earlobe.

Kerry tilted her head closer to allow his lips better access to the spot behind her ear. "What, you want to gather the others and go over it together?"

"Not bloody likely."

The tip of his tongue was circling the inner rim of her ear. Kerry thought she would slide off his lap onto the floor in a puddle of melted nerve endings.

His hands were moving across her belly, aiming lower for the softness between her legs. His fingers stroked in a teasing gesture, lower still and Kerry shifted in his hold. His teeth bit lightly at her neck until she turned her head toward him and captured his mouth with her own.

The shrill ring of the landline phone cut through their fog like a chainsaw through lumber.

Kerry moaned in disappointment.

The second ring thrust more of the real world between them. Kerry kissed his lips lightly and began to wiggle off his lap.

"No." Max's arms tightened. "Not this time. Let the voice mail pick up."

Kerry softened, settled back onto his lap. "What if there's an emergency?"

He licked her throat. "There's always an emergency." His voice was guttural. His lips searched for hers and, finding them, deepened the kiss until they breathed as one.

She pulled away and turned her head, pressing her ear against his chest. At the slow thump of his heartbeat she fell into his rhythm. They held each other in a long span of wordless conversation.

Finally Max loosed his arms and tucked her head under his chin. "I want you."

"Me, too." His arms encircled her and Kerry let out a long sigh. This was the closest she'd ever felt to heaven.

"But I know us, darling." He nuzzled her available ear. "Guilt-ridden over-achievers, the two of us. If we seek our bed we'll have fun, but the shadow will be there."

Kerry smiled. His mixture of pedantry and romanticism was beyond wonderful. "You're right, damn you. The long arm of responsibility beckons."

"When this is all over, I'll take you to Ireland, to one of those snug little inns and we'll stay in bed for a month." He tilted her chin up and captured her lips. He pulled back to look into her eyes. "No ghosts," he whispered, "no shrieks in the night, accept when you come." He kissed her again. "Just you and I and a bed."

Kerry shivered. "We could buy tickets now."

Max groaned at the thought. "Long arm...responsibility..." He turned his head, holding her to his heart. Again their separate breaths melded in one rhythm and Kerry felt a pang of pure happiness.

When Max went still, Kerry whispered, "It's all right, love. We'll enjoy ourselves more if we've done the work."

Max was scarcely breathing, and his arms were clenching her too tightly. "Max?"

"Look," he said, voice guttural again, but not with passion. "Over at the counter by the sink."

She turned her head in time to see a stack of books rising toward the ceiling light fixture, separating and floating down to land, one by one, on the table.

"Shit." Kerry blinked and looked again. Another stack was moving directly toward them. "Somebody's impatient at our leisurely pace."

The books fell to the floor, near their chairs. "Crikey!" Max pushed her off his lap and jumped to his feet. "Let's get out of here." Grabbing her hand, he tugged her toward the door. Kerry snatched up the journal and tried to keep up with his rapid pace.

Max flung open the door and pulled her out, slamming it behind them. Rapid thuds of objects hitting the door followed.

"Our books?" Kerry whispered, as if someone was listening.

"What else?"

The doorknob rattled violently and they ran down the hallway toward the outer door as if pursued by devils.

When they reached the main house, they silently looked at each other. "Are you okay?" Kerry asked Max softly. She reached up to caress his hair into a semblance of order.

Max grabbed her hand and planted a kiss on her palm. "More than. And you?"

Kerry sighed. "Cast out of heaven by the spirits of industry." When he laughed, she hugged him to her. "We got out alive, that's all that matters. Question is, should we tell them right away or check the lay of the land first?"

Max grimaced. "I'm for easing into it later. Too much has happened lately to be ham-handed now."

"Agreed." She reached up for a kiss. "Let's go in."

When they opened the door, the perfume of food drifted to them and they exchanged a glance. "Chicken and dumplings, I'd reckon." Kerry inhaled deeply. "My God, I'm starved."

"Me, too." Max shivered. "And cold. Those bastards ran us off before we could get our coats."

"I'll bet everyone's in by the fire. Let's go."

They entered the living room, making a beeline for the fireplace. Kerry shuddered as the heat hit her. "Don't hog all the heat, luv," Max murmured as he nudged her over to one side. Eve watched them from the sofa, giving a fleeting thought to the easy bond between them. She'd never experienced that. The idea of Charlie flashed in her mind and she wondered if being inside someone's head could be the greatest intimacy of all. The notion gave her pleasure and her lips curved in a smile.

When she glanced up, Kerry and Max were staring at her oddly. *Wait till they hear what I have to tell them. They'll probably call in a shrink. Or laugh me out of town.* "Pull up a chair."

Kerry sat on the sturdy wingback across from her and Max pulled an ottoman near it. Kerry eyed her with sympathy. "Did Jerri come see you today?"

Eve nodded. "She's great. I thought sure she'd swoop in and put me in the hospital. Instead she just checked me over and told me to pig out on Aura Lee's food. Tough duty, right?"

Max's smile was brief. He leaned against Kerry's chair and crossed one ankle over the other. "Are you ready to talk about what happened?"

Eve closed her eyes for a moment, using her old trick of

imagining words on a page to organize her thoughts. "Do you know someone named Charlie?" she asked him. Danica jumped onto the sofa beside her.

Max smiled. "She's a lovely cat. I didn't get to see her when you arrived." He considered her carefully. "Do you have a surname for this Charlie you mentioned?"

Shrugging her shoulders, Eve looked away from the curiosity lighting his eyes. "It was a casual introduction." She noticed how he groped for Kerry's hand. "Charlie is a common name."

Evidently Max could read something in her face, or her voice. He leaned forward, his hand still clasping Kerry's. "Tell us, Eve."

She studied him for a moment. What did she have to lose? Both of them might think she was delusional, but the whole place was crawling with apparitions, to say nothing of snakes.

"He's been talking to me."

Max nodded slowly. "Charlie."

"Yes." Eve glanced at Kerry and was taken aback at the growing understanding spreading across her face.

"How?" Max asked. "By telephone? Online?" he added when Eve raised her brows in question.

Eve braced herself. *Here goes nothing.* "In my head." Danica bumped her head against Eve's arm and she petted her reflexively.

Kerry shot a look at Max. When he didn't say anything, she frowned at him.

Eve took a breath and let it out slowly. "He talks to me inside my mind." She waved in an offhanded gesture. "He was with me when I was trapped under my apartment."

"He's been helping you," Max said.

Nodding, Eve added, "When Brenna and I were in the tunnels, he woke me up to warn me about the drill Neal and the others were using to cut into the earth over our heads." She smiled a little. "Charlie always seems to catch me when I'm asleep."

Max leaned back against Kerry's chair. "Well," he said on a long exhale, "one never knows how things work out, does one?"

"What do you mean?" Eve was confused by the gleam of humor in his eyes. "You do know him, don't you?"

"Yes." Max paused for a moment. "As it happens, a colleague named Charlie sent me a message telling me something about your flat was dangerous."

"How would he know that?"

Max shrugged. "That's the least of our issues. All right then, tell me about this Charlie of yours."

Rubbing her hands together, Eve thought back. "He might have, uh, approached me as early as before I arrived here at Wisdom Court. Looking at it now, he probably wakened me several times when odd things were happening. As I said, he usually shows up when I'm sleeping."

"Do you hear his voice or think what he's saying?" Kerry paused. "I guess I'm asking how you communicate with him? Or he with you?"

Eve considered how to accurately describe what she'd experienced. "The first thing I remember him telling me is to wake up." She caught the glance between Max and Kerry. "I didn't hear him so much as I jerked awake because he was in my mind saying it several times. *Wake up, Evie.*"

"He knew you were asleep."

Eve shrugged. "Evidently."

"And you were in New Jersey then?" At Eve's nod, Kerry said to Max, "That's quite a distance."

"Where does this colleague of yours live?" Eve asked.

"Near London." His lips twisted at the surprise in her face. "It's not a question of distance."

Eve leaned toward him. "What isn't?"

Max ran both hands through his hair. "I'm getting ahead of myself. Let's continue with you and I'll fill in from my end after that."

"Okay." Eve recounted the times she could remember when Charlie had awakened her, and told them how he'd helped her regain control of herself in the hidden chamber beneath her rooms in the associate house. "He sounded stressed," she said slowly. "As if he was under pressure of some kind, but he kept trying to keep my spirits up. It was during that when he told me to talk to you, to give you a message."

Max raised a brow.

"He said he was getting close, was trying to get through." Eve frowned. "He was having some difficulties, he said."

"So he wasn't sending the message directly to you, Max?" The irritation in Kerry's voice was clear. "Quit the fuddy-duddy discretion and just tell her."

Eve looked from one to the other. "What do you mean?"

"I mean that—"

Max interrupted her. "She thinks I'm not being forthright with you. Charlie and I work together and we communicate with each other the same way you and he do, Eve. Until this moment, however, I didn't realize he was able to do so. We've always been the only two."

"Who could be in touch mentally." Eve gave him a long look. Then she frowned as a thought occurred to her. "So why are you and I having to talk out loud?"

"I haven't a clue." Max pondered the thought. "We know so little about psi functions and the range of talents individuals have within them. You and Charlie apparently have an intensely strong link allowing you to have complete conversations with one another. Charlie and I do fairly well, but our communiqués aren't nearly as detailed."

Kerry stirred in the chair. "The amazing thing is that Charlie knows when you're in danger and can send his thoughts to you. It makes me wonder. Do you have any kid of visual impression of him? Because he might have of you."

Eve shook her head. "The only awareness I have is of his voice. I feel it. As I told you, I knew he was under pressure that one time. I could tell by his voice he was worried about me. He seems to get me, if you know what I mean."

Kerry nodded. "That's so cool, as long as he's a good guy. It would be scary as hell if he weren't."

"There's a thought." Eve's voice weakened.

Max shot Kerry an annoyed glance. "So reassuring."

Kerry's cheeks reddened. "Sorry. We start talking about this stuff and it's hard to fight off questions, you know?"

Eve nodded. "Basic reality has turned upside down ever since I got here. You're not the only one asking questions. I have one for you. What's Charlie's last name?"

"Pierce." Max smiled. "I don't have a photo of him, but I can tell you he's a bit over six feet tall, has auburn hair he keeps short. His eyes are blue-green and his humor is wicked."

Eve's gaze fell to her hands. "Um, that's very interesting." At Kerry's laugh, she glanced up at the two of them. "Don't get any ideas. But you try having someone wandering around inside your head and see how you react."

"I'm sure it's difficult to get used to." Max looked to Kerry. "I'm sorry, but if I keep smelling that food without eating any of it, I'm going to fall into despair." He stood up and headed for the kitchen.

Kerry rose as well, looking down at Eve. "You've been through a lot, even for life at Wisdom Court. Take it easy and we'll help you get caught up on what's been going on. Maybe you'll feel like reading Caldicott's journals tomorrow."

"I'd like that." Eve nestled down under the blanket. "Once I get the lay of the land, I'd like to help with what you're doing to deal with all this stuff."

"We can use all the help we can get." Kerry gave Danica a pat or two and then waved a hand as she went in pursuit of Max.

That went well, Eve thought, her eyes slowly closing. It helped a lot to know some of the things going on at Wisdom Court. She took a deep breath and let it out. She was still afraid, and had good reason to be. But for the first time she felt a part of the group. That would make it easier to contend with whatever was behind the madness. On the thought she fell into a peaceful sleep.

Eve didn't hear the snatches of discussion from the kitchen as Aura Lee supplied Kerry and Max with food. She didn't feel the gaze of the glowing eyes watching her from the shadowy corners. She slept and did not dream. Danica growled low in her throat at the shifting of the drapery over the large window at the end of the room.

CHAPTER 17

B renna turned her head back and forth on the pillow. Her eyes were closed and images moved behind the lids. Tiny creatures, millions of insect-monsters were cascading, swarming, trying to climb the legs of her bed, coming to get her.

We are coming for you. We are coming for you. We are coming for you.

Stir the cauldron, feed the fire.
Masses spawning in the mire.
Speed the message, whet the knife.
Flesh under torment, end the life.

The chanting voices beat against her eardrums, the rhythm pounded out with a drum. An unknown stench floated by her nose and her face crumpled in disgust. Back and forth went her head as she fought the clinging vines of sleep.

I know I'm dreaming. Let me out, let me out.

The face behind her eyes was cut from stone-hard ice. Sharp angles, hot eyes half-lidded and alight with vicious glee. Black hair framed features twisted by hatred.

Long mouth opened, showed bloody teeth, the voice of doom chanted: *We are coming for you. We are coming for you. We are coming for you.*

Savage drums thundered. The fire flared higher, its smoke reeking of burnt flesh. A vortex of flame and rising voices and throbbing shapes spun in madness.

Melody cut through her mind, a baby's lullaby.

Hush-a-bye, don't you cry, go to sleepy little baby.

When you wake, you will find all the pretty little horses.

A tear escaped from the corner of her eye and trailed down her cheek.

Chickie, sweet girl, you're safe. You're safe.

Brenna heard the beloved voice and her eyes shot open. "Gran?"

She was in a shadowed room where a dim light eased the darkness. It reflected from an oval mirror and she remembered. Andrea had lent her room to her. She'd come back from the MRI prescribed by Jerri Williamson and had gone directly to bed. Aura Lee had been checking on her all evening.

Brenna let herself ease back into the pillow. It had been a horrible dream, and yet she'd heard her grandmother's voice. She could almost hear it still. It was the first time she'd dreamed of her as she'd been before Alzheimer's disease had destroyed her. "Oh, Gran," she whispered, her hand over her mouth, trying to keep tears at bay. "I miss you so much."

A sob escaped into the silence. *I will not cry again. I won't.* She inhaled to calm herself and froze. Exhaling slowly, she paused and took a deeper breath. There it was again. Floating over her face, riding the barest movement in the air was the scent of Wind Song, her grandmother's favorite perfume. "Gran?" Her whisper was little more than a sigh.

Brenna reached toward the left pocket of her jeans, then the right. Where had she left her cell phone? Through the aching of her head she tried to remember. She'd had it in the tunnel; she'd taken pictures but had no service for calls.

Pushing against the mattress, Brenna turned onto her side and looked at the bedside table. The dial of the landline phone was outlined by a blue glow. Slowly she extended her hand and picked up the receiver. She punched in Dink's number and waited through three rings.

"Hello?" His voice was rough, tired.

"Dink?"

"Bren?" Surprise edged his voice. "Is that you?"

"Yes." She swallowed at the lump in her throat. "Listen. I need you. Things are bad here, scary. I need you to be here with me." Her voice was breaking under the rush of small sobs rushing to get out.

"Hey, wait a minute, what's going on?" He listened to her attempts to stop crying. "Tell me what it is, babe. Talk to me."

"I'm messed up. Hit my head in the tunnel." Brenna paused, the weight of trying to explain everything too heavy for her to deal with. "Has the restaurant reopened? Can you get here without making problems for Sandoval?" Her voice trembled.

"Screw that." Dink was scared for her; she could hear the concern clearly. "I'll try to get the next plane out of here. Things are under control, but I'd come even if they weren't. Do you have someone taking care of you?"

Brenna nodded her head and the movement sent pain down her temples. "Yes, Aura Lee keeps creeping in to see if I'm okay." She felt a pang of guilt at asking him to upend everything to come to her. "I'm not dying, it's just that I needed to have you here. So much has happened."

"It's okay, don't worry. Tell them not to let you out of their sight. I'll be there as soon as I can."

"What about pickup?" fretted Brenna. "I can't drive, everyone else is up to their eyebrows—"

"They've got shuttles, right?" He paused. "Bren, don't worry about me, just take care of yourself. I'm coming, okay?"

Brenna struggled not to cry again. "Okay, okay. Love you."

"Love you, too."

The connection ended and Brenna replaced the receiver. "He's coming," she whispered. "He's coming."

* * *

Max and Kerry stared at each other blearily over the nest of throws tucked around them. The living fireplace glowed with red coals and the only sound was Eve's deep, even breathing.

"I guess everyone went to bed," Kerry whispered. Beside her Max nodded.

"What woke you up?" Max murmured. He tucked her head under his chin and tightened his arm around her shoulders.

"Don't know." Kerry's stomach growled and she suppressed a laugh.

"Want me to get us a snack?"

Kerry smiled into his eyes. "That would be great. Don't make any noise, though."

"What d'you want?"

"Brownies and milk," she answered promptly. "If there are brownies left."

Max rose from the sofa slowly and stood beside it until he could move easily. Kerry reached for his hand. "Your leg stiff?"

He nodded. "It's not a problem."

Kerry's smile was off center. "You wouldn't tell me if it were, would you?"

Max kissed the back of her hand. "I'm not so noble as all that. My sister tells me I complain more than anyone she knows."

Kerry stared at him in surprise. "You have a sister?" She realized how short a time it had been since his arrival. He could be the youngest of a dozen children and she wouldn't know it. They'd shared so little of their stories.

Max's expression was rueful, aware of her thoughts. "We just haven't had time, have we?"

She shook her head sadly. "I'm tired of going through all this. And of being scared all the time."

"I as well." He turned but looked down at her. "Coming across you has been the plum in the pudding."

"Don't you mean pie in the sky? You're just sweet-talking me."

"Not in the slightest."

Max headed for the kitchen and Kerry slid down under the covers. She was almost asleep again when he came back. He paused at the big couch where Eve slept and listened to her breathing for a moment. When he reached Kerry, he put a saucer on the coffee table and handed her a glass filled with milk. He set a book beside the glass.

"Thanks," she whispered and sipped at the cold liquid.

"My pleasure." He crawled into their nest and tucked the blankets around them.

Kerry nibbled her brownie and washed it down with milk, relishing the mix of flavors in her mouth. When she was finished she handed him the dishes and he returned them to the table.

"Are you sleepy?"

Kerry shook her head. "I was, but not now. Wish we could read for a bit."

Max slid the book on the coffee table his way and handed it to her.

"Cottie's journal?" Kerry started to open it. "It's too dark to read in here."

"I brought a torch." Max slipped it from behind his pillow and flicked it on. "We can't read aloud, but we can share this and go through it together."

"You're a genius."

Max kissed the tip of her nose. "I continue to tell you that."

"Okay," Kerry breathed, skimming over the pages they'd already read before Eve arrived. She glanced up from the journal page. "Quick summary," she whispered near his ear. "Caldicott renamed herself Anna Collins and went job hunting so she could provide a cover for the money she had coming from the German bearer bonds. After the first job with the furniture manufacturer ended in her being sacked, she was out of work for six months and then met the Russian bookshop owner, Arnie Zdretzer." She looked down at the journal once more. "We stopped reading at the point when she decided to get Arnie to help her create a new life."

"All right. Let's see what she has to tell us about that."

It was difficult for me to tell Arnie about my past. I trusted him because I had witnessed how careful he was in his efforts to help the immigrants who continued to approach him. His reputation would not be so sound if he'd betrayed any of these poor people.

No, while I wanted to tell him everything, a strong part didn't want to share anything with him or anyone else. I'd been hiding for a long time, and I'd lost a great deal. As long as I kept it hidden, I didn't have to see myself as one of the wounded refugees who sought out Arnie for guidance. I didn't have to admit to myself that I, too, had been a victim of the monsters who had nearly destroyed our world.

However, I underestimated Arnie. He recognized in me the similarities with his other clientele. The day he decided to broach the subject with me was filled with petty frustrations and I was upset at not being able to finish a mailing.

"Miss Anna," he said as he came into the small room that served as my office. "I have need to talk with you."

I barely looked at him, merely shoved a pile of papers toward the corner of the desktop and opened one of the large drawers holding the envelopes and labels. "What is it?" I'm certain the tone of my voice was barely civil.

Arnie sat down heavily in the chair beside my desk. "You have trouble?" he asked kindly. When I looked at him in surprise, he surveyed me closely. "You are pale from too much time with dusty books." He pointed at the open drawer with his deformed hand. "You do not smile and you do not talk to me over coffee as before." He poked his chest with his thumb. "I do not see reason for this so I must ask you." Then he sat silent, waiting for me to answer.

I waited, too, for the courage to reveal myself, to put myself in his hands. I sneaked a peek at him and let myself recognize the compassion in his steady gaze. "All right." I cleared my throat. "All right. I have some things to tell you. Will you have dinner with me tonight? I will explain."

He nodded, his thick lips curving in a smile. "I would be honored to break bread with you." He pushed himself out of the chair and stood looking down at me. "You need not be afraid." He turned and left my office.

For once I went home early, stopping at the butcher shop to buy a beef roast. Potatoes, parsnips, and apples, along with a loaf of rye bread, all from the nearby grocery, filled my bag. I took the time to bake an apple tart. And when Arnie knocked on my door, I greeted him and helped him out of his overcoat.

As he sat on my sofa, a glass of burgundy in hand, I hurried to the kitchen to lower the heat in the oven. We would talk and then we would eat.

As I came back into the small living room I said, "I'm not who you think I am, Arnie."

"No one is, dorogaya." He drank wine and put the glass on the coffee table in front of him. "Tell me."

I told it all, the story of Clara, the barmaid's daughter always being told to improve herself. I recounted my love affair with Duncan and when I dabbed at the tears in my eyes, Arnie used his large handkerchief to wipe at his. And as I told him about my escape from the little English village where Duncan was born, Arnie sat a little straighter and the interest in his eyes intensified.

"You were smuggled out in Gypsy wagon?"

I nodded. "Along with a fortune in German bearer bonds." I waited for his response, but he stared at his deformed hand and said nothing. Finally he lifted his head and met my eyes. "You have lived much for one so young," he said in a low voice. "I am honored you share your story with me. You are very brave."

Those few words released a storm of tears. I found myself beside him on the sofa, one of his tweed-covered arms around my shoulder. He murmured to me in Russian as I cried out my fear and pain, feelings I had hidden even from myself for long, lonely years.

As my crying ebbed, he reached for the glass of burgundy and held it to my lips. "Drink a bit of this, dorogaya. It will help you."

I finished the glass and thanked him with a kiss on his cheek. When I rose from the sofa he started to protest, but I waved away his words. "It's time for dinner. Come into the kitchen and we'll eat."

Arnie ate as if he hadn't for a long time. I had taught myself to cook roast beef after I settled in New York. We'd never had enough money to eat meat often and my mother wasn't the cooking sort. For a sharp, sad moment I wished I could fill a plate for her and watch her eat the food I'd prepared.

Mopping up the last of the gravy on his plate with a chunk of bread, Arnie shot a smiling glance at me across the table as he stuffed it into his mouth. He chewed with enjoyment and wiped his lips with his napkin. "You are good cook." He placed the napkin beside his plate and reached for his empty glass. "Let us have more wine and share further about your life." At my nod he rose from his chair and carried his glass with him into the living room.

I took the bottle and my own glass and we settled in to talk. I expected him to explain to me how he could help protect my money and guide me do something with it, but that was not what he was thinking about.

"You tell me more about the Gypsies you met in England, yes?"

I stared at him, not understanding why he would focus on that part of my story. Frowning, I told him the truth. "I met Andras and then his father and mother. Her name was Miriam, and she was the one who set the protective spell on the talisman that was in the bag Duncan gave me, the bag with the bearer bonds. That evening was the only time I've ever had anything to do with Gypsies. Why do you ask?"

He looked at his glass, brooding silently. When he raised his head to meet my eyes, his face was lined with pain. "All of us who remain have gone through terrible things. During the war, I lost members of my family as my wife did. Killed by the Nazi swine. Her people were Russian Gypsies."

I stared at him in surprise. "I'm so sorry."

"Several of her cousins in Germany died in the camps. One family crossed the border into France and, I learn later, made their way to England. I search for them since war ends, but what I find of them..." He dusted his hands together. "Neechevo."

"Do you think Andras and his people might have met them? Or perhaps offered them shelter in their group?"

Arnie drained his glass and set it on the table. "This I do not know. But I hunt for small details, any connection, hoping I will learn of them." His smile was sad. "Vadoma is gone, yes, but her questions are here. So I look."

I wracked my brain for anything Duncan had told me. All I could remember was the haunted expression he wore that last night we had together, when he told me of the Gypsy girl who had been killed in a ritual sacrifice, a cousin to Andras. I related this to Arnie. "His father was deeply involved in the occult. I assumed the girl's death had to do with one of their evil ceremonies. One of the reasons I've been so afraid of attracting the earl's notice is dread of being caught and punished by him and his followers. Duncan said his father planned to use the talisman to affect the course of the war."

The suffering in his face stopped me. What if the dead girl was one of his family members? "Arnie," I said in an uneven voice, "you don't think—"

"That this girl was one of mine?" He shook his head. "I do not know. The Romani are never treated well, but to be killed by this crazy nobleman...no, I think not so." He shifted his weight uncomfortably. "But I think you came into my shop for a reason. I think we work together on this problem of the money and your hiding place. I work many times to help people to disappear. You are another of these, I think."

I folded my lips together to stop their trembling. I had come this far, and now it appeared I would have to travel *again, to find another place to go to ground in order to avoid the evil man who would have been my father-in-law. "What do you suggest?"*

"First, you and I go over your books and then we look for new home for these bonds of yours. Is doubtful your English earl could find them as you set up two trusts, but I do not like that large sums move to New York on dates so near when you escape from England. This we must change."

Max laid his hand over the page to stop Kerry's reading. "Let's stop now, luv."

Kerry blinked, realizing how dry her eyes were.

"I can barely keep my eyes open." Max shifted against her and slipped lower on the pillow. "We can finish tomorrow, don't you think?"

Kerry yawned. "My eyes are tired. I could use some sleep."

He leaned toward her, his mouth capturing hers. He kissed her thoroughly and turned her toward the back of the sofa so he could wrap himself around her.

"Goodnight," she whispered, but he was already breathing in the deep pattern of sleep.

Kerry snuggled against him and drifted off.

The room settled into stillness, only the small sounds of the fireplace and the breathing of the three people in the room breaking the peaceful atmosphere.

The slow movement of the journal across the surface of the coffee table made no sound until the volume fell onto the rug. The little cat Danica awakened and watched as it continued, a legless creature, in a straight path down the corridor created by the placement of the items of furniture. It eased between the hearth and the sofa, eventually sliding soundlessly through the open door to the kitchen. Danica lowered her head to her paws and slept.

TIME OUT OF TIME

Seventh son of seventh son,
Blood of ages, held in one.
Force of evil, force of power,
Before thee must the weakened cower.

"Words from the grave, words from the grave." Severn murmured as he thumbed through the worn pages of the book in front of him. His life had been lived by this book. His first memories were triggered by its scent, a papery, dusty smell brushing his nose. It had opened his mind every time. And then came the pain.

Revulsion surged inside him. From his earliest days he had followed the strictures set down by his grandfather. No—his father. The man who had posed as his father had really been his brother, the sixth. He, Severn, was the seventh son.

Severn's hand tightened on the page, almost tearing it, and he smoothed it carefully. His lineage was impeccable, his birthright unassailable. His *pretend* father had hidden the hate provoked by the evil old man's dark passions, vented on him. The only thing they'd both received equally was the message: find the money, find the woman, and *find the talisman*. He was told only these achievements could make up for his illegitimate birth. He hadn't know the truth until the old man's death.

How different his life might have been if his wastrel brother had followed the old man's orders and gone in search of the three vital things. Instead he had reveled in sabotaging their inherited task. He'd ignored the work, had sought the lowest pleasures of the flesh: spreading his seed and drinking himself into oblivion. He was successful at both.

How many nephews and nieces did he have in the county? None of them had surfaced from the mire asking to join the family business.

The short, harsh laugh spat from his throat. *No matter. Laughter was strangled at an early age.*

Severn straightened his spine and bent again over the book. Days had passed since the defeat of his creation. "Such an elegant spell." His whisper rustled in the silent room. The fire was near dead, the coals able only to cast weak shadows.

He tried to focus on the arcane symbols marching across the vellum page, but his head pounded and his vision blurred.

Severn pushed himself up, inwardly cursing. What kind of weakling was he, to care deeply for a spell above all so short-lived? The intricacy he prided most likely was the flaw leading to the nest's demise.

Cold fear forced new questions. What if he were unable to complete the task? What if her powers blocked him from identifying the true location? What if he hadn't the strength to destroy the protections?

If only he had someone to help him.

The memory of his father's—no, his brother's—features filled his mind, the open, handsome face, symmetrical and surrounded by a thatch of curling hair. No one had ever appeared to notice the emptiness in his heavily fringed eyes. He'd been blessed with the fondest desire of every female: perfection of form, taken as a promise of virtue and truth. He, the seventh son, was dark of hair and eyes, features narrow and sharp. Women edged away from him, damn them.

"I wonder how many of the women he killed." The words pulsed in the air. *I wonder how many I've killed.* He'd kept no count but…many.

The woods had been allowed to swallow any paths, obliterate several cottages, to spread over the evidence of rites and rituals. If any of the bodies were ever found…

Irritated with his own disordered thoughts, Severn slumped back into the chair. Perhaps he needed a bit of his brother's favorite remedy. A woman and a bottle, judiciously mixed. They would provide a few hours of escape. He reached for the telephone on the desk. He tapped the button on the receiver and waited for a voice. When it came, he was puzzled as to its identity. *Is it Fitch?* He cursed at forgetting. *Fitch is no longer a part of the plan.*

"Who is this?" he demanded brusquely.

"It's Pierce, sir."

Severn thought quickly, mind sorting names and physical characteristics. Ah, the man with the auburn hair. "Pierce, I have need of the Mercedes. Bring it round."

"Certainly, sir."

Severn scowled at the dead receiver and replaced it onto the base. Very little deference came from that one.

CHAPTER 18

———◆———

Clouds had consumed the sun and shadows were spreading through Wisdom Court. Neal walked down the corridor to Rose's workroom and hesitated outside it. Aura Lee had told him she was resting and shouldn't be disturbed, but he had no choice. The courtyard was a danger and they had to decide what to do about it before someone fell into one of the holes.

Neal knocked gently at the door. "Rose? It's Neal."

"Come in," came the muffled reply as the lock clicked. The door swung open.

Rose peered out at him and he was shocked at her appearance. Dark circles ringed her gray eyes and her mouth was tight with tension.

"This won't take long," he said quickly. "I need a decision from you about the tunnels and then we can get other okays from the board. I'll be out of your hair in five minutes."

Rose pulled the door further open and waved him in. "Don't be silly. I may look like hell but I'm still running things around here." She gestured toward the chair across from her desk and plopped down into her own seat. "What's the estimate?"

"Sam started at fifteen thousand, but I think he's optimistic on that." Neal glanced at the clipboard he'd brought. "Most of the tunnel system is okay, though we need to inspect all of it thoroughly. The portions under and east of Eve's apartments are the most damaged, and the basic question has to do with how—or if—we go about fixing it. The good news is, the foundations appear to be in good shape."

Rose rolled a pencil between her palms, her eyes on a framed photograph in front of her. Neal couldn't see what it represented. "You said *if we fix it.*" She glanced up at him and he was struck at how…lost she looked. "Are you suggesting we fill it in and call it good?"

Neal rubbed his chin and the bristles made a scratching sound against his fingers. "I've tossed the idea around, but to tell you the truth, I think Cottie would haunt us if we did it. Though she probably already is." He leaned the clipboard against his chair legs and leaned forward to rest his elbows on his knees. "She has to be the one behind the building of those tunnels, and I imagine she had a good reason for it. I don't want to be the one to destroy what might be part of a defense system against our ghost problems."

Rose nodded, but didn't say anything. Neal straightened in the chair and waited.

After a few minutes, Rose stirred and sighed. "I'll propose to the board that we treat this as a restoration project. Remember, we've already formed a committee to get the main house on the historic registry. I think most will agree." Her eyes were weary. "After, that is, they've had a good time trying to figure out what Caldicott was thinking when she had them built."

"It'll spice up the next meeting." He met her gaze, his smile fading. "Have you told any of them what's been going on?"

Rose shrugged. "I had to fill in Jerri when she was here. After she checked out Eve and Brenna, she insisted on details. Couldn't blame her for that."

"No." Neal pushed himself out of the chair and stood looking down at her. "Sooner or later they'll have to know.

The way things are going it'll be damned soon." When she nodded, a rueful expression on her face, he headed for the door.

"Is Andrea staying with you again tonight?"

"Yeah." He caught the worry in her eyes. "Is that a problem?"

"Not really. It's just that I'd like us to go over the rest of that journal Brenna found. There hasn't been time and I've been wondering if there's anything in it that would help."

Neal rubbed the back of his neck and bit back a yawn. "We could stay for dinner and either read during it or wait until after. Gotta admit, I could use some sleep."

Rose stood up and pointed at his clipboard, still on the floor next to his chair. "Don't forget that." She waited as he bent to retrieve it and followed him to the door. "Are you talking to Sam again tomorrow?"

"Yeah. I told him I'd call him late morning. I'll have him do two estimates, one for a fill-in, one for rebuilding the tunnels. That way we can take both to the board meeting."

"Sounds good." Rose closed the door behind them and locked it. When she saw Neal watching her, she shrugged. "I haven't seen any more circles lately, but I want to be sure no one else has had access in case there are some. Plausible deniability."

Neal had the familiar feeling they were sinking into a swamp of paranoia. "I hear you."

The distant chime of the front doorbell sounded as they walked into the kitchen. Neal glanced at Rose. "Is Aura Lee still here?"

"She was going on a grocery run last I heard." Rose picked up her pace and trotted toward the dining room. "I'll get it."

The bell rang again and Rose called, "Coming." When she arrived at the door, she turned the latch and swung it open. There on the step were Elizabeth Schuster and Dolores Rivera. The two had ended their Wisdom Court year almost two months before.

"My God, what are you doing here?" Rose said over Elizabeth's shoulder as they hugged each other. "And you?" Dolores was clutching her like a limpet. Rose pulled back and took a closer look at both of them. They, in turn, exchanged a grimace at the sight of her.

From behind her Neal greeted the two. "Man, it sure is good to see you." He caught hold of Elizabeth's hand and pulled her to him for a kiss on the cheek. Putting his other arm around Dolores's shoulders he asked, "When did you get here?"

Elizabeth pulled her suitcase inside and shoved it under the coat hooks by the door. The brown slacks and gold sweater she wore set off her cocoa-brown skin and her gold hoop earrings gleamed against the small braids tumbling over her scarf. "We met each other in the baggage section at DIA."

"Honest to God." Dolores trailed in after Elizabeth and set her bags near the others, fumbling with the buttons of her black raincoat. Her loose coil of her ebony hair fell from one shoulder and she swung it back when she stood up. "Weird, huh?"

Rose shook her head in disbelief. "You could say that, though I don't know if weird is the word anymore."

"Tell me about it." Elizabeth took off her stylish cape-jacket and helped Dolores with her coat. "Considerin' the dreams I've had every night for the last month, weird is the new normal. And this one," she motioned toward Dolores. "She's been making some things out of clay that I don't even want to think about." She put her hands on her hips and gave Neal and Rose the once-over. "What's been goin' on here, people?"

As if a signal had gone through the place, several of the others wandered in, gravitating to the living room where greetings were exchanged and introductions made. Snacks were thrown together and arranged on the coffee table. They clustered around the fireplace, catching up with Dolores and Elizabeth, both a little awkward at having returned so soon.

"Where's Kerry?" Dolores asked suddenly.

Rose glanced around the circle. "She and Max have been working on something most of the day. They said they'd be here for dinner."

Dolores nodded, satisfied. "Good. That way I don't have to ask who Max is." She turned to Rose. "I meant to call you, but I kept putting it off until I couldn't stand it anymore."

Andrea narrowed her eyes, puzzled. "What do you mean?"

Dolores flipped her long black hair over one shoulder. "It was the weirdest thing. I began a series of sculptures—the idea was to make a tree of life—only instead of animals and plants, I was going to put hands doing all kinds of things on the branches. Holding a book, gardening shears, a pen with a piece of paper."

"Cool." Brenna leaned forward a little in interest. "Different looking hands?"

Dolores sipped her wine and set down her glass. "Yes. Old, young, baby hands in a couple of places. Problem was, I kept making things I wasn't even thinking of." She reached for her glass again. "One morning I formed a hand that was holding an axe. Next was a hand holding a severed head." Her large brown eyes widened and she put one hand to her throat. "Madre de Dios, I was shaking so hard after that, I didn't even try to make anything else until the next day."

"You poor thing!" Aura Lee said in horror. "You must have been scared to death."

"*To build a wall and have one's mind lay it waste in the next breath is a hallmark of madness.* Jane Purcell Toombs, seventeen ninety-eight to eighteen forty-two." Noreen regarded Dolores gravely. "How's your mental health, my dear?"

Elizabeth's rich laugh rolled over budding tension. "I have missed your quotations," she said with feeling. "Life doesn't feel right without you punctuating every conversation." She winked at Dolores. "Don't forget, I'm here, too, also without an invitation. Go ahead, ask me what got me on a plane to Denver."

"I'll bite." Andrea popped a cherry tomato into her mouth and waited with interest.

"I was cooking my granny's jambalaya recipe a week ago and when I started to turn the heat down, I glanced into the pot." Her fingers tightened on the carrot stick she held.

"And?" Rose asked softly.

Elizabeth took a deep breath and let it out. "And I saw the carcass of a rabbit cooking in its own blood."

At the appalled silence, her lips twisted. "Aren't you gonna ask about *my* mental health?" She nodded toward Noreen.

The small woman ruffled her hair, brows drawn together. "No," she said finally, "I'm going to ask if you really saw that rabbit or if it was an illusion."

"It was real enough to make me sick," Elizabeth said grimly. "I threw it out. It didn't disappear when it hit the garbage can."

Noreen shot an apologetic glance toward Dolores. "And I'm asking you. Did you find the items you described to us were actually those shapes, or had you merely seen them that way?"

Dolores shook her head. "I wish it was like that, but, no. I made those hands and more, a knife slicing a human foot. A necklace of fingers." She turned toward Brenna's gasp. "I don't even know how I could have made that. The technique, I mean. I sculpted things I didn't know I could make." She shook her head. "I have a whole new understanding of what you went through when you were drawing and painting without knowing it, *jita*." She reached her hand toward Andrea, who clasped it tightly.

"It got to the point that I didn't want to go near the clay or any other medium. On some level I knew it had to do with Wisdom Court. So today I flew home."

Aura Lee was so touched at the sentiment she got to her feet and came around the table. "You dear, sweet girl." They hugged and when Dolores pulled back, tears were on her cheeks.

Rose wiped her eyes with her napkin. "I wish I didn't have such mixed feelings about seeing the two of you. It really is like having you come home," she said, putting one hand on her heart, "but the danger here keeps mounting and you both mean so much to us." She dabbed at her eyes again. "Sorry, it's been rough for a while. I hate to see you walk back into it."

Elizabeth wiped her eyes with the backs of her hands. "Don't get me goin', I'll cry all night." She sniffed mightily. "The danger doesn't matter. If what's been goin' on doesn't prove anything else, it shows we can be touched by this crazy ghost thing no matter where we are. I had to come back because I know I'm supposed to be here to see it out."

Dolores nodded solemnly. "Me, too. I couldn't stop thinking about you, Rose. And Aura Lee." She grabbed her wine and chugged some down. "You've been more like a mother to me than my own."

Neal groaned. "Cut it out, you guys. I've never cried in front of you and I don't want to start now."

Andrea's giggle was watery. "You're such a dork."

"Excuse me but what's going on in here?" Max was standing at the door, Kerry beside him. They were bleary-eyed and listing with fatigue.

Kerry took a step into the room and caught sight of the two women on the sofa and squealed. She pushed through the others to get to them. She pulled Dolores up for a one-armed hug and held onto Elizabeth's hand at the same time. "It's so good to see you." She leaned back to consider them more closely. "I'd like to say you both look wonderful but you don't."

Andrea laughed and Kerry glanced at her. "Well, they don't." She turned back to them. "I guess we don't either. What's going on?"

Elizabeth stood up. "We can talk about that later. Who's this gorgeous young man here?"

Kerry's cheeks reddened and she sent a quick glance at Max, who was listening with interest. "He's my, uh, he's the paranormal researcher that—"

"Her boyfriend, Max Steadman," he said smoothly. "And you?"

"Ooh-la-la." The laugh in Elizabeth's voice brought a smile to his face. "I'm Elizabeth Schuster, chef extraordinaire and the author of a brand new cookbook coming out next year." She reached around Kerry to shake his hand. "This is Dolores Rivera, outstanding sculptor, also recently of Wisdom Court. We've come back to fight the ghosts and ghouls around here."

"Wait till you hear what they've been going through," Aura Lee added in a meaningful tone. "It's amazing."

Kerry frowned as Elizabeth resumed her seat. "We've had so much amazing around here lately, we've gotten beyond the point of amazing." She held out her hand to Max and he stepped up beside her to take it in his own. "We were at my place, looking for the journal we were reading last night. In this room."

Eve leaned in from the ottoman where she perched like a bird on a large rock. "I thought I remembered seeing some light in here."

"I'm sorry if we bothered you." Max smiled at her. "You should have joined us."

"I wasn't really awake, just aware of a lightening of the dark. What time was it then?"

Max sat on the blue wingback chair and pulled Kerry down beside him. "I don't know, really. We'd wakened and wanted a snack. Then we read a while." He pointed to a spot on the coffee table. "I set the journal right there just before we turned off the torch. It was gone this morning."

Kerry glanced at them. "Please tell me one of you took it to read."

The silence was punctuated with shaken heads and shrugged shoulders. "I haven't seen any of the journals lately, except the ones in the library where we've been working on them." Brenna frowned. "You looked under the couch, right?"

"Everywhere." Kerry sighed. "Haven't a clue as to where it could be."

"Where what could be?" Brenna stood in the doorway in her pajamas with a fuzzy robe tied at the waist. She caught sight of Dolores and Elizabeth and took a step back. "I'm so sorry to interrupt."

Before she could move further out the door, Aura Lee bustled over to stop her, and chivvied her into a chair. "You must be starving. You've been asleep forever."

Elizabeth winced at the size of the goose egg on her forehead. "What happened to you?"

Brenna leaned toward the plate of cookies on the coffee table. "We were caught in the collapse of the secret tunnels under Eve's rooms."

"We'll tell you all about it," Kerry assured her. "For now we're concentrating on getting the journal back."

"Which one is it?" asked Noreen. "What were you reading about before you quite last night?"

"It's the one we started a few days ago, including Anna's looking for a job, finding one at the Russian bookseller's shop."

"Sorry to interrupt the flow," Dolores said in a hesitant voice. "But why were you sleeping in here?"

"We were run out of my place by, shall we say, *active spirits*?" Kerry glanced at Max.

"They threw books at the door as soon as we decamped. Neither one of us believed we'd get a good night's sleep there."

"Dios," murmured Dolores. She turned her head to meet Elizabeth's gaze. "Guess we came to the right place."

"Mmmm-hmmm."

Rose got out of her chair. "I suggest we observe the cocktail hour and share what information we have. Then we can come up with a plan." She nodded at Aura Lee. "Do we have something easy for dinner? I'll get the wine."

"I'll help," said Neal. "I'm starving."

"All right, then. Let's pull it together." Rose left for the kitchen, Aura Lee following.

Elizabeth leaned her head against Dolores's shoulder for a moment. "I've missed this so much. Not that I'm sad to be at home with Lovell and the girls, but one of the best things about this place is how, at the drop of a hat, we always put together a feast."

Dolores nodded. "And the company is always the best."

Noreen smiled at them both. "That's true, my dears, and having you back will add immeasurably to the mix." Her smile died and her eyes darkened. "But I'll warn you there are dark doings here, much more severe than what went on before you left. Give a moment's reflection to whether you want to submerge yourselves in it all again."

The two women glanced at each other, smiles gone.

"That's why I came," said Elizabeth.

"I'm in," added Dolores.

CHAPTER 19

The living room was warm from the fire and at least two conversations were criss-crossing each other as more refreshments were brought out from the kitchen. Max had settled in the big blue chair, a throw held in one hand.

Kerry grabbed a chunk of dark rye bread and pulled it through the bowl of dip on the coffee table. The flavors of olive, curry, and sour cream woke up her taste buds, and her eyes closed in bliss. "Who came up with this dip?" She scooped up more and stuffed it in her mouth. "Heavenly," she murmured.

Elizabeth raised her hand. "I just threw in whatever I could find." She tasted the mixture and smiled. "It worked out okay, didn't it?"

"You know it." Kerry sidled around the corner of the table and headed for the kitchen.

Brenna reached for a pickle and swirled it in the dip. She crunched as she chewed. "Yum. You must've been the most popular associate at Wisdom Court. And the food's always great now."

"I've always considered myself the most popular associate." Noreen's eyes twinkled. "And by preserving my façade as kitchen idiot, I never have to lift a hand at cooking."

Neal carried in several more bottles of wine and set them in a row along the edge of the sideboard. "This ought to keep us going for a while." He turned to find Andrea directly behind him, a bowl in each hand, one heaped with tortilla chips, the other with crisp pita triangles. "I'll take those." Neal leaned over to kiss her and put the bowls on the coffee table.

"Cheese platter coming through." Dolores edged through the gap toward the table.

"Wait a minute." Andrea bent to rearrange the dishes to make space for the cheese. "Is this the last of it?"

"Eve's chopping up veggies." Kerry shot Max a look. "You want that toddy you were talking about?"

"You don't have to wait on me."

Kerry touched his shoulder as she passed by. "No biggie. The kettle's hot so I'll mix it up. Feel any better?"

"I feel wretched." Max leaned his head against the chair back and closed his eyes. "I don't like the sound of food, but that toddy might be therapeutic."

Kerry frowned at him. He'd been tired earlier, as was she, but not sick. "When did you start feeling bad?"

"It's not been long." He opened his eyes. "My head began to ache a bit while we were reading the journal last night."

A sense of dread crept over her, evoking a shiver. "Remember how tired we both were? And my eyes were so dry I could hardly stand it."

Max sat up straighter. "Do you think both effects were because of our reading the journal?"

Kerry sat down beside him in the chair. "Is it possible?"

He reached for her hand and pulled her closer to him. "I've never heard of anyone becoming ill from encounters with the other side, but the sorts of things happening here put the lie to nearly everything I've learned over the years."

She leaned her head against his chest. "Every time I think I'm as frightened as can be, something else ups it a notch."

Max sighed. "It's not that dire yet, luv. We're working well together and we're bound to find out more now that Charlie's involved. He's one of the best."

Kerry became aware of the silence in the room. She lifted her head and caught the interest in Noreen's expression. Another glance revealed that Neal and Andrea were listening, too.

"Well," she said lamely, "We didn't mean to put a damper on the conversation." Aura Lee stopped beside the chair and handed her a cup of steaming liquid.

When Kerry questioned her with a look, Aura Lee said, "The toddy you wanted for him." She nodded at Max.

"Oh, Aura Lee, that's so nice." Kerry handed it over and he warmed his hands with it.

"So what happened last night?"

Kerry kept an eye on Max as she answered. "We were asleep in here and I woke up wanting brownies and milk."

Max took a drink of the toddy and his eyes brightened. "This is good."

"I added some herbs," Aura Lee said. "Go on."

"We finished the snack and wanted to read for a while. Max had brought a flashlight from the kitchen. We used it so we wouldn't disturb Eve."

"What did you learn from the journal?"

"She explains how she came to tell Arnie, the bookseller she worked for, about her coming to America. She laid it out to him: the Nazi sympathizers and her trip in the Gypsy wagon…" Kerry made an inclusive gesture. "The whole bit about the German bearer bonds. But, as we said, now we can't find the journal. It was right here on the coffee table. Now it's not."

Andrea reached for a chunk of cheese. "So where is it?"

"That's the question." Kerry frowned at the table. "If no one here took it, does it mean one of our ghostly friends disappeared it? Do we know if that's even possible?"

"Maybe it means we should drink ourselves into a stupor." Eve limped to the table and set down a plate of crudités. "It would be like a vacation after all the stuff going on the last couple of days."

"When we've read the rest of the journal," Noreen replied. *"The mind may put on its slippers only after the day's work is done.* Bethany Perkins Andicott, eighteen ninety-two to nineteen thirty-nine."

Eve grinned as she settled onto a chair. "What a lovely metaphor. Or is it simile? Who cares?"

From the kitchen came the buzz of the oven timer. Rose stood up and wended her way through the crush of bodies. "First we eat enough to keep us going. Pizza coming up— gluten-free included," she told Brenna, who'd started to ask.

"I'm beginning to love this place," Eve announced.

"Of course you are." Aura Lee's smile was only slightly crooked. "Even the ghosts want to hang out with us."

As they ate where they sat, Kerry briefly sketched in what she and Max had read. "Arnie had been looking for his wife's people since the end of the war, but hadn't found any of them. Caldicott was worried the dead Gypsy girl Duncan told her about might be related to Vadoma, but Arnie said probably not."

"Vadoma?" Eve asked. She took a big bite of her pizza and caught several vegetables threatening to slide down her chin.

"That was Arnie's wife's name. Wonder what it means?" Pulling a pen from the spiral of her notebook, Kerry wrote a note to herself to check.

Rose reached for her glass. "That's as far as you got?"

Kerry nodded. "We haven't read the rest."

"So what do we do now?" Elizabeth asked.

"Dunno." Kerry chewed steadily. "We've looked around here but haven't found a thing."

Max patted the chair cushion clumsily. "Can't remember where I put it." He aimed a sloppy smile at Kerry. "Didn't you put it in your satchel to keep it safe?"

Kerry stared at him, mouth open. "Max. We had it here, remember?" She turned to Rose, her face frightened. "I swear, we read it right here."

Rose was frowning at Max. "Could he have taken it back to your place?"

Kerry glanced back at him, and the strange expression on his face shook her. When he closed his eyes, she said in a low voice, "We went to sleep. I guess he could've gone to my place once I'd dropped off, but why would he?"

Rose got to her feet and came to Max's side. She bent over him and kissed his forehead. When she stood up, her eyes were dark with worry. "He has quite a fever. There's no way to know whether he took the journal somewhere else."

Max made a sound and their eyes went to his face. Frowning, he moved his head back and forth. "Get away," he mumbled suddenly. "Bloody door."

From the kitchen area came an unearthly howl.

"What in the world?" Aura Lee jumped to her feet as another cry split the air. "Is it Strudel?" She rushed out of the room before anyone else could react.

"Wait a minute." Andrea struggled to push herself out of her chair, hampered by the blanket wrapped around her. "I can come with you."

"Don't forget the rule." Noreen slid her paper plate onto the hearthstone and trotted after Aura Lee.

"What rule?" Dolores asked in confusion.

"Don't go anywhere alone." Andrea tugged the tail of the blanket from under one hip and draped the whole thing across the back of her chair. "We keep running into weird things, so we travel in pairs to protect ourselves and each other."

"I suppose we could all go." Rose glanced down at the small piece of pizza on her plate and picked it up. "Or we can wait here to see what happens next." Slipping the pizza into her mouth, she chewed. At Brenna's choke of laughter, her eyes narrowed. "I'm tired of all the dark and stormy night stuff."

Neal stretched his feet toward the fire. "I hear you." Elizabeth's gaze veered toward Dolores. She raised her brows and shivered.

In a few moments Aura Lee returned with Strudel under one arm. The little dachshund was panting gently, eyes swiveling to note the numerous treat options available. "She must have been lonely," Aura Lee explained in a tender voice. "When I got to my room, she was on the other side of the door, waiting for someone to come get her."

"It sounded as if she was being flayed," Noreen muttered as she reseated herself. "I was certain we'd be faced with at least one ghost. Or a musical number from Aura Lee's organ."

Aura Lee sat down, gently setting Strudel beside her. "She feels things in the air. We can't blame her for getting as scared as the rest of us are." She tore a bit off her pizza and offered it to the dog. It was gone with a swipe of pink tongue.

Kerry stopped at the chair holding Max. "Should we go back to my place and at least try to get the journal?" When he didn't answer, she bent to look at him more closely, putting her palm against his forehead. "Max?"

A light snore was his only response.

She stood up, chewing on her lower lip as she watched him sleep. "He's getting hotter." She turned to the others. "Any of you want to go with me to see if the book is at my place?"

Brenna wrinkled her nose. "Not all that tempting a proposition, you know?"

Kerry nodded. "Tell me. Chamber of horrors-ish."

Neal let out a sigh. "It'll only take a minute. It's probably not there anyway, but I'm betting if it is, the spirit reading it got bored and went home." He frowned. "Wherever that is." He stood up and Andrea shifted her weight to join him, but he pressed her back down. "Stay here. Kerry and I will be brave and noble, right?" He slanted a look at Rose, pushing his thatch of hair off his forehead. "The rest of you can weave laurel wreaths for us. Or bake brownies," he added pointedly to Aura Lee. "Hero's welcome, and all that."

"You certainly have a high opinion of yourself." Noreen grinned at Rose. "We mere females will more likely sit in awed silence until you get back."

"Dammit, I always crank up the awe button too high." Neal winked at her and grabbed Kerry's arm. "Let's go see if Max made it over there last night." The two of them went out through the kitchen and the back door shut a few moments later.

Aura Lee got out of her chair.

Rose stirred. "Don't tell me you're going to bake brownies for him."

Aura Lee smiled smugly. "I've never told him I keep a batch or two in the freezer, just for him. He might get a swelled head." She eased by the coffee table and entered the kitchen.

"A swelled belly, more likely." Andrea yawned and propped her feet on the edge of the table. "I don't suppose anything will try to hurt them." Her gaze strayed toward Rose. "Do you?"

"No." She looked worried. "They'll run in, they'll look, they'll run out. No time for anything to harm them."

Brenna leaned toward the coffee table for chips and dip. "It'll be fine, I'm sure."

A low, hoarse voice sounded behind her. "It'll be fine, I'm sure."

Brenna shrieked, scrambling off her chair and whirling to find the source. Eve was making her way around the sofa toward Andrea, who gawked at her with eyes as wide as they would go. The laptop Eve carried was held out like a tray, and as she bent to sit on the rug, she used it to clear enough space to set it on the coffee table, pushing dishes to the floor. Andrea lifted her feet off the table and scrambled out of her chair.

Eve's face was blank as a mannequin's, her eyes glassy and unfocused.

"What's happening?" Dolores whispered. "Is she possessed?"

"I don't know." Rose's voice cracked on the words. "Noreen?"

She cleared her throat with difficulty. "Close enough for government work."

As they stared at her, Eve opened the laptop and began to type, her fingers moving smoothly and steadily across the keyboard. Her gaze was fixed on the screen, her eyes rarely blinking. She barely breathed, staying in an upright position, legs bent under the table in an ankle over ankle pose.

"Her leg must be killing her," Brenna murmured. "She can't bend it like that when she's…when she's awake." She cupped her elbows with her hands, trying to keep herself warm.

Aura Lee appeared at the doorway to the kitchen bearing an ornate plate filled with steaming brownies. "Wait till Neal catches a load of these." Her voice rang with satisfaction. "He'll never believe—"

Eve's hands stilled on the keyboard and she slowly turned her head toward Aura Lee.

Rose stiffened as her gaze passed over her, feeling ice form in her belly. "Hush."

Aura Lee raised a brow and noticed the others were staring at Eve. As she followed suit, her gaze locked with Eve's and the plate started to tilt toward the floor. Noreen lunged to grab it, just saving the brownies. Her hands were shaking as she set the platter on the hearthstone.

"Cottie?" whispered Aura Lee. "Is it really you?"

Eve shifted her eyes back to the laptop and resumed typing. "What's going on?" Aura Lee asked painfully. "When did this start?"

"After you went to the kitchen." Elizabeth's voice was low. "Eve went and got her laptop and brought it in here. She started typin'." Her voice wavered and she took a deep breath. "Why did you call her Cottie?"

Aura Lee didn't answer and Noreen turned to her. The dishtowel she'd used to protect herself from the heat of the brownie plate was serving as a handkerchief. "The look in her eyes," Aura Lee whispered finally. "It made me think of Cottie."

Brenna was edging toward the fireplace, shaking with nerves. "What are we supposed to do?"

Rose clasped her hands together to keep them steady. "Let her type until she's finished, I guess." She had no color in her face and her eyes had dark circles around them. "Feel the cold?"

Brenna sat down beside the brownies. "It's getting worse. Can we turn up the flames?"

"I don't know if it will do any good." Rose reached for the knob set in the stone and turned it. The orange and blue flames grew higher.

"It's a little warmer," Brenna whispered, holding her hands in front of the glass.

"How can we keep on like this?" Rose's voice was barely above a whisper. "How can we—"

Eve's cat Danica walked into the room from the kitchen. She tiptoed toward Eve and stopped suddenly. Lowering her chin to the floor, arching her back, she hissed and growled. Eve's hands went still and she cast a look at the little cat. Danica yowled and ran from the room.

"You don't need to be in awe," Neal said from the doorway. "We couldn't find the journal."

Kerry eased past him and started toward Max.

"Wait!" Rose spoke quickly and loudly.

Eve stopped typing and looked up at the two newcomers.

Kerry took an unsteady step backward, nearly treading on Neal's foot. "My God."

Neal could have been turned to stone for all the motion in his body. He revived to shoot a glance at Andrea, relaxing a fraction when she nodded at him. "When did this start?"

"Right after you left."

"What's she typing?"

Brenna took a shaky breath and, incongruously, giggled, a sharp little sound. "We haven't asked."

Eve took her hands off the keyboard and let out a long breath. She dropped sideways to the floor.

Kerry darted to the chair where Max still slept. Andrea stepped around her and knelt beside Eve.

"Is she okay?"

Andrea held her hand against Eve's face, bending to make sure she was still breathing. As she lifted her head, Eve's eyes opened and she stared up at her. "What's going on?" she asked in a reedy voice. "What are you doing?"

"You passed out," Andrea said. "We're trying to help you."

Neal came closer and bent to put one arm under her shoulders. As he lifted her into a sitting position, her face creased in pain. "My knee, oh, God, what did I do?"

"Here," Andrea said, "let's get you on the sofa so you can stretch it out." They got her arranged and tucked a blanket around her. "Do you want us to call a doctor?"

Eve shook her head. "Not yet. Let me settle."

Brenna had lowered herself to the floor and was scrolling through the pages Eve had typed.

"What is it?" Noreen asked finally.

Brenna looked up from the screen with a frown. "I'm not sure. Here's part: *I folded my lips together to stop their trembling. I had come this far, and now it appeared I would have to travel again, to find another place to go to ground in order to avoid the evil man who would have been my father-in-law.*"

Max's voice sounded groggily from the chair. "That's what we read, Kerry and I. Where did you find it?"

"Find what?" Neal asked.

"The journal. That's part of what we read."

Kerry turned toward Brenna. "Does it keep going?"

Brenna nodded. "For pages and pages."

Neal sat back on his heels and stared at the laptop in amazement. "So we couldn't find the journal but Eve typed it while we were looking for it?"

"I told you it was Cottie," Aura Lee whispered. "She wants us to know it all."

CHAPTER 20

E ve took another gulp of the brandy Neal gave her. "Go ahead," she gasped as the liquor burned down to her stomach. "Ask the question of the day." She glanced toward the windows, where no light shone. "The night."

In the big chair Kerry stirred and Max tightened his arm around her shoulders. "Why were you—*how* were you able to type the journal on your laptop?"

"You're sure what I typed was the same as the journal pages." Eve held her glass with both hands as if she feared having it taken from her.

Max nodded somberly. "As best I can recall. As for the part we hadn't yet read, I'm ready to believe it's an exact copy. Why go to the trouble if it weren't?"

Aura Lee stopped rubbing her hands together and looked straight at Eve, something she hadn't yet managed since the spirit had left her. "You don't remember anything about the time while you were…typing?"

Eve bit back irritation. She'd been asked the question over and over again, each repetition making her want to scream and run from the room. Or limp from the room, she thought sourly. She glanced at the ice pack strapped to her knee, now swollen to the size of a cantaloupe. Aura Lee's defeated air, surrounding her like one of her robes, was the real reason she kept still. "No memory of it at all. I was absolutely blank, didn't even feel my leg." She lifted the glass to her lips once more. Brandy was proving to be a surprisingly effective pain medication.

Rose adjusted the blanket draped around her shoulders. "We need to focus. Yes, the notion of Caldicott's taking over Eve's body—" She paused to clear her throat. "And typing skills, is hard to deal with but I suggest we make use of what Caldicott wanted us to have access to. The journal. Let's read it."

Andrea leaned against Neal and lifted her feet onto the sofa cushion. "How about it, Eve? Do feel up for that?"

"Wouldn't make any difference if I didn't," she said, her voice thickening. "We need to find out all we can, right?" She leaned her head back. Her smile felt sloppy but she didn't care.

"Okay, then, who wants to read it?" Rose turned to Kerry, who shook her head. "Brenna?"

Brenna pulled her chair a little closer to the coffee table and reached for one of the water bottles Aura Lee had carried in. She slid the laptop off the table and set it on her lap. "Here goes." She glanced at the screen. "Okay, we have her talking about the evil man who would've been her father-in-law. She asks Arnie what he suggests."

"You and I go over your books and then we look for new home for these bonds of yours. Is doubtful your English earl could find them as you set up two trusts, but I do not like that large sums move to New York on dates so near when you escape from England. This we must change."

And change those details, along with many more, is what we did. Arnie had helped many a refugee launder his funds upon arrival in America. With my money he created an umbrella corporation, which ultimately became the ornithological society where I supposedly worked after immigrating to the U.S. Why birds? Arnie liked birds of all kinds, but he was particularly fond of owls. One afternoon he pulled from his vest pocket a small leather pouch. Inside it was what he identified as an owl foot, with sharp talons.

"Owl claws we carry with us, that our souls use them to climb to heaven when we die."

Eve nestled more deeply into the throw wrapped around her. "Wonder if that has anything to do with the owl I saw in the chamber under my apartment."

"Climbing to heaven?" Neal asked.

"Climbing to somewhere."

Brenna resumed reading.

I changed my name again, this time to Caldicott Wyntham. Arnie shook his head at it, but I wanted something distinctive. And the medal bearing the name appealed to me. I spelled it with an 'i' instead of an 'e' to set it apart. When we had the money covered, I began to look for a place to live. I rode on trains across the country, trying to decide what elements would please me most. Did I want to live near the ocean? Beside one of the Great Lakes? In mountains? Near a desert?

Arnie told me about an article regarding a bird conference in Colorado, at the university in Boulder. What better way to smooth over my tracks than to attend such a meeting as a representative of my ornithological foundation?

And so it was I came to Boulder, then a small town at the foot of the Rocky Mountains. It was so beautiful and I felt such a sense of homecoming. When the conference finished, I stayed on to explore the place. I walked through the town, across the university campus, up the trails of Chautauqua Park. The air was unlike any I'd ever known: thin, clean, and challenging. When I found the old Thornton farm for sale, I was almost troubled by the draw I felt to it. I telephoned Arnie and we talked about the asking price, the land included—all of the details I had no one else to share with.

Arnie was excited for me and he urged me to hire a lawyer to handle the deal. In a month I was the new owner of the place. In two, I was living there, trying to let my life catch up to my decisions.

Summer was on its way and I began to venture out to discover the community. One late afternoon I happened upon a carnival at the county fairgrounds. The colorful rides and brassy music brought memories of fairs I'd seen with my mother. The intent was the same: to provide distraction and to part people from their money. As I walked through the tiny midway, I found myself humming to the raucous tune of the carousel.

The sun was beginning to set. Behind the horses and zoo animals whirling round and round, I caught sight of a tent. Fortunes 25 cents said the sign. I drew close enough to note the worn edges of the canvas structure, to detect the heavy incense escaping into the evening air.

I'd almost walked past it when a woman appeared in the gap between the canvas panels that was the door. She was young and wore a peasant skirt with a muslin scoop-necked blouse. She smiled at me and waved me toward her. "Miss wants to know her fortune?" How many times had I accompanied Mum into such a place? Always she wanted to hear of love and riches to come.

I shook my head but she took a step toward me. "Only twenty-five cents, and you will ask me questions I can answer."

Something in her voice struck a chord. I walked toward her and as she lifted one of the flaps, I slipped into the darkness of the tent. It was so like all the tents I'd been in. The round table had a worn velvet cloth; a glow came from the crystal ball; thickening incense limned the air with mystery.

"I am Madame Lizetta," she said, her voice deep now. "Be seated. Give me your token and I will tell your fortune."

I gave her a quarter and she held out her hand. When I placed my own in it she bent to study the lines on my palm. I waited with a smile. Would her forecast include a tall, handsome man? Would she predict how many children I would bear? At that thought my smile died. I would never have children because my love was dead, killed by his own father.

As if she could hear the sorrow in my thoughts, Madame Lizetta lifted her head to stare at me intently. "Who are you?" she whispered, but before I could answer she looked down again at my hand.

By the time she released it her skin was ashen. "I know you," she whispered. "Mother Miriam told me you were coming."

"What?" I felt I'd been knocked sideways. "What are you talking about?"

The mysterious Madame Lizetta was gone, replaced by a young woman who was terribly frightened. As I stared, saucer-eyed, she spoke barely above a whisper, and so quickly that I had to bend toward her to catch every word.

"You are a legend among the Romani. You carried the stone of evil and you escaped from the danger threatening our people. Mother Miriam told us few who read the stars about you, that you would find one of us someday. Never did I think it would be me." She broke off to look over her shoulder toward the door. "You are in great danger. The wicked lord has died but another is in his place. He seeks you and he lusts for vengeance. Most of all, he wants the stone."

At this point I was shaking more than she was. Her hand tightened on mine. She was so pale I thought she might faint. "I will tell the people of you; you will have help to find protection. Mother Miriam held our promise to serve you. I am to tell you this: build tunnels and caves under the houses. Plan your escape before you need it. Hide the stone well." She closed her eyes and took several deep breaths. Then she opened her eyes and looked deeply into mine. "You must find the women who will be your allies. Many will come, one by one. Among them you will find those you will need to protect what you have built."

"But how will I—" I began, but she went on, holding fast to my hand, her eyes frightened. "The battle will come near the end of your life. The brave women will arrive over a short time. Then the evil will come to all of you. You must be valiant. You must win. Much depends on this."

Her eyes were as dark as wells. "The stone must be destroyed." Her whisper thrilled along my nerves like an electrical current. "If it is not, someday it will win. Many will die."

I pulled my hand from hers and stood up on shaky legs. "I don't—I don't—" I stepped backward from her and turned to leave the hot, heavy air of the tent.

"You are not alone," she whispered. "But you must be as if you are. Do not trust. Judge each one yourself. Find the ones who will stand with you." Her head bent as she slumped more deeply into her chair. "We will do what we can, but the burden is yours."

I heard nothing else as I plunged out into the air of the carnival. Nearly gagging on the stench of rancid butter and caramelized sugar I walked as fast as I could to the edge of the fairgrounds. It took forever to find my car, forever to fit the key into the ignition. My hands were shaking so hard I could barely hold onto the steering wheel.

Somehow I returned to the house and locked the door behind me. I felt as if I had traveled through time, coming face to face with Clara, the foolish girl who fell in love with the son of an earl, only to lose him to evil. My whole life had been changed by that encounter. It had made me into another person. In the years since, I had papered over the cracks in that life, had continued onward to something I couldn't conceive of. Now, tonight, I had met with the plans someone—something had made for me. Miriam had spread my story across her world and now it had touched me again. Had I come full circle?

I thought about that question as I proceeded methodically through the house, locking doors and windows, leaving lights on in this room and that. Never had I felt so alone in this place.

When I finished barricading myself inside, I went into the old-fashioned kitchen and poured a glass of milk. In the silence I could hear an owl from the mountain and I had a sudden image of myself holding an owl's claw, struggling to make my way to heaven.

Tonight was only one step, and I'd already taken so many. My story was not done. My task was not finished.

This was the night when all the versions of myself, from the girl Clara to the woman I was now, became Caldicott Wyntham.

Brenna set the laptop onto the coffee table. "That's all."

Kerry let out a long breath. "I don't believe it," she said in a stunned voice. "But I do! How could she have been so—so sanguine about what was waiting for her? How could she have been who she was to all of us, knowing what was hanging over her?" Max wrapped his arm around her shoulders and she bent her head to rest against him. "She was more than valiant."

The doorbell chimed from the front of the house and Strudel jumped off Aura Lee's chair, barking raucously. Rose groaned.

"Who could that be?" Aura Lee asked in a scared voice. "It's late, isn't it?"

Rose got to her feet. "I don't even know. Who's coming with me?"

Neal stood up, his knees cracking. "Oof, the wear and tear is getting to me."

"You're not alone in that." Rose led the way through the forest of chairs and tables, Neal at her heels.

Elizabeth leaned back in her chair. "I always knew this place was special." She waved one hand in frustration. "More than special, outside the ordinary, but this story she tells is flat-out strange." She sought Dolores, and spoke directly to her. "We've been away for a couple of months and everything has gotten deeper, more dangerous. What's your take on this?"

Dolores's rich brown eyes reflected the movements of the flames in the fireplace. "In my culture we have *brujas*. Witches. They live in a heightened realm, aware of the things in life most people know nothing about. Caldicott lived in that world, too. Because we all came here to Wisdom Court, we've been welcomed into it as well."

"Look who we found." Rose announced in a lively voice. She pulled a young man forward.

"Dink!" Brenna surged to her feet and scrambled toward him. "You came. You're here."

Dink grabbed hold of her as she threw herself against him. "I told you I would." He pushed her away to look into her face. "Are you okay?" His gaze rested on lump on her forehead. "What did the doctor say?"

Brenna pulled him close. "I'm fine. I'm so glad to see you." His arms tightened around her and he pulled her close.

Rose looked at the others and made an attempt at a smile. "I suggest we all have a nightcap and then adjourn to bed. We'll tackle everything tomorrow."

Kerry looked troubled. "I'm all for some sleep, but I don't want to go back to my place. Max and I have already had a couple of go-rounds with the spirits who've moved in. Can we stay here tonight?"

"I concur with Kerry," Noreen said firmly. "I have no desire to be alone in my room waiting for ghosts to appear for a midnight visit."

"All right, you've made your point." Rose appealed to the group. "Shall we camp out here for the rest of the night?"

"Definitely." Andrea got to her feet and began to distribute blankets. "I'm not sure Neal and I would get a visit from the other world at his place tonight, but I don't want to test it."

Aura Lee smiled in relief. "If you'll save me a pillow and a blanket, I'll go make some hot cocoa for us. Would anyone like cookies? All the brownies are gone."

Elizabeth laughed quietly. "Seems like old times, doesn't it?" She got out of her chair and grabbed a batch of blankets. "Here, I'll help."

Eve settled more deeply into the sofa cushions and waited as Danica went through her nightly ritual of rubbing her face against Eve's, circling on her chest until she found just the right spot to curl into a ball. Her purring vibrated against Eve's neck.

As they bustled to make the area ready for sleep, the slight back-and-forth swaying of the heavy burgundy drapes at the big picture window went unnoticed. Nor did the blinking eyes above the curtain rods attract their attention. For good or ill, all of the Wisdom Court inhabitants made ready for bed.

Silence stole over the room and Danica opened her eyes. As the humans sank into sleep, she kept watch.

CHAPTER 21

Having spent the night sleeping in the living room, they decided to stay at the main house for the day. Dividing tasks, Rose created teams to handle the most pressing needs. "Max and Noreen, you hit the library and see if you can find any references to a Romani community here in Boulder. Check the smaller mountain towns, too. Gold Hill, Pinecliff. Coal mining towns might also be worth looking into. Like Superior and Erie."

"Neal and Andrea, would you double-check the tunnel area? We need to know what state they're in, if they're deteriorating any faster."

"I think Dink and I ought to go with them," Brenna suggested. "Having been inside the tunnels, I can tell you we need to stay near each other and keep in touch."

"What about your head? Didn't Jerri tell you to chill for a couple of days?"

Brenna frowned. "But I feel a lot better."

Dink grabbed her hand. "You could rest while you fill me in on what's been going on."

Brenna nodded reluctantly.

"That sounds good." Rose's gray eyes were clouded with worry. "Breakfast first. We'll reconnoiter and check back with one another. Agreed?"

"You've got it." Neal glanced down at Andrea. "I'm going to get flashlights for us, and maybe some rope. I'll be back in a bit."

"Eve," Rose added. "You'd better stay off that knee. Will you help Noreen and Max? I'm sure you've done enough research to find your way around the notes we've accumulated."

Eve nodded. "I'd be glad to."

Kerry, Dolores, and Elizabeth were on breakfast duty and stepped around each other as easily as if they'd been performing their tasks in a dance of long standing. The aroma of fresh coffee filled the room.

Kerry was slicing strawberries at the sink. The sun peered through the window, adding a shine to their deep red. "I feel like someone's looking over my shoulder," she said with a shiver. "I keep expecting something to jump out at me." Holding the full colander under the faucet, she rinsed the strawberries thoroughly. "It's like a simmering pot around here, and the air itself is going to start boiling."

"You got that right." Elizabeth wielded a spatula to flip hotcakes off the griddle. "My skin feels like it's gonna itch any minute—on the edge of itching. It's driving me crazy. Here, Dolores, take these." She handed the platter of hotcakes to her.

"It's the dreams that are getting to me." Dolores set the plate in the middle of the table and picked up the roll of paper towels nearby. As she tore them off for napkins, she looked around the room warily. "Once I got to sleep last night, I kept dreaming of crawly creatures, especially here in the kitchen. Moving over the wallpaper crawly."

"Ack." Elizabeth dropped circles of batter onto the griddle, pausing to wipe her forehead with the back of one hand. "Took some time to get to sleep. Then I was too tired to dream."

Dolores fetched butter and syrup to the table and stopped at a cabinet to gather coffee mugs. "Is the kettle hot? Aura Lee's tea," she added.

"Un huh." Elizabeth flipped the pancakes. "We've got three men with us. How many of these things should I make?"

"You're the restauranteur. You oughta know."

Kerry carried the large bowl of berries to the table. "More than you've got now. Max looks like a starving academic but he eats like a maniac, wears a fedora."

"What?"

"Private joke." Kerry set down the bowl and stretched her back muscles. "I'm pretty hungry, too. Don't stint on the hotcakes." She dropped to a chair. "Seriously for a minute…"

"Yeah?" Elizabeth divided her attention between the griddle and Kerry.

Dolores dealt forks and spoons like cards in a poker game. "What?"

"Don't you think things are getting scarier? More dangerous?"

"How would we know?" Elizabeth tested a pancake and began to chuck them onto another platter. "Everything feels different—worse—thicker than when we were here before. Don't you think, Dolores?"

Nodding solemnly, Dolores opened the door to the dish cabinet. She shrieked and jumped back.

"What?" Kerry demanded. "What?"

Dolores waved a hand at the cabinet. On the bottom shelf were plates arranged vertically on their edges, one after another in a line across the width of the shelf.

"Look, they're trembling." Dolores took a small step forward and turned a shocked face toward Kerry when she pushed her out of the way.

"Hurry, hold out your hands." Kerry began to slide plates out as fast as she could, stacking them on Dolores's forearms. "Elizabeth, you, too." She continued until all of the plates were out of the shelf and piled on the counter. "I thought sure they were going to start flying like Frisbees."

Dolores cast a wary eye toward the dishes on the other shelves. "Maybe someone was trying to help." She choked on a small giggle and lifted her hand to shut the cabinet door.

"That's what scares me." Kerry helped her set the dishes around the edge of the table. "I think we can blame some of the things happening here on spirits that don't have control over their powers or what they're using as props. They can hurt us without meaning to."

"Kerry, girl, *you're* talking about spirits? What happened to your skepticism?"

Kerry gestured toward the plates. "You see enough stuff like that and you stop talking about oddities and start looking for the ghosts."

"That's pretty scary all by itself, *jita.*" Dolores grabbed a cup and headed for the coffeemaker.

"Well, at least you got a good man to go lookin' with." Elizabeth turned off the stove. "If we don't have enough of these things, we'll eat somethin' else." She went to the doorway. "Y'all better get in here before we eat it up!" She grinned at Kerry. "That always gets my girls to the table."

Soon the room was full. Plates were passed, coffee poured, and the first wonderful bites consumed. Rose had just glanced around the table, asking in surprise, "Where's Aura Lee?"

The beginnings of a frown pulled Neal's brows together. "Isn't she here?" He started to push his chair back when he relaxed. "There she is."

Aura Lee came into the kitchen with a stack of folded dishtowels draped over one arm, stopping to drop a small package in front of Eve. "This was falling out of your pants pocket. Praise the Goddess I found it before I threw them in the wash."

Eve stared at the rough black material tied with leather twine. She frowned at it, trying in vain to place it. "I'm sorry, I don't remem—" And then it popped into her mind. "I'd forgotten all about it." She began to unwind the string. "I found it in a hidden drawer at the base of the wall, in that room where you found us."

"What is it?" Kerry held out a hand. "May I see?"

"Not till I do." Eve pulled a roll of paper from the packet and flattened it on the table. "Huh. Looks like a map."

"Map?" Kerry leaned closer. "Map to what? More journals? Maybe more information about what's going on around here?"

Eve peered at the figures on the thick paper. "Sometimes a map is merely a map, Dr. Freud."

"Ha-ha. Fork it over. Let me see it."

Eve flashed on a memory of her sister being just as irritating as Kerry was now. "Cut it out. Let me actually look at the thing."

"Kerry." Max's mouth was full and he could hardly be understood. "Give the woman a chance."

Kerry growled at him.

A screech came from across the room. "No!" Dolores lurched away from the kitchen sink and ran toward the door.

As she ran out, Brenna darted to the sink. When she looked into it, she froze. "Oh, man." She held onto the edge of the countertop. "What in hell is this?"

Dink joined her, one hand going to her shoulder. He checked the sink and looked at her. "Are you doing that?"

"Doing what?" Her voice was high-pitched and scared. "No way!"

"What are you nattering about?" Noreen approached the sink and stretched up on her toes to see what was going on. "They look like—they look like—" She watched for a moment and then turned from the sink. To the horror of all of them, she grabbed a dishtowel and began to retch into it.

"Noreen!" Rose ran to her side and held her shoulders until she was still. She steadied her and escorted her to the nearest chair.

Noreen waved a hand toward the sink. Rose walked to the counter as the others crowded in behind her.

The sink held creatures in motion, green, living things, crawling on what looked like leafy legs as they tumbled over each other in a swarm. From what appeared to be their heads some spat a red substance, and others turned on them, tearing at the leafy legs until more of the goo covered the victims.

"That looks like—" Kerry paused.

"Blood." Max stared at the teeming mass with disgust.

Kerry's mouth twisted. "I didn't put the leaves down the disposal. And they turned into *that.*"

"But why?" Rose stared at them both. "For what purpose?"

"To scare us," Kerry said in an angry voice. "Look at us! It worked on me. How about you?"

Max grabbed her hand and started to lead her back to the table. "So we'll stop reacting."

"Don't just walk away." Kerry pulled him back to the counter. "Give me that spatula, the one in that jar of tools." She took it from him and turned to the sink. "I'm going to shove them into the drain and I want you to turn on the disposal."

"Ewww!" Dolores had come back into the kitchen. "How can you stand to do that?"

"It's a damn sight better than watching them crawl out of the sink." Kerry shoved the soft plastic blade of the spatula into the mass of leafy creatures and pushed them toward the drain. She twisted the faucet handle. "Turn on the disposal."

The machine began to grind as Kerry continued to push the bodies into it. To her horror, some of the red substance splashed onto one sleeve of her sweatshirt. "Ugh, hand me a paper towel."

Dolores gave her one and Kerry wiped frantically at her sleeve. Then she peered into the sink and slumped against the counter. "Turn off the disposal. They're gone."

"So was this magic?" Aura Lee demanded. "Squirmy things that make you sick to look at?" She shuddered. "How can we go on if we have to deal with things like this?"

Rose sank back into her chair. "How many times have we asked that question? We either go on or we walk away."

"When you think about it, they just looked like bugs." Brenna shrugged when Kerry glared at her. "It's a dumb sort of magic spell, don't you think?"

Max flashed a smile. "Dumb but effective. And separating magical elements into the benign and the malignant, I think we could label the strawberry leaf spiders as malignant."

"I'd agree with that." Rose reached for her coffee.

"We've found there are different amounts of good and evil in magic," Max said. "The strawberry leaf spiders are lightweight conjuring. Old, deep magic, like the talisman Caldicott described, is formidably strong. You can scare people with the shallow stuff, but you can change the world with the deep, dark stuff. That's why the old earl who killed Caldicott's Duncan wanted that talisman—to alter the wishes of millions of people and present England to the Nazis, wrapped in a bow."

"It's scary as hell to think how devastating the talisman would've been if it hadn't been taken away from him," Rose said.

"No wonder he and his followers continued to look for it." Andrea clutched her coffee mug. "We're babes in the woods. How can we possibly fight his followers, if they are the ones doing these things to us?"

Rose sighed. "We can't afford to look at it that way." Her gaze challenged each of them as she looked around the table. "We can't withdraw. I admit to a certain amount of anger that we never had a real choice about becoming engaged in the battle. But I'd rather we be involved in ending it than imagining people less prepared than we are having to deal with it."

"I don't feel like charging the barriers yet," Kerry said in a rough voice, "but I know we're on the front line. Here we are. It's us or nobody."

"We go into battle ill-prepared, but we go. Our tattered banner will stand for imperfect glory. But glory it will be." The light in Noreen's eyes was militant. "Anna Fordham Willis, circa eighteen twenty-two to eighteen seventy-nine."

"Oh, I wish Cottie were here to join us." Aura Lee sniffed mightily.

Rose let out a breath. "I think she is."

One by one they clasped each other's hands until the circle was complete.

Eve's eye was caught by the bulge at the end of the packet on the table. She picked it up and shook it gently toward the opening on the other end. A small bundle wrapped in a handkerchief fell onto the table. As she unwrapped it, Brenna asked, "What is it?"

Eve held it up. "An owl's claw." Her throat worked. "Our way to get to heaven."

CHAPTER 22

Pausing at the open door to the library, Noreen looked in to see Eve sitting at the end of the long table, her head bent. Her fine blonde hair curved on either side of her face, creating a curtain hiding her features. The packet she'd discovered in the hidden tunnel lay open before her.

They'd spent the morning compiling a list from the journals of every magical activity mentioned in them. "We'll create a profile to use for strategies to fight what's happening here," Max said. "When we add our findings to the notes we've kept on our paranormal encounters, we'll have access to each other's experiences as well as Caldicott's. Then Charlie and I will add anything we've encountered that appears useful. We just need to find the right prism."

As the hours passed, Noreen concluded she'd never met anyone who seemed more alone than Eve. She'd used her imagination and reactions to Caldicott's words in defining the enemy they fought but hadn't seen. She was gifted in making intuitive leaps as they catalogued and recorded the information they'd accumulated over the last six months or so. She even shared some of her own experiences, but still she had an air of being apart.

Noreen rubbed the knuckles of her right hand, where a constant ache had taken up residence. She needed to locate some of Eve's writing to better understand her. Maybe she shared herself primarily in her work, leaving little available for interaction with people.

Noreen sighed soundlessly. That was a small problem in the scheme of things. They were trying to arm themselves to go up against something well beyond their strengths. It was becoming more difficult to muster any confidence they'd be able to defeat whatever hounds of hell were marshaled against them. Caldicott had hidden her secrets too well. For every discovery they made, more secrets were suggested.

A movement at Eve's back drew Noreen's gaze. She blinked and looked more intently at the space behind her chair. As she watched, the air near the base of Eve's neck began to shimmer. Noreen took a step into the room, eyes focused on the area becoming infused with light. "Eve," she croaked, and her voice froze in her throat.

Eve turned to see Noreen crumple onto the floor near the open door. She pushed back her chair and stood up, stopping dead when she felt the ice along her back. Desperate to get away from the slicing pain of it, she fell forward onto the table, covering the packet she'd been examining. Her back felt inflamed now, the freezing sensation overcome with heat. She tried to shift her weight to the side of the table, to escape from the pain, but she was unable to move her body.

Max yelled from the doorway and Eve felt a surge of relief. When he grabbed her arm, she whispered, "Noreen. On the floor."

Max's hand fell from her as he turned toward the small body behind him.

Strong, hard fingers clutched her arm where Max had held it, and began jerking her to the end of the table. At first Eve was too shocked to move, but abruptly she *knew* that whatever held her was after the contents of the packet. Eve slid her arm over the bundle with the owl's claw and she grasped it reflexively. She felt warmth against her palm and a surge of power went through her.

She closed her eyes and saw the image of the open trap door over her, as it had been the day she'd fallen into the secret room beneath her apartment. With all her strength she used her mind to push the hanging door up until it slammed shut and she was plunged deeply into darkness. She had defeated *it* that time in darkness.

She thrust a message into that total blackness in her mind: *Charlie, Charlie. Help me. HELP ME!*

She couldn't feel him.

Eve breathed deeply in and out, in and out, ignoring the sharp pain in her back, visualizing the fingers wrapped around her arm. She imagined the sinews of each digit tightening, the bones increasing their force moment by moment. When she felt the clamping increase around her arm to as strong a hold as she could bear, she set her will to forcing each finger back, bending back the bones, holding the muscles immobile, then pushing them past the knuckles, making each one lie flat against the back of the hand. At some point in the middle of this process a mighty scream broke inside her head, shaking her free of the power immobilizing her.

"Eve? Are you all right?"

Max was nearby. She could feel the waves of concern flowing from him. She opened her eyes and looked up into his face, slowly returning to herself. She was lying on her back just under the edge of the library table.

"Noreen?" she whispered.

Max knelt beside her. "A bruised shoulder. Kerry took her off to Rose for treatment. And you?"

Eve was aware of a nagging irritation, an unpleasantness tightening her shoulders. She turned her head to see what could be causing it. Her hand crept up her side to clutch her amulet. Three feet away was a book. She could see the title on the spine. *The Punishment of the Disbeliever.*

"Help me up. Please."

Max took hold of her hand and elbow gingerly and eased her into a sitting position. The he brought her to her feet and seated her in a chair. "There, is that better?"

Eve summoned him closer with a wave of her hand. "Get me out of here now," she whispered. "Hurry."

Without a blink of surprise, Max pulled her up and steered her out the door.

As they reached the hallway, Eve realized how cold the library had been. "Stop, please." She closed the door carefully behind them and said, "Let's go to the living room to talk."

"Very well." He held her hand loosely and led her down the picture gallery hallway. "Was there a spirit in there you wanted to get away from?"

Eve was beginning to notice how depleted her energy was. "Slow down, will you?"

Max stopped and peered into her face. "I'm sorry. You must be exhausted." He put her arm on his and supported her the last distance into the living room. Once she was seated and he'd given her a glass of water, he sat down across from her. "Can you tell me now?"

Eve swallowed the cold water gratefully. "Tell you what?"

"What happened in there?" He got up from the ottoman and fetched two glasses for them. Once they were filled with brandy, he sat back down and presented one to her. "You must tell me before the details get fuzzy. *Something* unusual was happening, that I could tell."

"Seeing me spread-eagled on the table had to be a pretty good clue." Eve knocked back a swallow of brandy.

"Indeed." He clicked his fingers nervously. "Tell me."

Eve described Noreen's sudden entrance into the library and her subsequent collapse. "She called my name and then fell to the floor. I started toward her but something stopped me. It felt like ice on my back and I couldn't move. You came in and I was grabbed after you'd left to check on Noreen. I got it to let go of me, and I ended up on the floor and saw that filthy book I found in my office the day I fell into the secret room."

Max considered her with a frown. "You got it to let go? What do you mean by that?"

Eve closed her eyes and rolled her head, trying to loosen the muscles in her neck. Then she stopped and met his gaze. "I took charge of the situation. Deep breathing and then I just imagined the fingers of the hand on my arm letting go of me. And they did."

Max sat back in amazement, having to save himself from tumbling onto the floor since he was perched on the ottoman.

Eve's lips twisted in a smile.

"I hardly know which question to ask first." He stared at her. "Is this the kind of thing you've always been able to do?"

Eve shook her head. "Something happened to me when I was stuck in that secret room. A creature with red eyes and an unfriendly attitude was heading toward me. I was scared out of my mind and I started yelling at it, screaming and swearing. Casting it to hell. And it worked. The eyes faded, it moved away from me, and then all I had to do was wait for you guys to pull me up."

Max cocked his head, clearly unconvinced. "Don't forget the snakes."

She shrugged. "Can't do everything at once. This time I caught hold of the owl claw. It made me stronger," Eve added. "Anyway, I realized the thing holding onto me was after the packet." She froze, her eyes opening wide, her breath wheezing inward. "Oh, God," she gasped, "I left it there, and the claw, too. On the table."

Max slid his hand into his jacket pocket and pulled out the packet. "It didn't feel right to just leave them sitting there." He took out the owl claw and handed it to her.

Eve let out a shriek and threw her arms around him, holding tightly to the claw, upsetting the glass of brandy onto the rug.

"So this is what you get up to when I'm not around to keep an eye on you." Kerry sauntered in from the kitchen doorway with a giant economy bag of potato chips and stopped beside Max, patting him on the cheek. "It's a good thing I'm not the jealous type or you both would be toast."

Eve eyed the chips. "I'll trade him for some of those."

Kerry laughed and sat down beside her. "Deal. Don't look so grumpy," she told him. "These are really fine potato chips." She took one and bit into it with gusto. "So how's your day been?"

Max leaned forward and kissed her on the nose. "You'll hear all about it this evening. I think we've had a breakthrough."

Kerry glanced at the brandy glasses, full and spilled. "So you're celebrating? That's fabulous!" She caught sight of the owl claw in Eve's hand. "Did you figure out what the map's all about? Will it help us defeat the bad guys?"

"I don't know yet." Eve looked down at the brandy stain on the rug. "I guess I'd better do something about cleaning that up." She took the cloth from the floor and rewrapped the claw, returning it to the packet. "I may have figured out some things about it, but mainly we're celebrating surviving another encounter with weirdness."

Kerry turned to Max. "You're okay. Right?"

Max slid an arm around her. "Yes. And we may have discovered a superpower in our friend here. All told, I think it's been a good morning."

Kerry shot him a surprised expression. "You mean morning and afternoon. I came hunting for you because Rose wants to have cocktails in about a half hour."

"What time is it?" Eve asked.

"Getting on toward six. Geez, did you guys lose time, or what?"

"Maybe so," Max said blankly. "Which is another strange thing we've had to deal with. Now I wonder how much that has to do with our haunting encounters."

"We'll need drinks for that discussion." Kerry got to her feet and handed the potato chip bag to Eve with a flourish.

"I suggest you go splash some water in your face and lie down for a few minutes. Sounds like we'll have a post mortem tonight."

Eve felt a spasm of rage inside her, but it wasn't her own. Somewhere their enemy was suffering a great deal of pain. His next step would be to reciprocate. "*Gather ye rosebuds while ye may,*" she said quietly and dug into the bag of chips.

TIME OUT OF TIME

"Sir, your hand. Are you all right?" Simms shut his mouth as if realizing what he'd done and stepped back from his employer. "I beg your pardon, sir. My words were spoken in haste."

Severn was in too much pain to appreciate the quandary in which his butler found himself. It was all he could do to continue walking toward his study. The corridor around him was blurry, the furniture outsized and deformed. As Severn arrived at the door, he paused and Simms reached around him to open it. When Severn looked at the butler he paled and his hand fell from the knob. Simms turned and lurched back down the hallway, touching the wall several times to steady himself.

Severn's shoulder hit against the door as he entered the room. He shoved it closed behind him and reached the desk just as his legs lost their strength. Falling into the chair, he all but curled his body around his core in an effort to protect himself from the pain. He reached blindly for the bottle kept on the shelf behind him. Pulling the cork from it with his teeth, he tilted the bottle against his lips and drank, choked and drank again.

In all he studied, all he'd sought in the moldering books stored in the cellar workshop, he had never come across as direct a cross-spell as the one she'd used on him this day.

He forced himself to look at his hand. His stomach churned at the sight. His fingers were swollen to twice their size and they lay just above the back of his hand like dead creatures floating in the sewer gases of hell.

How did she do it? How did she take my strength and turn it against me?

What magic did she have? What would he have to do to kill her? He'd gleaned nothing from the book. *Punishment of the Disbeliever* indeed. It was dead, its power stilled. It had been useless, nothing more than an elaborate parlour trick.

A tear burned down his cheek and fell onto a half-open sheet of paper. It sizzled as it burned through and he could not stop the other tears from falling.

CHAPTER 23

They cleared off the dining room table after dinner and brought in what they had to share from their research. The air was scented with cinnamon and cloves, and the flames of the candles in the multilevel pottery centerpiece shifted in the air, creating a heartbeat rhythm of motion, as if the room itself breathed.

As Aura Lee carried in a package, placing it on top of the sideboard, the clock chimed eleven.

Rose frowned. "What time is it? What's that?"

Aura Lee wiped her hands on a napkin. "That dreadful book about punishment. We need to check it out thoroughly. And it's a little after eight."

Eve looked at the bundle. "We can't have that book in here. There's something very wrong with it. Put it in the kitchen. Or outside."

Eve spread the map out flat on the table. On it was a flat rendition of Wisdom Court. The old farmhouse and two associate houses were sketched with enough detail to be easily identified. The fountain was in the middle of the courtyard and fine drawings of trees and bushes were included, as were the wrought-iron fence along the north side of the property and the hedge along the south. Baseline

Avenue was labeled, along with its offshoot up the mountain, Flagstaff Road.

Rose leaned over her shoulder to take a closer look. "What are all the little marks along the boundaries? They almost look like crosses."

Elizabeth carried in a tray full of coffee cups, pausing to see what she was talking about. "Do not tell me this place is some kind of a graveyard. My heart won't take it."

"I don't think it is." Eve pushed down the right upper corner and set a saltshaker on it to keep it flat. "There's a key in the square at the bottom." She pointed at the left corner. "It labels them as 'holders,' whatever that means." She touched each one as she counted. "Twelve. Three on each side." She leaned closer to the paper. "Do you have a magnifying glass?" she asked Rose. "I've been looking at these things till my eyes cross and I swear there's something printed on them. I can't make out the letters. They're probably nothing, but…"

"But you want to know. I think there's one in the library." Rose wandered off to look. Brenna followed her but was back in the dining room almost immediately, heading for the kitchen. Kerry came in clutching several notebooks to her chest, Max close behind her with his old leather briefcase. They carried in the scent of leaves and fresh air, both of them windblown and pink-cheeked. Max was pushing his hair out of his eyes. "What's a holder?"

"I'm not sure." Eve glanced up when she heard Brenna whisper, *"Stop it!"* from the kitchen entrance. Dink followed her, pretending to steal the pie she carried. "What kind of pie is that?"

"Pumpkin." His hand hovered near the plate, drawing a warning shake of the head from Brenna. "My favorite."

"Then it's a good thing I made four of them." Pleased, Aura Lee favored him with a smile. "You could bring in the bowl of whipped cream next."

"Without sampling it along the way." Brenna shot him a frowning glance and Dink focused on her face, his eyes wrinkling with concern.

Dolores elbowed Andrea and patted her hand against her chest. "He's a goner," she whispered. "Where's Neal?"

"I don't know." Andrea reached into the canvas bag she'd brought, putting a couple of sketchpads on the table and then fishing out a box of pencils. "He said he might be a little late." She took a quick look over her shoulder at the windows, wincing as lightning flashed in their frames.

Muffled thunder soon followed and Andrea grimaced. "I hope we don't get any real rain. Those tunnels are fragile enough as it is."

Rose came back from the library and Brenna set down the pie she was carrying to approach her. "I need to talk to you about something."

"In a moment. I'm still looking for that magnifying glass." She pulled open one of the drawers in the sideboard and pawed through the detritus inside. Brenna turned with an impatient toss of her head. Her short dark hair lifted in a current of air, touched at the tips by candlelight.

Noreen set a pile of books at her place and headed toward the kitchen. She scooped up the pile of forks from the counter and grabbed a stack of napkins as well, carrying them into the dining room. "Are we about ready to begin?"

"As soon as Neal shows up." Andrea crossed to a window and peered out into the evening. "I hope he didn't run into any problems."

Elizabeth came to her side and looked out at the wind assaulting the trees and vines. "Honey, he probably had some work to do. It's not like life stops altogether just because we've got a bunch of ghosts actin' up around here." Lightning cracked again.

Andrea shivered. "I got spooked, roaming around the tunnels this morning."

Rose patted Andrea's shoulder as she walked past her. "I'm sure he's fine. He's been trying to get a backhoe over here from one of his construction sites. He said it was going to take some doing." She set a magnifying glass beside Eve and moved on toward the kitchen. "Did anyone make coffee?"

"I did." Kerry was stacking papers into four different piles, squaring the corners. "That's the only way I'll make it through the night."

"Thanks. I'll get the plates. Maybe Neal will arrive by the time we get our pie and coffee."

Every light on the lower floor went out. Gray remnants of daylight spread over the windows, leaving the candles to transform the table into a flickering island of intrigue. Shadows pushed in from the room's corners, ready to take over.

"What's up with that?" Kerry got out of her chair just as booming thunder rattled the windowpanes. "Oof! I do not like lightning." She scuttled to the window, dodging Aura Lee, who was gathering more candles from the sideboard, and looked out at the agitated branches hurling their leaves at the wind. "It's getting nasty out there." Peering more closely at the storm, Kerry hissed, "*God,* what *was that?*"

Dolores darted to the casement and stared outside. "What? What did you see?"

"Did you see a ghost?" asked Aura Lee, crowding against Kerry to see outside.

"Why would any self-respecting ghost be outside in a storm?" Noreen asked gruffly, though she headed over to join them. "There's no reason to be haunting out there."

Rose put the plates on the table, easing around the chairs to come up behind Kerry. "What did you see?"

"It looked like someone moving along the edges of the fountain." Kerry leaned her forehead against the cold glass. "It reminded me a little of the storm we went through up on the mountain, when we went up with Neal to rescue Andrea."

"Kerry!" Dolores viewed her with horror. Noreen's dismay was obvious, and Rose's hand crept up to find her amulet.

Turning, Kerry saw their upset. "I'm sorry. I don't mean I saw shadows walking on the courtyard bricks, or anything like that. It just had a…*sidling* motion; it looked distorted, moving oddly, not like the way people really move."

Dink stood stiffly beside the table, a cup in hand. "You're freaking me out, lady." He shot a glance at Brenna. "It could be Neal, right?"

Kerry laughed a little in surprise. "You're right. Of course, it's Neal checking things out near the fountain. You even said that's what he'd be doing." She ruffled her hair and produced a smile. "Geez, my bad, you guys. I guess I've just got a wicked case of the creepy-crawlies."

Andrea's pocket made a buzzing sound and she groped in it for her cell phone. She squinted down at it for a moment. "It's a text from Neal. He's stuck in a line of cars near Broadway. A lightning hit took out the signal lights and the cars are doing the four-way-stop shuffle. He'll be here in a half hour or so."

Everyone seemed to freeze for a moment as that sank in.

Dink let out a breath. "Okay, back to wondering what you saw out there, Kerry."

"Swell."

"Oh." Eve's voice was threaded with fear. "What can this…oh…"

"By the Goddess," Aura Lee exclaimed. "I'm beginning to suffer from the creepy-crawlies myself. What is it now?"

Eve had put a candle near the map and was peering down at it through the magnifying glass. The wavering light lent her an ethereal glow, and her blonde hair and pale complexion combined with it to create an almost angelic effect.

She looked up from the map, and they could see the fear and confusion on her face. "It's on the map. You know those holders I mentioned."

"What about 'em?" Elizabeth asked. Carefully she sat down at the table, waiting.

"Your hand's shaking." Dolores came to her side, patted her arm. "Take a breath, *jita*."

"Okay, okay. I'm just really scared now." Eve inhaled, coughing a little. "Rose, our names are on those little cross things. The 'holders' is what the key says they're called." She shook her head. "I guess I already told you that."

Rose sat down in the chair on Eve's other side. She took her hand in hers and held it tightly. "What do you mean, our names are on them?"

"All twelve of us," Eve said numbly. "Starting at the top left corner is you. You can see it on the vertical line of it if you use the magnifying glass. Look." She picked up the glass with her other hand.

Rose let go of her and held the glass near the paper. She moved it up and down a few times to get the clearest image. "It *is* my name. Rose." She dropped the glass on the map. "Who else?"

"All of us." Eve touched the second mark. "Elizabeth. The third is Dolores. Andrea is the first on the side, going down." Her finger moved down the right edge of the map. "Neal is next. Aura Lee. Across the bottom, going left is Kerry, then Max. Lucas is next—"

"It says Lucas?" Brenna asked in surprise. "His real name?"

Eve nodded, frowning in thought. "You call him Dink."

"It's my stupid nickname." Dink tanned cheeks reddened in embarrassment. "How many of you even know my real name?"

Rose raised her hand with a wan smile.

Kerry jumped to her feet in a surge of anger. "So how the hell and who the hell and what the hell?"

"Have you run out of hells, luv?" Max tugged her down onto her chair and put his arm around her. "Keep going, Eve."

"Brenna is at the left corner going up. After her are Noreen, and then me. Eve."

The silence was broken by another burst of thunder.

Max sighed. "These 'holders' are on the map from the packet you found in the tunnel?"

"In the safe room off the tunnel." Eve felt a twinge in her back where the icy paralysis had happened that afternoon. She moved her shoulders in an effort to stem the discomfort. "Brenna was asleep and I had the flashlight on for a minute. Caught the flash of metal and went to look. It was a drawer about four inches by four inches and the packet was in it."

"So you said before." Max frowned in thought. "Did it look as though anyone had been in that room, or could have put the packet in that drawer?"

Eve shook her head, not understanding what he meant. "It's a hidden tunnel, a hidden room. Who would've gone down there?"

"As it happened we did." Neal was standing in the kitchen doorway. His jacket had rain beaded on it and his hair was wet.

Andrea rushed to him, and ignoring his jacket, threw her arms around him. "Am I glad to see you. Are you okay?"

Neal kissed her soundly and pulled back to search her face. "Sure. Why wouldn't I be?" He took the towel Aura Lee handed him and wiped his face and hair.

"We've been scaring ourselves while waiting for you." Noreen said in a querulous voice. "A time-honored practice here at Wisdom Court."

"Maybe so," said Rose from her chair at the table, "but this time we've got a little extra oomph in our source. Come sit down, Neal, and we'll get your take on this."

While he discarded his jacket and finished drying off, the others cut and served the pie. Dink showed his skill at piling whipping cream on each piece and dumped it into the coffee as well.

"Okay," Neal said finally after a large bite of pumpkin, "what's the big deal?" He peered down at the map Eve slid in front of him. "That's Wisdom Court for sure, and in plenty of detail."

Rose handed him the magnifying glass as Eve explained what she'd found. "The question is," she summed up, "if this map has been hidden in the tunnel for however many years, how can we explain our names being written on it?"

Neal stopped chewing. "There's no way. Caldicott died what, seven months ago? Before that she was too frail to climb into those tunnels, although," he said in a lower, preoccupied voice, "she could've accessed them from the pantry. And there were the stairs. But she didn't have the strength to go all the way to that room and pull out the map for last-minute adjustments."

Eve had pulled the map back in front of her and was sliding the magnifying glass her way. "I want to look at the legend again."

"Aura Lee would've known if she sneaked off into the tunnels, right?" He looked to her for confirmation.

"She hadn't even met Andrea when she died!" exclaimed Kerry. "Or Brenna, let alone Dink. Eve just got here. There's no way Caldicott had anything to do with this."

"Wait a minute. There's a tiny line just under the drawing of Wisdom Court. The farmhouse, I mean." Eve picked up the glass again and looked through it. *For a perilous journey, persons of strength hold the directions for the seeker to keep her from losing her way.* Eve looked up, her hand shaking. "Have you heard of holding the directions?"

Aura Lee nodded. "It has a ceremonial meaning. The concern is for a person undertaking a vision quest. She goes out searching for identity and purpose in her life, and she encounters dangers along the way. Trusted people are given tokens to keep on her behalf. Each token represents a direction, like on a compass. The person holding it chants for the seeker and keeps it as a beacon for her. All of the beacons work together to guide the seeker. It's considered an honor to be asked." Carefully she flicked a lighter and lit the row of candles arranged on the sideboard.

Eve grasped her cup to warm her hands. "Apparently we've all been honored, then, because we've been asked."

"Who else has something to share tonight?" Rose asked abruptly.

Brenna raised her head. She'd been staring down at the table, rubbing around the edges of the bump on her forehead. "I've been trying to. Remember how I asked if I could photograph our trip into the tunnels?"

Neal nodded.

"Well, I finally looked at what I recorded." She leaned against Dink's shoulder. "I've been a little out of it.

Anyway, I want to show you what I found. I've turned up the contrast as much as I can so you can catch the details." She typed in a command and turned her open laptop around for them.

The picture was grainy and in so much shadow it appeared to be shot in black and white. Brenna had been behind the others as they started out from the hidden room below Eve's apartment. The banter between Andrea and Neal, and then Eve's comments along with Kerry's and Max's additions lasted as the group went forward through the narrow corridors. When Eve and Brenna stayed behind, however, the tenor changed.

The sound was obscured as they sat on the stones in the first room they'd found. Eve stretched her legs and Brenna said something, the only sound now an electronic buzz. A figure moved behind Eve, easing across the rock face out of the frame.

"What was that?" Rose was leaning toward the screen. "Did I actually see that?"

"Yes, hold on." The camera angle jutted upward, reflecting Brenna's fall in the cave. A figure hanging from the ceiling stared down, and reached across Brenna toward Eve, malevolence in its shadowed features. The edges of it began to break up and, with a quick leap, it skittered away across the rocks, flowing over the uneven surface and disappearing into a crack between two large stones. The laptop screen went dark.

"By the Goddess." Aura Lee's face was frozen with fear. "You didn't see that at the time?"

"No. Remember, I'd fallen, too, and it was the camera that looked up. I'd landed on my side and was trying to get up."

Max looked at the empty screen. "Were there any other shots of that creature?"

Brenna nodded and typed another command. "After I hit my head on that filthy stone, I dropped my phone. I set this in slow motion. Take a look."

A jumble of rocks and wood supports were blocked as a shadow figure moved toward the camera and then away as the camera itself jerked as if kicked. In the light they saw the outline of a man with long arms and legs. His hands cast grotesque shadows on the smooth wall directly behind him. Eve bent over Brenna as the shadow reached for her. A screeching sound filled the air and he backed up to the wall and was slowly absorbed into the stone.

CHAPTER 24

The room was hushed but for the wind whipping at the house. Eve felt the beat of her heart, was aware of pain in her knee, but shock had blasted away every thought in her head. As she waited for what would happen next, an idea trickled into her mind: they formed a tableau, a group of motionless people representing a scene for the amusement of an unseen audience. Did they symbolize amazement? Horror? People overwhelmed by the ongoing assault of paranormal events? Who was the audience?

A second later Elizabeth sighed, and the spell was broken. "What did we just see?"

"And was it real?" asked Noreen. She appeared even more wizened than usual, her skin gray against the contrast of her black sweater.

Rose was holding her arms in an attempt warm herself. "That's one of the most frightening things I've ever seen."

"How could it happen?" Aura Lee's face was creased in bewilderment. "How? A person who can melt into a rock? Who can move across a rock like a shadow?" She shuddered.

"What if it *is* a shadow?" Eve winced at the pain in her knee, trying to erase the aching with her fingertips. "I didn't see anyone else in that tunnel, but so much was going on and the flashlight was fitful, to say the least. If the camera captured the shadow of someone who stood watching us, then..."

"That's pretty scary." Kerry hunched her shoulders. "But what I saw couldn't be just a man and his shadow. The way it moved—God!—the way it hung from the ceiling of the tunnel." She leaned into Max, seeking his warmth. "It was an *other*. Something outside my understanding."

Elizabeth's eyes widened. "An Outside Man," she whispered. Shivering, she looked over both shoulders, expecting something to jump out at her. "My auntie told us about a tribe in the Aleutians that banished men who did evil things—murder, rape—stuff like that. No one would accept them and they existed alone on the fringes, stealing food and other things. Children were warned to stay in at night so they couldn't be stolen."

"Like the bogeyman?" Brenna asked in a small voice.

"Uh-huh, but the Outside Man sounded scarier to me. Auntie said over time they became more than men, worse than men, and did steal children to eat them or turn them to evil."

Neal zeroed in on Brenna. "I assume you've inspected your camera."

Brenna nodded. "I tested it this afternoon and everything checked out fine. There wasn't much light down in the tunnel, but it recorded what you saw. It looked like a man, or the shadow of a man who could sink into his background."

"*Dios,* it looked like one of those special effects movies," Dolores said with feeling. "To think of someone like this sliding around under the house will drive away sleep tonight."

"Thanks, Dolores." Kerry rubbed her face with a scrubbing motion. "The longer all this goes on, the weirder it gets. Where the hell would something like that come from?"

"That's one question. The other is to what end?" Max tapped a pencil on the edge of the table. "Every culture has its bogeyman, some of them bone-chilling, but even after the research we've done on every paranormal manifestation you can imagine, I can tell you we haven't come across anything like what we saw in Brenna's recording."

"Could it be that man in England who's looking for the talisman?" Andrea asked. "Could he have refined remote viewing to include travel to the place he's been observing?"

He shook his head. "I don't know how to answer that."

Aura Lee looked down at her hands. "What about magic?"

Rose raised a brow. "What about it?"

"Oh, you know what I mean." Aura Lee pursed her lips in irritation. "Cottie's journal said the reason the evil earl wanted the talisman was to create spells that would further the Nazi cause. What if he continued working toward that without the talisman? What if he practiced black magic, the kind I've barely found out about because it's evil?"

Brenna was holding tightly onto Dink's hand. "So you're saying it's possible that what my camera picked up was something sent by this mad Englishman's coven to spy on us?"

Dink frowned at her as he mulled over the idea. "That's quite a leap, isn't it? Don't get me wrong," he added hurriedly, "Bren told me about her grandmother's ghost and all that, and I'm not saying I don't believe her, but how skilled are these people? How crazy are they, too?"

The lights went back on.

Like sleepwalkers abruptly awakened they blinked and looked around at each other in light that suddenly felt too bright.

Neal ran his hand across his beard in a bewildered gesture. "Has anybody seen anything else like this shadow figure since the tunnel fell in?"

Rose shook her head. "We've been spared that, I suspect."

"Maybe not," Kerry said suddenly. "The figure I saw out in the courtyard. You know, the one we thought might be Neal?" She turned to Max, eyes wide. "What if that was the same creature?"

"What was it doing?" Neal asked.

Kerry leaned against Max's shoulder. "It was moving around the fountain, but what bothered me was *how* it moved. It sort of slid over the courtyard bricks, moving faster here and there, almost gliding."

Neal frowned. "Is that how I move?"

"No, of course not, but Andrea was getting upset, so we all said it could be you." Kerry shot an annoyed glance at Andrea. "See how mistakes are made?"

"Bite me." Andrea picked up one of her pencils and tapped it against her sketchbook.

Absentmindedly Neal patted her on the shoulder. "Andrea said something happened in the library this afternoon."

Max glanced across the table at Eve. "I came in at the end. She's the one to ask."

Haltingly, Eve told them about the icy pain she'd felt along her spine, then Noreen's collapse as she'd tried to come to her aid. "Max went to help her and something grabbed onto my arm. Hard. It tried to pull me down to the end of the table and I had the strongest feeling that whatever it was doing it wanted the packet. I'd fallen on it." She paused and took a breath. "I don't know exactly how it happened. I thought of the figure in the hidden room, the one with red eyes, and how I drove it away by screaming and cursing it."

"Oh, mercy, do you think they're related?" Noreen exclaimed.

"I don't know." Eve frowned as she considered the idea. "Maybe. But today I focused on recreating the dark. I imagined how the open trapdoor looked and I closed it in my mind. And I visualized the hand on my arm, letting it hold me more and more tightly." She paused and then shrugged helplessly. "I just imagined peeling those fingers off my arm, one by one, and because I was angry, I saw myself folding them back as far as I could push them. When I heard his scream in my head, I knew I'd done it."

Elizabeth slumped in her chair. "Are you saying it actually happened? The invisible hand got its fingers bent back?"

Eve closed her eyes and sighed. "The hand let go of my arm." She pushed her left sleeve up and someone gasped. Deep purple bruises on her bicep looked like nothing so much as fingers wrapped around her arm.

"Oh, Eve." Rose came around the table and knelt beside her. "I have some arnica and we can make a poultice with it." She glanced up into her face. "Is it terribly painful?"

"Not too bad." Eve pulled her sleeve back down. "I've been more freaked out emotionally than feeling a lot of pain."

Rose steadied herself with the table as she stood up. "I can understand that." She noticed Dolores staring at her hands. "What is it, Dolores?"

When she looked up at Eve, tears spilled from her eyes. "You are hurting, *jita*, and that makes me sad, but if I am honest, what I also think is a question scaring me so much."

Beside her Elizabeth reached for her hand. "What question, honey?"

Dolores seemed to shrink into herself. "This Outside Man, if he was here at Wisdom Court...when he comes again, how angry will he be because his fingers are bent?"

On her way back to her chair, Rose patted Dolores on the shoulder. "All will be well."

Eve straightened in her chair. "I hope he's royally pissed off. And frightened, because I made him let go." She glanced at Max. "We may be mixing up things that don't belong together, the Outside Man, the red-eyed creature in the hidden room." She looked at them with serious eyes. "What we need to worry about now is the map with our names on the little holder labels."

"If we're the direction holders, who's our vision seeker?" Kerry shot a look at Max. "Is it one of us or is some one trying to come here?"

Max shrugged. "You're good at asking questions, luv, but I don't have the answers. I feel we're moving toward a confrontation, but I don't know with whom. I've been attempting to contact Charlie, but he hasn't responded for the last few days. I'm worried about him, but afraid to further try contacting him to avoid alerting others around him."

Eve felt her nerves tighten. "Do you think he's in danger?"

Max's eyes were kind. "I don't *feel* he is, but I can't be totally confident I'm right."

Rose spoke softly from the end of the table. "Look at Andrea."

They turned toward her and saw her hand was wielding a pencil swiftly over her sketchpad.

"Her eyes are closed," Brenna whispered. "How can she see what she's drawing?"

Noreen cleared her throat. "She may not be the one sketching this picture."

Eve was watching closely, barely breathing as the lines on the paper began to take shape.

"She's drawing a face." Kerry leaned over the table a little to get a clearer view. "She's amazing."

Rose saw that Neal was stone still, his eyes dark with pain. "What is it?"

"She hates the loss of control." His voice was gravelly. "I hate her having to go through this again."

"It's coming together, the image, I mean." Dolores looked up from the page and stared at Eve. "I think it's you." She turned toward Rose. "Why would she draw a portrait of Eve?"

"Wait." Noreen narrowed her eyes as she saw the letters forming under the picture of Eve's face. "I suspect you have an answer to your question, Kerry." She waved her small hand at the sketchpad.

Kerry peered at it and looked across the table at Eve. "It's you. You're the one."

Eve felt her stomach roil. "What?"

"Says it right here. Look." Eve got up to limp around the table. On the sketchpad in front of Andrea her own face stared up at her, unsmiling, eyes steady. Under it were the words, *Vision Seeker*.

TIME OUT OF TIME

◆

"Words from the grave, words from the grave." Severn muttered hoarsely, over and over. He struggled through the worn pages in front of him, pushing them with his good hand. He had to find a weapon against the woman. There had to be something he could use to stem her power. *To end her.*

Had she been playing with him this whole time? His face burned as the thought ripped through him. She had shown herself the fearful victim. He'd followed her signatures thinking her helpless. How had she so thoroughly hidden her true nature? Were all her powers greater than his? He howled inwardly with rage.

Somewhere here were the spells his father had used to sway his English cronies to the side of Hitler. And somehow he'd kept himself out of prison as post-war revelations of his efforts to sabotage the British fight against Germany began to be known. He had to have used the old ways to save his corrupt hide.

There. He pulled the volume to him, eyes closing in agony as a fresh wave of pain crackled along his nerves. His fingers…his useless claw of a hand, maimed forever by a whore of a woman who laughed at his spells, who mocked his careful efforts. Growling with rage he leaned over the pages.

> *Blood of retribution summon.*
> *Hatred writhes, and insult taunts.*
> *Justice hereby swears destruction,*
> *Past transgression looms and haunts.*
> *Sharpen knives to razor edge,*
> *Milk the venom, fill the arrows.*
> *Rouse the hellhounds, cloud all reason,*
> *Hell will rise to suck life's marrow.*
> *Her life for mine, my soul for thee.*
> *As seventh son, so mote it be.*

The words died into gurgled laughter and Severn heard nothing of the man entering his study.

"Sir, the doctor is here. I've put him in the sitting room." One of the servants stood before his desk, his eyes noting every throb and jolt.

Severn surfaced enough to recognize Pierce. "Damn you, leave me alone." He groped with his uninjured hand across the desktop, finding a paper filled with writing. The coven list. He fumbled with it one-handed, jamming it into his pocket. "Tell Fitch to contact his number two man. He'll know why."

"Fitch is dead, sir."

Fitch dead? Images filled his mind, of the luckless fool, of his eyes bulging as Severn squeezed the life from him by way of a charmed snake. He saw Pierce, serious and pale like a well-dressed schoolboy. He began to laugh, raw, bubbling laughter catching in his chest and hemming in his breathing.

"Sir, come with me now."

Severn let Pierce help him up, even leaning on him as they made their way down the hallway to the sitting room.

"Leave us," Severn ordered as they paused in the doorway. "Follow my instructions, do you understand? Tell them to ready themselves."

Pierce nodded and turned, hearing Severn say, "How good of you to come, Dr. Jarrett. I fear my people may have been too anxious, getting you here..." He began to cough.

When he reached the study door, Pierce looked left and right, making certain no one watched him. He slipped into the room and searched the desktop for what he could find. As he pawed through the jumble, he caught sight of an ancient book, open and shoved halfway under a pile of papers. Its pages were dog-eared and stained. He bent over it to read what was written. When he had done so, he left the room and shut the door. He sped down the hall and took the stairs to the kitchen two at a time.

The wall phone was dead, as was his cell. Had Severn cast a protection spell around the property?

CHAPTER 25

They put Eve in Andrea's room for the night, and Brenna and Dink in Caldicott's.

"Cottie wouldn't mind," Aura Lee told them earnestly. "Eve, your leg will feel better in a real bed instead of the sofa. And if you have any disturbances," she added to Brenna, "You'll know that Cottie would never hurt you."

Eve had expected to toss and turn, but when she climbed into Andrea's bed, she arrowed into sleep like a cormorant diving for minnows. She swam in dreams, all haunted by a man with auburn hair who walked ahead of her on a rugged trail. His face was obscured, but a wicked smile flashed as he looked back at her with sharp blue eyes. If only she could reach him, so far ahead of her.

He was leading her through grassy hills, and though she called to him, he did not respond. His long legs ate up the miles on a path toward tall mountains in the distance. No matter how she pushed herself, she fell further behind.

My heart, she thought. *You'll make my heart stop if you don't wait for me.*

He didn't hear her.

At the edge of a lake prisoners were chained together, waiting to be taken to the caverns under a massive castle. She knew they would be tortured there but she could do nothing until she caught up with the man who walked away from her so steadily.

How can I have hope if you won't listen? Fatigue blurred her vision and she stumbled over the rocky path. *Without hope I'll die, and you will die.*

"The blackness of eternal night encompasses me," she heard him say clearly. "It's hope that triumphs on the rack…"

It's hope that triumphs on the rack…

Eve sat up in bed, her eyes open wide. "Poe. It has to be Poe." She fought to catch her breath, her heart hammering an urgent rhythm. She pulled the blankets more closely around her against the chill. What was it from?

She frowned, trying to recall the details. The castle could represent Wisdom Court, but she couldn't think of a particular Poe story featuring a man who walked away from someone. The nearby prisoners waiting to be tortured in the caverns sounded like Poe. "He had a thing about prisoners," she murmured, not realizing she spoke. "And torture."

"The blackness of eternal night…hope that triumphs on the rack." She took in a deep breath. The rack. Torture. The Inquisition. "The Pit and the Pendulum," she said with certainty. "Has to be."

Nature's call interrupted her thoughts. Eve rolled out of bed to use the bathroom. When she'd finished she looked at herself in the mirror, and saw someone behind her. She spun round, her heart in her throat, catching an impression of movement, but no one was there.

"I'm losing my mind." *I'm talking to myself; what other proof do I need?* She opened the door slowly and peeked around its edge. The room was dark and she could see nothing until a light glimmered around the edge of the cheval mirror near the tall chest of drawers. Mustering her courage, Eve stepped closer to it. She saw a face, not her own, but the face of a man she didn't recognize. Her breath came more rapidly. She was looking at a man *inside* the mirror. The glass was so dark she could barely make out his features.

Eve reached one hand toward the mirror's surface and saw her gesture replicated in the reflection. As her palm touched the cool glass, his did as well, and they stared into each other's eyes. His lips moved and she strained to hear what he was saying.

There was no sound.

He moved his lips again and she pressed closer to the glass, staring at his mouth. She couldn't make out what he trying to say.

"Damn," she whispered. "What are you saying?"

He closed his eyes. When he moved his hand, she saw he was pointing at her with his forefinger. Slowly he moved his finger across the glass, writing letters with his finger. As she looked at them they glowed against the dark backdrop behind them.

.gnimoc era yehT .eraweB She touched the letters, frowning.

"For God's sake, it's backwards." Eve used her own forefinger to trace the letters from the end of the line, murmuring them as she did. "B e w a r e. Beware. T h e y. A—are. C o m—they are coming?" She'd been told this before.

"Are you the one who sent me that message on the computer?"

As he stared at her, not comprehending, the letters faded and disappeared.

She looked into his face. He'd said *beware*. "Someone's coming to harm us." She exaggerated the movements of her lips. "We'll be attacked?"

He nodded.

His image began to weaken and then he was gone.

She'd been warned.

Eve was statue still for a moment, her mind tumbling with what she'd seen. It must have been a ghost, she thought, wondering why she wasn't terrified. The south window blazed with white light and she shrieked as thunder shook the glass.

What should she do first?

The map. The idea burst in her mind and she wheeled toward the chair where she'd put the items brought upstairs after last night's meeting. Her knee protested and she cursed it, limping quickly across the room. Fumbling through the clothes she'd worn, she found the packet and tossed it onto the bed.

It was the work of moments to dress, slightly longer to make sure her shoes were double-tied. Constant questions marched through her mind. And answers followed on their heels.

Who are coming? Has to be the ones who've been causing the disturbances at Wisdom Court.

How can we defend ourselves? The holders will take their places around the perimeter armed with spells and counter-spells.

What if they keep coming until they overwhelm us? We'll have the talisman.

Eve stopped at that, breathing faster at the temerity of it. When had she come to that conclusion? She felt her blood thrumming through her and electricity dancing along her nerves.

Where is the talisman? The dreams told me. I'll find it.

She braced herself against the ache in her knee and grabbed a pain pill from the bathroom. Swallowing it dry, she opened the door and hurried into the hallway.

You'll go after it alone? I'll tell them. They're all here. We'll work together.

"Rose?" Eve called as she neared her bedroom. "Wake up. Company's coming."

Eve roused the others, telling them to get dressed and meet her in the kitchen. While she waited for them she made several trips back and forth from the cupboards, gathering cups and plates. When Aura Lee came in, she took over the refreshments prep and Eve limped for the dining room to retrieve several books she thought they'd need.

Max slumped in his chair as Eve described the visitor in the mirror. The encounter intrigued him. "It could be Charlie."

"It could be anybody," Kerry interjected from the coffeemaker. She'd added enough ground beans to deny them sleep for a week. "Are you sure you were awake?"

Eve looked up from the map, her impatience clear. "For the third time, yes. I was awake, I got the message, and I'm giving it to you. Now let me tell you the most important part."

"Okay, okay," muttered Kerry. "Just checking."

Max's brows knitted in concentration as Eve repeated the aspects of her dream.

"I can see how the castle could be Wisdom Court, but I don't entirely understand the significance of the prisoners and the torture. Do you think the members of Wisdom Court are imprisoned by the hauntings? Are tortured by the impact of the paranormal events you've witnessed?"

Eve poured cream into her coffee and stirred it thoroughly. "No, I told you. I think my subconscious was reminding me of a story by Edgar Allen Poe. *The Pit and the Pendulum.*"

"But why?" Andrea asked, yawning. "All that makes me think of is the Vincent Price movie."

"That was great," Brenna chimed in.

Eve noticed her red sweater was turned inside out.

"He had such a good voice for the spooky stuff. Did you ever see *The Simpsons* version of *The Raven*?" Brenna added. "Outstanding."

Eve closed her eyes and summoned patience. "Listen, I know it's early and we're sleepy, but this is important. The dream was telling me something about the clock. It has a pendulum, the business about the clock always being seventeen minutes fast, the way it's been off with the number of chimes lately."

Rose clasped her coffee cup and stared into its depths. "I'm not getting what you mean."

Elizabeth shook her head, setting the little braids in her hair into motion. "You and me both, sister."

Aura Lee's head snapped up and she gawked at Eve. "All in bad time." She turned to Rose. "*All in bad time.*"

"Yeah." Eve pushed her hair behind her ears and rested her chin on her hands.

Dink scrubbed at his face with both hands. "What are you people talking about?"

"It's what Caldicott used to say." Rose yawned. "Somebody would ask her a question and she'd say, *All in bad time.*" She frowned in confusion. "So you're saying your dream was about a saying she used?"

Eve felt a pang of uncertainty. She'd been so sure. What if she was wrong? "I think she was giving a hint about where the talisman is hidden."

Kerry's mouth dropped open and she stared at Eve as she worked it out in her head. "So you're saying you think the talisman might be in the old clock?"

Eve nodded. "On the pendulum."

Dolores was resting her head on her crossed arms. "Why don't you go look for it and then we can go back to sleep."

"Not a bad idea." Neal stood up and put his hand out for Andrea, tugging her to her feet. "Shall we?"

They left the kitchen and filed in a bedraggled pilgrimage through the dining room and into the foyer. Max stopped them before they got close to the clock. "I think we'd best keep our distance. After reading what Caldicott had to say about the talisman in her journal, we need to proceed very carefully."

Neal nodded. "I'll get a flashlight and tools." He started off and looked back over his shoulder. "And some heavy gloves I keep in my pickup. Be right back."

Even though he didn't take long, Eve was biting her nails by the time he returned.

Noreen frowned at her in concern. "*When bated breath is all one has to fill the lungs, make each count as more, for held breath may mean death, and hesitation may signal the clear edge of defeat."* She started to cite her source but caught sight of Eve's face. "Um, what's bothering you?"

Eve had to bite back a groan. Where did the woman *get* these quotes? "The man in the mirror said they're coming. He didn't say when. We're using time we need to get ready for them."

Neal pulled out a couple of screwdrivers and an adjustable wrench. He put on his gloves and headed for the clock. "Let's see what we've got." He walked to the alcove beside the stairs and approached the old grandfather clock as it ticked in stately rhythm. Opening the glass door to the pendulum, he clicked on the flashlight. "Let me shine this back here," he murmured and reached for the shaft of the pendulum. As he touched it an electrical crack produced a flash of light, knocking him away from the clock and across the foyer.

"Neal!" Andrea ran to kneel beside him. "Are you all right?" She felt his head and leaned down to put her ear to his chest. "His heart's beating. Neal, can you hear me?"

A long groan came from him and he opened his eyes.

The windows glared with sudden light. At once the rumble of thunder shook the house. The lights went out.

"Oh, shit." Elizabeth's voice was filled with dread.

"It's October," Aura Lee screeched. "We don't have electrical storms in October."

As if to argue the point with her, more thunder clapped above them.

Eve limped across the floor to Neal's flashlight, the cockeyed beam illuminating the newel post of the stairs. She stooped to pick it up and pointed it at Neal. "Is he okay?"

Andrea had his head in her lap and was smoothing his hair back from his forehead. "I think so, but he had a hell of a shock." Brenna entered the circle of light carrying a glass of water, handing it off to her. "Thanks."

Eve shone the light around the group, most sitting on floor now, seeking Aura Lee. When she found her, she made her way through the throng to her side. "Do you have any idea of how to disarm the protections on the pendulum?"

The woman was gray with fatigue and Eve wondered how old she was. She put her arm around Aura Lee's shoulders and looked into her face, trying to keep the flashlight at an indirect angle. "Can you do this, come up with a counter-spell, I mean? If it's too much for you, we'll find another way."

Aura Lee stiffened her spine as the light of determination filled her eyes. "Cottie had to be the one to create the protection, and she would never have left something to hurt me." She saw Eve's involuntary glance toward Neal. "We didn't think to make it safe for him. I'll do a simple counter-spell now and we'll try to get the talisman."

"Wouldn't it be a more complicated spell, to keep out the ones who are coming for us?"

Aura Lee shook her head. "I have a feeling. The lightning's the key. Dolores?" she called.

As Dolores pushed herself off the floor, Aura Lee drew a pencil and a small piece of paper from the pocket of her robe. She was writing feverishly when Dolores sat down beside her.

"What is it?" Dolores looked warm in sweatpants and a hoodie over a tee shirt. She'd pulled her glossy black hair into a tail held by a scrunchie. "What do you need?"

Aura Lee grasped her hands. "Two things: my magicks journal on the bedside table in my bedroom and the leather valise in my closet. It's toward the back, behind my shoes."

Dolores stood up and nodded toward the flashlight. "Do we have anymore of those?"

Rose held out a small LED light and Dolores flicked it on. "What if the ghosts have come out to play?"

Eve could feel the minutes ticking away. "Tell them to come help us. We're going into battle."

Dolores shot her a doubtful glance but headed toward the dining room, which would lead her to Aura Lee's apartment.

"What's the plan?" Rose asked softly.

Before Eve could answer, the clock began to chime, culminating in the hour strokes: one, two, three, four, five.

"Minus seventeen minutes." She'd put the flashlight in front of her on the floor, and in its limited light Rose's face was gaunt. "I'm going to take the talisman and go down to the secret room under my apartment." Her throat was dry and she coughed to clear it. "I figure the attack will come there. The rest of you will take your places along Wisdom Court's border and you'll all chant protective spells to keep us strong."

The others were beginning to crowd around Eve and Rose. "Where will we get the spells?" Elizabeth asked.

"Aura Lee." Eve smiled at the older woman. "Simple protective spells chanted over and over again. No matter what, you all keep chanting."

"What about Neal?" whispered Andrea. "He's asleep."

"He'll wake up. There'll be one unguarded spot: the one I'm supposed to hold. But we'll have to make do."

Max held Kerry's hand and had closed his eyes, his lips moving.

"Are you praying, Max?"

He shook his head. "Some of that chanting you mentioned."

Dolores came back into the circle, a book in one hand and a valise in the other. "I found them."

"Did you see anything unusual?" Eve eyed her in concern. Her hands were trembling and she kept glancing over her shoulder.

"The mirror in Aura Lee's room was…humming." She shook her head as if to dislodge her fears. "I didn't stop to find out why. I just told…them…what you said about the battle. Nothing tried to mess with me."

Aura Lee had opened the valise and was digging inside it. "Many of the protective substances are already in your amulets," she said, "and I have small amounts of others for us to put in our pockets when we go out." She looked up at

Eve. "Give me a few minutes and I'll have a counter-spell to try on the clock."

Eve sat slumped on the stairs, trying to keep focused on the job at hand. When she heard a tiny sound, she opened her eyes. Danica sat on a step above her, licking one paw. She jumped onto Eve's lap and crawled up her shirt. Eve listened to the purring in her ear and gained strength for what lay ahead.

The sun was rising by the time Aura Lee came to Eve and reached for her hand. Into it she dropped a small leather bag.

"What's in it?" Eve asked. It felt heavier than its size would suggest. Her gaze followed Danica as she ran up the stairs.

"You don't need to know." Aura Lee turned a page in her magicks book and read through what was written one more time. "This is what you'll chant now. You'll chant the other when you go through the secret room. You'll keep chanting it, just as we will be chanting above you." She closed Eve's hand on the bag. "Do not drop this, no matter what. Your life and possibly ours will depend upon your holding this. Don't forget."

Eve shook her head. She wouldn't forget.

"Now." Aura Lee turned to Rose. "You come with Eve and me." She looked at the others. "All of you stay here regardless of what happens. Put the small charm bags in your pockets. Either Eve will obtain the talisman or she will not. If she can't, I don't know if the three of us will survive. If we don't, get out as fast as you can. Don't stop for anything. Noreen, make sure they follow my instructions."

Noreen nodded, quoteless at last.

"Strudel?" Brenna was on the edge of tears.

"She's safe in my apartment. Max, Dink, my knees are stiff. Help me up." Each grasped her arms and hoisted her to her feet. Beside her Rose stood, holding out her hand for Eve.

"Try not to look at the clock," Aura Lee told the others, "in case there's more lightning." She caught hold of Eve's free hand and with her other grasped the small bag atop the valise. "It's time."

The three of them walked to the back of the alcove and stood beside the old clock. Aura Lee let go of their hands. "Begin the chant," she whispered and Eve complied.

Edge of light creates the shadow.
Night's advance has threatened day.
Harnessed lightning firms the boundary.
Time itself will thus give way.
Now pull out the veiled corruption.
That work is done; new fights begin.
Let her take the hell-broth tool,
Help use the wickedness to win.
Wisdom Court must be made free,
As we ask so mote it be.

TIME OUT OF TIME

Severn found the page he sought. The Serpent Nostrum would take care of the woman. Finally. Forever. In agony. He would possess the talisman and power beyond measure would be his destiny.

He let his hand rest on the desktop and the contact triggered pain as severe as any he had ever known.

Mulier adolendum incensum coram oculis meis, he muttered through the small sobs shaking his voice.

"What did you say, sir?"

Severn looked up through narrowed eyes at the man standing before his desk. "Let the woman burn before my eyes!" he roared.

After a brief silence, the man—what *was* his name? Pierce—cleared his throat. "I beg your pardon, sir. I didn't mean to intrude." He turned to go. Severn let himself lean back in his chair. "Stay. I felt some…discomfort and spoke from pain."

"Yes, sir." The man stood, stiff as a lead soldier. *And probably as sentient*, Severn said to himself. "I have plans for the evening. Call the members of the group and tell them to be present by seven o'clock this evening. And dismiss the servants early."

An uncomfortable expression crossed Pierce's face.

"What is it now?" Severn growled. He had little liking for this servant.

"The staff has left, sir."

Cold fury rose in Severn's chest, threatening to overtake him. He fought for control. "When did this occur?"

Pierce shifted his weight from one foot to the other. "Over the last month, sir. The rumors about the bodies on the grounds affected some of them, and the others were nervous due to the visits by the police."

"And you?" His lips pulled away from his teeth in the travesty of a smile.

"I need the work, sir."

"Very well. Go make the calls, then."

"Yes, sir."

As the door clicked shut, Severn surged to his feet. He plucked a paperweight from the desktop and hurled into the fireplace. He pitched a cigarette box through the window, but its crash was not enough to sooth the wrath bubbling inside him. In a frenzy he threw whatever he encountered, into the fire, against a painting, crashing a mirror. As his energy ebbed, pain flared and determination grew. "She will die, she will die, she will die," he chanted. "Death to the woman, death to her sisters. Death to them all!"

CHAPTER 26

As the pendulum swung by her fingers, Aura Lee caught the rod and held it still. Eve felt Rose's hand tighten on her own. They braced for a lightning burst, but the pendulum rested in Aura Lee's hand. She shot them a glance of pure triumph and then bent to open the back of the bob.

Eve's breath stopped and her mind whirled with images she couldn't identify. Beside her Rose sighed deeply.

Aura Lee cupped the pendulum bob and then swiftly pulled her hand back. All the while her lips moved in a chant as she took a handkerchief from her pocket and, using it as insulation, twisted off the bob. A reddish light fought back the shadows in the alcove, and Aura Lee stared at it in dread. "Oh, Goddess. It isn't wrapped," she whispered.

Eve pushed past Rose and found the source of the glow.

The rough, triangular stone was black, at its center a reddish light that deepened as it was viewed. Hypnotically it pulled Eve's gaze into itself and she felt icy fear.

"No protections, Eve," Aura Lee whispered. "Chant and don't stop."

Eve drew in air. She was in thrall, unable to fill her lungs. She extended her hand and the stone was suddenly in the center of her palm. When her fingers closed around it her spirit plummeted and she was falling, whirling, closing her eyes against wind beating against her face.

How long she moved through turbulent air she didn't know. Time did not exist, only motion—and the words she heard inside her head:

> *Keep us clear of heart and goal.*
> *Guard us as our home we free.*
> *Lend us power to end attack,*
> *As we ask so mote it be.*

Eve gave a thought to the voice she heard and then began to echo the words as she fell.

After what could have been several lifetimes, Eve opened her eyes, expecting to see the far reaches of the world unfurled beneath her feet.

She was in darkness.

The foyer was dark and still. A clicking noise produced a long shaft of light from the torch, and it floated over the group huddled near the stairs.

Rose turned, stumbling against the old clock. "Where's Eve?"

Aura Lee sat on the floor, leaning against the wall. Her eyes were closed and her face gray.

"Aura Lee!" Rose set the light on the floor. "Here, let's get her to a chair." Elizabeth helped Rose steady her and they guided her to the bench by the front door. They eased her down onto the seat and Elizabeth groped for a coat hanging from the row of pegs nearby. She wrapped it around the older woman as Rose knelt at her side, patting her hand.

Dolores picked up the flashlight and, walking carefully around Neal and Andrea at the base of the stairs, crossed the floor to join them at the bench. "What happened over there?" she quavered. "You were chanting and then I saw a light swirling around. When it stopped Eve was gone and the lights went out."

The front door burst open, letting in wind and rain along with Kerry. She turned to force the door shut and leant against it for a moment, fighting for breath. "Max and I...followed the light...it shot out of here. Looked like it circled...around the house...into the hole...near the tunnel collapse. Max...still out there." She searched the room. "Why is it so dark? Where's Dink?"

Elizabeth waved at the dining room. "Brenna ran that-away just as things went all Twilight Zone. He took off after her."

"Are the rest of us here?" Rose stood up stiffly, using the wall to brace herself.

"It would seem so. Give me that light," Noreen said to Dolores. She aimed it around the room, counting heads as she did. The edge of the light caught Brenna as she came out of the dining room, Dink at her heels.

"Where'd you get off to?" demanded Noreen.

Brenna waved the packet. "The map—and the chants. I heard Eve in my head. She told me to get them and to keep them safe."

Noreen nearly dropped the light, grabbing hold before it could slip out of her hand. "The chants?"

"Copies for us when we get to the holding spots." She glanced down at the wad of papers in her hands. "Wait a minute, what?" She glanced back at Dink. "Did I pick up the wrong ones?"

Rose reached for the papers and took them from her. She stared down at them and looked up at Brenna. "There's nothing written on them."

"I know." As Rose dropped them onto the floor, Brenna appealed to her. "I had them, I saw them."

Aura Lee roused herself and pulled at Brenna's sweatshirt. "It's inside us," she whispered. "Listen. You can hear it if you listen."

Brenna's hand crept into Dink's and the two of them heard the words in their minds.

One by one they nodded as they began to hear the mantra

inside themselves. Andrea and Neal joined them and as one they began to speak aloud:

Keep us clear of heart and goal.
Guard us as our home we free.
Lend us power to end attack,
As we ask so mote it be.

Rose lifted her coat from the row of pegs. "We have to go out now. Do we need a quick look at the map?"

Neal glanced at Andrea. "You?"

"No," she said softly. "I can see exactly where I need to be."

Noreen's eyes widened. "I can, too."

"Who's doing this?" Dolores asked in fear. "Who's putting the words and images in our minds?"

"I think I can guess." Elizabeth wrapped her cape around her shoulders. "It feels like Caldicott."

"For me it's Gran." Brenna squeezed Dink's hand. "Can you smell her perfume?"

Dink nodded and raised her hand to his lips. "She's with us."

Noreen's smile died. "What about Eve's place? Who will be a holder for her?"

Kerry and Rose shared a look of understanding. "We have a lot of volunteers," Rose murmured.

Kerry nodded. "Maybe Jessamine and Kelvin will show up."

Elizabeth swallowed at the thought. "You mean…"

"I think we may have a lot of help with us today," Rose said firmly. "For now, let's be concerned with ourselves."

"And let's leave." Kerry turned toward the door and reached for the knob. As she pulled it open, light flared like fire and they saw flames coming through and falling onto the wood floor.

"Quick!" yelled Neal. "Run to your stations. Now! Don't stop."

"And chant!" Aura Lee swept out the door, her flowing robes catching fire at the hem. She marched briskly down the porch steps and across the grassy strip edging the courtyard. When she arrived at her northwest hold near Gregory Creek, the edge of her robe was wet from the soaked grass, all the embers quenched.

The front door slammed and Neal and Andrea ran to his space south of Aura Lee, who yelled, "The floor?"

"Fire extinguisher," he called back.

Andrea sped beyond him to the southwest corner area she'd seen in her mind. She waved as she caught sight of Dolores on the south side of the hedge along Baseline Avenue. Further east Elizabeth was tying a scarf over her braids, her lips moving with the words she recited.

Rose strode swiftly through the gardens toward her hold at the southeast corner of the lot. Noreen trotted behind her, reaching her location first. "Godspeed," she called to Rose, and resumed her mantra.

Rose waved and took her place where the hedge met the row of forsythia bushes. The space between her and Noreen was open, and Rose couldn't see that Eve's place was filled. At the thought, the outlines of the bushes blurred in a particular spot, a cloudiness dimming the outlines of the wrought iron fence. *Who it could be?* Rose wondered.

Dink held Brenna's hand until he'd reached his place along the front fence behind the east associate house. Brenna cupped his cheek for a brief moment and hurried on to her hold on the east side, south of him. She chanted steadily, quietly as she checked out the area. Nothing appeared different than usual. She turned in each direction to look for danger, but all was quiet.

Kerry raced to the fountain area and looked around wildly. "Max!" She shouted as loudly as she could. "Where are you?"

"Here." She saw his hand reaching for one of the fountain stones as he scrambled from the fissure over the tunnel, trying to pull himself up at the edge of the hole.

Kerry ran to his side, grasping his arm and straining to pull him onto the courtyard bricks. "Are you crazy?" she exploded when she found her breath.

"Something grabbed me as I walked past here." He pushed himself into a sitting position and she could see how shaken he was. "I've spent the last half hour trying to get out of there."

"What was it? Did you see?"

He shook his head. "I swear I was alone down there. But I had a hellacious time getting out."

Kerry grabbed his hand. "I'm sorry. I was so worried." She bent her head against his shoulder. "Are you hearing the chant? Do you know where your hold is?"

"I assumed that's what was happening."

He watched her lips moving in the chant and smiled. "I love you."

Kerry's eyes lit with joy. When she'd have spoken, Max put his forefinger over her lips. "Don't stop. We've work to do. Just remember, and don't let anything harm you."

He bent to kiss her, but before his lips touched hers, the ground beneath them shuddered. "Get to your station," Max snapped as he scrambled to his feet. He pulled her up and pushed her toward the foothills. "Run!"

"I love you, too," Kerry called as she ran to her hold. Already she was chanting with the words inside her.

Surrounded by darkness, Eve was aware of the words running through her mind as she dug in her pocket. She had to be ready for whatever happened. The bag Aura Lee had given her was halfway out. Heart pounding, she carefully tucked it into the zippered pouch lower on her pant leg. Aura Lee said she'd die if she lost it.

Trying again, Eve found the only thing she'd wanted to bring. Her fingertips rubbed against the sack of rough fabric around angles formed by bones and talons. She pulled out the owl claw, fingers registering the softness of feathers and the sharpness of nails and slipped it inside her bra, next to her heart. The pricking of the talons at her skin didn't bother her. She was imbued with a feeling of power, of force. She had to be able to grab it in an instant.

In her left hand the talisman pulsed. The heat of it hurt her, but it was fused to her skin and she didn't waste time wondering if she'd ever be rid of it.

Around her was silence, but inside her mind the words of the chant, recited by all of them, rolled through her mind. Each of the others was on guard, all of them the weapons Caldicott Wyntham had designated to fight this final battle.

Smoke limned the air, wrinkling her nose. It was unlike any she'd smelled before: caustic and threatening. The rustle of skin against rock brushed against her ears. That sound she'd heard before, when the secret room had writhed with snakes.

Hissing filled the darkness and her imagination bloomed with thousands of squirming bodies. They were coming toward her and she didn't know yet how she would fight them. Deliberately Eve caught up with the rhythm of the mantra and chanted along with it, pitting her voice against the sibilance surrounding her.

> *Keep us clear of heart and goal.*
> *Guard us as our home we free.*
> *Lend us power to end attack,*
> *As we ask so mote it be.*

The rustling grew louder and Eve took a step backward. It was so dark, the air itself black as a deep well and she was trapped here while the others got by with chanting. Fear grew in a deformed spiral. How was this fair to her? She'd come like all the others for her chance, only to be left alone with a futile challenge begun decades before. It had nothing to do with her. Anger licked along her nerves and she wanted to throw something, anything to make her feelings known. She balled her left fist, felt the lump on her palm and imagined hurling it across the room—across the universe. She would throw it with all the rage filling her body and let them see how they liked it. Her muscles trembled as she drew back her arm.

The chant filled her, louder in her ears now, the words moving slowly across a verdant meadow, calm words of purpose and connection. Her fingers relaxed as she joined the rhythm and her shoulders eased, her mind unlocked. *Yes, that's right*, a voice said, and its warmth was gossamer strength inside.

A wave of hatred flowed against her, and the rustling increased. The talisman heated against her palm, its hot light escaping between her fingers.

Eve thrust out her hand and pointed the stone toward the sound. A beam of light shot out from its center and what she saw made the blood freeze in her veins.

No swarm of squirming creatures here. A gargantuan serpent instead, its giant head brushing the ceiling and the thick length of it coiled for attack. Black scales gleamed as the light from the stone reflected off their polished surfaces. In horror she saw its searching tongue flick to scent the air. Fire flashed in front of it, revealing the deadly intent in its obsidian eyes.

Her hand clutched the talisman with fierce strength and she aimed it at those eyes. When the ray hit, she smelled burning flesh and she thrilled at striking the first blow. But the serpent wrenched its head up, smashing against the ceiling. Dirt and rocks rained down as the creature pulled further back to retaliate.

From the passage behind the snake burst a ball of flame and smoke, the flare of it forcing Eve to close her eyes. She stepped backward, tripping on loose rock, falling to the stone floor. A triumphant roar hit her like a blast of hot wind and her eyes flew open in time to see the serpent rear upward. From its bleeding eyes blasted hatred so intense she felt the flames of it against her skin.

Eve forced her arm up, aiming the talisman again and a beam of fire cut through the air and into the breast of the snake. Bending toward her, waving its great head back and forth, it lunged closer to her. Coughing, pushing herself back on the floor, Eve saw through the smoke great wings pumping as an immense bird streaked toward her. *The owl*, she realized as the snake turned toward it. The monster's mouth opened wide and the owl veered out of reach.

Eve groped for the owl claw inside her shirt. Her fingers closed around it and she yanked it out.

As the snake thrust toward the bird she screamed, "No!" and grabbed hold of the owl as it passed within inches over her head. She clutched its neck as it turned sharply to avoid the snake's strike, and then she scrambled onto the bird's back.

They flew toward the mouth of the tunnel, the owl's wings rising and falling. In the swirling smoke she gaped at the nightmare figure arched over them. The snake's mouth was open in threat, venom dripping from its fangs. She held tightly to the bird and pointed the owl claw out before her. In her mind the mantra was spoken, all the chants joining in one powerful voice.

Keep us clear of heart and goal.
Guard us as our home we free.
Lend us power to end attack,
As we ask so mote it be.

Light flashed toward the creature, again striking its wounded chest. *Throw the talisman,* said the delicate voice she'd felt before.

Eve braced herself, holding to the owl's neck with one arm. She flung out her left hand with all her might, scarcely aiming, feeling the skin rip from her palm as the stone flew true, into the pulsing fire at the heart of the serpent.

With a clap of thunder the ceiling fell in. The confusion of smoke and dust behind them, she leaned against soft feathers, felt muscles flexing, and heard a swooshing of air. They were moving up and out into the light.

They soared into the air over Wisdom Court and Eve looked down. Strands of glowing light linked the holders of the directions, forming a barricade around the entire site.

She leaned her head on the owl as they circled above the house and down to the ground.

EPILOGUE

When she became aware, Eve was lying on the ground and Rose was struggling to wrap a blanket around her. Above her the skies were darkening from gray to black clouds.

"Is it supposed to rain?" she asked.

"By the Goddess, you're all right!" Aura Lee thrust Rose out of the way and fell to her knees beside Eve. "You darling girl," she babbled, "we thought you were dead." Her frightened blue eyes were glassy with tears. "You weren't breathing and that man wouldn't let us check how you were."

"What?" Eve looked around, blinking to clear her vision. "Where'd he go?"

"Calm down, Aura Lee." Neal took her by the hand and helped her to her feet. "Let's get inside before this storm cuts loose. We can clear up everything then."

"If you'll allow me to assist you?" A man was standing nearby, dressed in what appeared to be black livery with silver tubing along his lapels. His curly hair was auburn and his blue eyes were amused. His smile was mischievous as he offered her his arm. "We haven't officially met, but I assure you, we do know each other." He had a lovely English accent.

Eve smiled back as she set her arm on his. "I appreciate the assist." Her limp was even worse than before.

The scent of garlic and sausage hit her as they came through the kitchen door. "I'm starving."

Rose was at her side. "Eve, let me escort you to the powder room while Aura Lee fixes you a plate. We're having pizza."

Eve followed Rose and was grateful when she saw herself in the mirror. Her hair was wild and her face was covered with soot and sweat. "What a mess."

Rose surprised her with a swift hug. "You saved the day, my dear. You could be wearing a clown suit and stilettos and no one would mind."

Eve felt heat rising in her cheeks. "We all saved the day. That was the whole point."

When Eve had finished washing her face, she heard a scratching sound. "Oh, no," she whispered. Hand shaking, she reached for the doorknob and yanked open the door. Danica looked up at her and meowed in complaint. Eve bent to pick up the cat, receiving a lavish lick on one eyebrow for her efforts.

A few minutes later Eve carried Danica into the living room and set her on the floor. The Englishman waited politely and handed her a glass. "Thanks," she murmured. She examined him carefully, smiling at the energy he exuded. "You're Charlie, aren't you?"

"I am." He sketched a bow. "And you are Evie."

"Nobody calls me Evie anymore."

"I do."

She lifted her hand and he drew in a breath, taking hold of it. "Your palm, it's burned."

"It doesn't hurt." She touched his shoulder. "Thank you for what you did. You got me out of there just in time."

"You blasted that abomination first. I think we're even." They studied each other's faces until he bent to kiss her cheek.

Kerry slid her arm around Eve's shoulder. "Come and sit down, you two. Your plates on the table."

By the time Eve had eaten two pieces of pizza, she was on her way to feeling normal. She described the standoff in the secret room, and Charlie recounted what had begun in England.

"Severn Barlow claimed to be the seventh son of a seventh son," he said matter-of-factly. "The man he thought was his father was actually his brother, giving Severn the honor. The old earl was the Nazi sympathizer and most likely killed his son Duncan. Severn cut his teeth on the legend of the stolen talisman and the missing bearer bonds. He was insanely interested in the occult and was behind the efforts to breach the walls of Wisdom Court in order to find both."

"Charlie was sent under cover as a servant about a year ago to keep an eye on him," added Max. "He was dangerously unstable, and while the local police couldn't prove anything, bodies were found fairly regularly near the estate. It's all still being investigated. When he wasn't honing in on you, Eve, he was quite the serial killer."

Eve took a swallow of the wine given to her. "But why did he focus on me? How was he able to create the odd sightings and send such blood-curdling messages?"

"My theory is he picked up on the connection between you and me." Charlie took her empty plate and set it on the coffee table. "Every time you and I communicated his pyrotechnics grew stronger. And the lot of you incited many of the various messages. This place is still crawling with spirits, many of them from long ago."

"What happened today...the giant snake. That was this Severn's doing?" Eve shivered at the memory.

"He was ahead of us at the Paranormal Society when it came to remote viewing," said Max. "Where he truly excelled was in discovering ways to transpose himself into other creatures."

Eve's eyes widened in shock. "*He* was the snake?"

"He was." Charlie lifted her hand to his lips. "And when you threw the talisman into that hole in his snaky chest, you put an end to him."

"You mean I killed him?"

Charlie put his hand over hers. "You did. Thank you."

"How did you transform yourself into the owl?"

Charlie leaned back to rest his head against the sofa. "We'll have to know each other much better for me to tell you that."

Eve sipped at her wine and was content to just sit.

Brenna and Dink hurried in from the kitchen, she with her Kindle in hand. "Wait till you hear this! There's a report from England about an old manor in Surrey imploding today. The owner, Severn Barlow, was killed when the old place just fell in on itself. It's been in the news anyway because of a police investigation. They even mentioned stuff about the noble family who established it being pro-Nazi during the war."

Aura Lee clapped both hands over her mouth and looked at them with wide eyes. Rose sagged in her chair. "Does this mean the whole thing could be over?"

Max frowned. "I doubt the ghosts will be going anywhere, but it seems the persecution from the nasty neo-Nazi buggers might have come to an end."

Laughter bounced off the walls. Rose's eyes filmed with tears. "All of you have made it possible for Wisdom Court to continue. Cottie's dream will enrich the dreams of others thanks to you."

Noreen stood up, a little tipsy from wine. "I want to make an announcement and a toast. At the end of my tenure here, which happens next month, I'll be moving into the house I've bought two blocks down the hill." As Kerry jumped up to envelop her in a hug, she added, "I have no family but this one, and I want to stay near it. And my toast," she added, "is to Caldicott Wyntham." She lifted her glass to the portrait above the fireplace where Caldicott looked on her creation. "With gratitude for the chances you've given us, with love for the spirit of the place which nurtures us all."

"To Caldicott!" Neal said deeply and they raised their glasses. As they drank, they heard a crashing sound.

Aura Lee hurried to the kitchen, but was back in a moment. "The door to my room is open. Will one of you come with me?"

Andrea and Neal followed her and the others looked at each other. "I'm stayin' right here," Elizabeth said firmly, rubbing Strudel's belly. "No more hauntings today for me."

"Might it be ghosts?" Charlie asked Eve with some excitement. "May we see, too?"

Eve set down her glass and stood up. "Let's go."

Max and Kerry followed them into Aura Lee's tiny living room, where Andrea and Neal were searching for any disruption. Aura Lee cocked her head at an odd humming sound.

"It's coming from my bedroom."

They trailed behind her, catching sight of the mirror over her dresser. The frame was glowing around the edges, but the mirror was black as onyx. The low humming was growing in volume.

As they watched, a light began to coalesce at the center of the glass, and the features of a woman with chestnut hair formed. At her side the image of a tall black-haired man took shape, one of his hands on her shoulder. He looked into her smiling face, love shining from his deep brown eyes.

Kerry reached blindly for Max's hand.

"It's Cottie," gulped Aura Lee. "When she was young."

"Do you think that's Duncan?" Rose asked, voice trembling.

"I think it has to be." Aura Lee was crying softly. "She's telling us they've found each other again."

The images in the mirror brightened and then were gone.

As the glass went dark, they heard a gossamer whisper fill the room.

Thank you.

AUTHOR'S NOTE

Many thanks, dear readers, for your interest in Wisdom Court. To keep in touch with the characters living there, please contact me at the following links:

Website/blog: Writer in the Garret at yvonnemontgomery.com

Facebook author page: @ayvonnemontgomery

Twitter feed is   @authorYvonneM

THE
WISDOM COURT
SERIES

Edge of the Shadow
A Signal Shown
All in Bad Time

Yvonne Montgomery became afraid of the dark, after her parents allowed her to see Psycho at the tender age of twelve.

Now Yvonne lives in a shadowy three-story Victorian house in Denver's historic Capitol Hill where her imagination rises to the challenge when the old floorboards creak for no reason and the window panes rattle without wind.